Göthique

Ravenscraft Anthology of Horror III

K.A. Schultz

Yes, indeed! A rather darkly romantic theory.

What was that? Yes! I love it. Romantically dark. I *knew* you two would be perfect. Sir, my I offer you a cigar?

None Are Sold Before Their Time

†††

Göthique

Ravenscraft Anthology of Horror III

K.A. Schultz

Dakeha Taunus LLC, publisher

GÖTHIQUE is a collection of works of fiction. Any resemblances to actual people, living or dead, places or events, are coincidental.
No AI was used in the creation or execution of this literary work.

Inquiries may be addressed to butterflybroth@gmail.com

Cover art *Mrs. Shroom* by Roberto Diaz
@roberto_diaz_arte_del_caos

https://linktr.ee/K.A.Schultz

Amazon
ISBN 979-8-9867569-5-0 paperback

Library of Congress Control Number: 2023916990

Other Amazon editions:
ISBN 979-8-9867569-6-7 kindle
ISBN 979-8-9894856-0-4 hardback

Also available via Ingram:
ISBN 9798986756974

*Also by Lilah Ravenscraft**

I And You

The Echo Tundra Series, vols. I, II, III

Classicke: Ravenscraft Anthology of Horror I

Inspirited: Ravenscraft Anthology of Horror II

Also by K.A. Schultz

Khrystmass – Holiday Horror Collection
Neitherium – Prose & Poetry from the Neither
Jacob – A Denouement in One Act

Rugs on Puddles Coats Over Oceans – Poems & Lyric Poetry

Unpublished, with content edited & absorbed into Neitherium:

Anathelogium

Milia Verboru

www.butterflybroth.com
www.jacobmarleystory.com
www.shewhowas.com

@kaschultz_writer
@butterflybroth
@lilahravenscraft

*for more on Lilah Ravenscraft, read "Ravenscrafted"
NEITHERIUM by K.A. Schultz

In Memoriam

Pax Panic

Graphic, possibly offensive & triggering content
Reader discretion is advised

TABLE OF CONTENTS

I.	Looking Back		11
II.	Forward	*Lilah Ravenscraft*	13
III.	A Killing Repose	*Kimann Schultz*	15
IV.	At One With Mere Ashes	*Philomena L. Byrne*	21
V.	Joined with the Seas	*Kimann Schultz*	29
VI.	Penchants of the Prize	*Francesca Caine-Ewan*	35
VII.	Postmortem Symbiosis	*Olivia T. Harmsworth*	43
VIII.	Book of Lucombe	*Anonymous*	51
IX.	All the Peace and Quiet	*M. Leigh Lynton*	57
X.	None Are Sold Before Their Time	*Heston Mueller*	89
XI.	Santa Domnia II: Hellscape Wrought	*Kimann Schultz*	111
XII.	We Thalassophiles	*E.V. Segel*	121
XIII.	Farther Up That Hill	*Ephram Bloome*	133
XIV.	Rectified (v.2)	*G.G. Sulliman*	137
XV.	Absolutely Everything	*Winifred Preiss*	159
XVI.	Infantile Troglodyte	*Woolston Memling*	173
XVII.	Gossamer Beast	*Jean-Luc de Luene*	177
XVIII.	100 Word Horror	*Millifred Snodgrass*	187
	Choose Wisely | Vengeance | Hardest Goodbyes		
	Brothers, Sisters | Well Spoken		
	Black Butterfly | Bride's Head		
XVII.	Poems	*Kimann Schultz*	195
	My Lord | Midnight Café | One Short Hour		
	Orphic Lament | Say It | Delectable Light		

Looking Back

A message from the Publisher

GÖTHIQUE is the third and final horror anthology curated by the former Milifred Snodgrass, better known and mourned the world over as the late, great Lilah Ravenscraft.

GÖTHIQUE would have no doubt been published under the auspices of Ravenscraft Publishing LLC, but tragic outcomes being what they most sadly are, this publication has been taken up by Dakeha Taunus LLC with permission of Ms Ravenscraft's estate.

GÖTHIQUE comprises a series of short stories and poems that fall tidily into the gothic horror subgenre in which Lilah specialized as both writer and publisher. While she is well known as author of the Echo Tundra Series, volumes 1-3 *(out of print, as mandated in Ms. Ravenscraft's will), Lilah is best known by way of her final work,* I AND YOU, *which, since its publication, has spent the last four years on best-seller lists the world over, and netted her – albeit posthumously – six literary and two motion picture awards. It is very possibly safe to say, Lilah was welcomed with open arms into the pantheon of past literary greats upon her departure from this world.*

The gift of Lilah's literary legacy – the impact I AND YOU *has had on the literary world and beyond – cannot be overstated.* I AND YOU *transfixed – nay, transformed – countless readers, further cementing its place in popular culture by way of the spoken vernacular and allegorical imagery adapted directly from the book's remarkable narrative.* I AND YOU *will continue to affect all who have read this novel – and even those with whom its fans interact, it is that revelationary a read. Lilah's swansong will continue to give long after we in our fleeting here and now are gone.*

The following Forward was transcribed from an unfinished draft, hand-written onto a pad of legal paper that was left, presumably by Lilah, on her writing desk, in the apartment where she lived. All agree, Ms. Ravenscraft was its author, and that it was intended for this anthology. The following essay, her Forward, was collected along with a folio that contained the manuscript which comprises this anthology. Both it and the short stories and poems found herein have been reproduced verbatim for this edition. [The originals, once copied in toto, *were returned to Ms Ravenscraft's residence, which the Ravenscrafters Society is in the process of registering as a historic home, with plans to eventually open it to the public as a museum.]*

It is surmised, the Forward may have been the final words Lilah wrote.

As is the case with her previous anthologies, but for two writers included in this collection (Kimann Schultz and Ms Ravenscraft herself, née Millifred Snodgrass), no other member of this book's roster was findable for purposes of basic contact or active inclusion in post publication promotion. A file of signed contracts was, in fact, located with the manuscript, which this publisher has relied on for permissions as having been granted. Lilah was known for seeking out reclusive creative types who, for reasons known only to them, remain to this day under all radars and therefore bereft of any post publication accolades. Granted, they are likewise spared of any untoward criticisms. . . The majority of contributing authors will remain therefore unknown but for the inclusion of their (pen)names, as listed alongside their contributions in the Table of Contents.

This publisher's office remains on alert and in active search for the participating authors, and grateful for any leads whatsoever, which may guide us to these writers. Tips or information can be emailed to:

goethique.author.search@gmail.com

. . . and if an underlying sadness tugs at your sensibilities as you read the stories contained in this volume, or if you discern a whisper of pending doom in the wake of Lilah's Forward, this editor respectfully, sadly submits, you are reading quite accurately between her lines.

Here now, looking back, is Ms. Ravenscraft's introduction to GÖTHIQUE.

Rest well, Lilah.

Forward

(undated)

I suppose you might construe this message as some sort of attempt to infect you, dear reader, with a melancholy. I see the purported sharing within this introduction as a form of expansion, and it lends least of all me some semblance of relief. My rejection of the ordinary has taken myriad forms. It has shaped what I sought to embrace, to embody. Inside, outside. It has come to reside within each and every line I have written to date as author, and I do believe it lurks within the stories that found me as their publisher – submissions which have consistently insisted by way of their clandestine messaging, *Take me, use me, make me yours.*

It *is* about possession. All that one has, is what one *does*.

And we are, whether we like it or not, the sum of our deeds.

Let no one be fooled, we do indeed ask for that which we ultimately receive, which we *become,* whether by way of spoken word or deed.

So, allow me, dear reader, to offer you this forward as a way of looking back. That is what I am left with at this particular point in time; and I confess, I am content with it. My lot is my destiny, and whatever else becomes my legacy, it will have to speak for itself, for my words have long existed outside of myself. They were mine but for a moment. I was their conduit.

As someone quite close to me once said,

Carpe lucem intra tenebras

On this, I have acted, as I imagine an entire cadre of literary contributors have acted, whose works now comprise this collection, an anthology I have simply entitled *Göthique.*

Yes, the umlaut is intentional. It is not a typo or the tinkering of some mischievous Draftmite, however random it might appear to be. As others before me have stood upon this standing down, so do I wish to suggest the negation of anything related to virtuous lift or snobbish loft by way of this fanciful, single-word title. Must we all try to be wonderful? Perfect? Some sort of proverbial best? Does that strike you as wearying as it does me? Presuppositions far too inter-connected with the mundane tropes of Humankind incessantly seek to link themselves with a universe that is in reality so vast and indifferent as to make, in all honesty, a fucking joke of existentiality. Hence, such as an utterly random umlaut. It's my little button push for anyone who, in taking themselves too seriously, might wish to self-elevate by way of a petty criticism.

Does that irk you? Does it make you smile, shake your head just a little?

Still, rather than laugh in the face of all the futility that exists out there, I turn once again to the written word, as I suspect the contributors of this anthology did, too. Nihilism has its poetics. Enjoy the stories as you see fit, take what you want or need from them. But take note also of the spaces between the lines, the minute fissures between the very letters of the words themselves. Look, if you dare, past the narratives as on their surfaces they have been presented – you just might begin to sense the frequency, "hear" some of what bleeds from the cracks, from the front edges where the Neither meets with life as we know it, live it, try to love it.

I, we, stand facing an invisible shoreline where, had I the option, I myself would like to stay a while longer. As it is, I will remain here, in my room, at my desk, hopefully long enough to see the sun rise in a couple hours. This, my perch, from which I have endured glimpses of the universe, is where for now I am calling it good enough.

And so, as I sign off, I wish you a

†††

A Killing Repose

Ice gathers visibly on the glass, crystalline rimes exploding, frosted dandelions gone to seed. The twins are fixated by the sparkling script as it charts its path across the window. The Grandmother peers beyond the distracting beauty, to the snowy vortexes spinning in the mead, just beyond the front stoop. A premature night is descending, lavender grays failing fast to an inky, opaque wash. Soon, but for the scattered peppering of the thick flakes as they spin about, it will be, as is said, black as midnight – and the clock has yet to chime the five o'clock hour.

Shaken by the harsh winds, the snowflakes tumble riotously. They will, like the waning day, give up, settle in, interlock, take hold, go dark. The Grandmother can tell, in no time will there be a blanket so thick, it will breach the window's ledge. The snow will then rise to block what remains of her view onto the fields. Never but when the arctic anomaly descends upon this portion of the world does the fracturing on the glass foretell a wintry cataclysm of this magnitude. The Grandmother has long wondered, not if but when it would occur, and when it did, where would it find her, or her daughter, or her daughter's family. Storms like this have scripted many a sorrowful tale. . .

The chalet holds fast to its foundations, but shudders as it is struck by winds that surge like frigid tides come ashore from distant, cold oceans. The small house backs up to the black-curtained brace of an *Uhrwald*, a sea of pines tall as clock towers, near as old as the hills they pierce. Their limbs are so densely linked, they force each snow-laden squall to topple over and back onto itself, against even the back walls of that poor, little structure, rendering it twice struck by the storm's gales, so exposed as it sits there, on the edge of the ancient forest.

Oh, the Grandmother knows what this storm is about. She has read of it in the dog-eared journals of her ancestors, been told of these storms since she was a little girl, by tradition and trepidation both, evidently, mandated. Hushed and reverential voices had relayed the stories for as long as she or her forebears could remember, the reasons behind this, the harshest of seasons.

How can she begin to explain to her grandchildren, who had grown up in the urban collectives her daughter had journeyed to, amidst the utter absences of anything borne of the historical, or the mythical, or metaphysical, which might help explain what was playing itself out tonight? How can the Grandmother broach the topic, or that of their own role, as circumstantial collateral for what Mankind has wrought?

The Grandmother turns her thoughts to the heavens, where the rent fibers of angels' feathers are making their way down through the skies, from what mystics might call the nethering realms, to journey far, so far, first into the uppermost reaches of mortal imagination, then into the stark realities of the present. And once entered into the planes of human existence, Grandmother knows, the silken petals eventually pass through what the more learned factions would call the troposphere, to dance amongst the nourishing vapors that fill and feed its living, breathing recipients, which hold a fortunate few of them aloft in their undulous arms.

The Grandmother wonders, how those precious, angelic remnants even made it this far, and how they could, when directed by the elements in such insidious fashion, coalesce into this, a winter's storm that will, by all predictions and ferocious display, like its predecessors become the stuff of both folklore and saddest irony.

The Grandmother and those who yet call the *Uhrwald* home had lost loved ones in the last, such storm. A taxed heart had given out as one tried to shovel a path to the well; a hunter, returning home with his catch, had instead become lost, then found the next day, mere meters distanced from his front door, buried in a drift at the base of a towering but unsheltering and indifferent tree. And the twins, a boy, and a girl who had been, it was whispered, lured outdoors to play in the snow by some childlike apparition, known to appear when the storms were at their worst, to entice the youngest and guilelessly unafraid away from the safe harbour of their homes. The children had disappeared without a trace, their footprints instantly erased by the blizzarding gales. . .

The Grandmother stands close behind her wards to make sure no apparition exists to catch the eyes of her little ones. Grateful for the preternaturally long night, she can soon draw the curtains on the children's curiosity, put them to bed. There is nothing else left to do.

No, the Grandmother thinks, safe as they seem to be, there is nothing left but to settle in to sleep.

The water in the bucket has frozen over; there will be no offering of a sip. The children, she ushers into bed fully dressed, then drapes every blanket she owns over the two, in hopes they can at the very least be granted the solace of sleep, perhaps with the parting gift of a sweet dream. The howling winds play the chimney like a flute, but with a melody so lonesome and discordant, it sings only of foreboding. A dirge: she knows its song. Even this grows muffled, the longer she listens.

The Grandmother also knows, the packed powder berm will only continue to build. By morning, it will reach above the roofline, drifting up and over the very peak of the chalet. In so doing, it will obliterate any visibility of the hovel. They are being buried alive. This, she will not tell the children.

As one accustomed to life off-grid, in which the modern world plays no part, the Grandmother knows well enough to keep goods stocked. Sustenance has always been attended to. But starvation is not at issue. Over the years, ever more distanced relatives had remembered less and less to circle back to her, relegating her to the peripheries of their own, hardscrabble lives. She has grown accustomed to living alone, with Grandfather having passed so many years ago, and her daughter and the young man she had partnered with having gone off to the big city, so sporadically heard from, her past having been set aside for a more modern-day present, presumed to be a better one. It has left the Grandmother feeling rather forsaken.

Tonight, it feels more like having been left behind. But now, with her beautiful daughter so tragically taken at such a young age – and that nice fellow of hers too – there is no one. The Grandmother's mournful isolation, after all those years on her own, has brought with it the inevitable – a regrettable forgettability. She, now with the grandchildren in her care, are all but forgotten. No one will even think to remember, let alone check in on the old woman, nor recall the fact that she had taken in the little ones after their mother and father had perished.

The storm holds entombment level potential. When the Grandmother arranges the last of the blankets around the three of them, she is mindful of how it will look come Spring, when perhaps their bodies will be discovered.

Tonight, she shall tell her grandchildren *the* story, if for no other reason than to not have let the storm's import be for naught. If unacknowledged, what is the point of the angels' sacrifice?

How else to honour what they have given up in the name of all the infant souls that will never possess wings, let alone fly with them, use them for their own accords, go somewhere, be somewhere, become a someone, forge the next links with which to connect to the next other?

†††

Time had come, for the angels to rejoin, silent and hands clasped, wings spread, and flexed.

Time had come for the angels to present themselves, to stand up alone, tall, and steadfast, still and stoic.

Time had come, for each angel to step up to the block, and to fall upon its knees, and for that angel to allow its wings to be lifted up and held aloft, be draped over the face of its brutally unyielding edge.

Time had come, for the Wielder of the Scythe, who unlike its brethren has not been cast down from the Heavens, but been permitted to subside there, in the shadows, in the periphery, in order to perform their one task, which is to raise up into the voids the razor-sharp arc of a mirror, and to cut with that blinding, bright and silvered blade into all doubt, all deception, all disorder.

Time had come, for that blade to strike with the force of ten-thousand brutes, all the strapping young men who knew no better.

Time had come, for the blade to strike with the force of fifty-thousand harpies, all the young women who knew no better.

Time had come, for that blade to sever from the angels' shoulders their wings, for which they had loved, had lived; for which they had fought, won, lost, had rendered from themselves the best they could muster.

Time had come, for the blood of those angels to spill onto the heavenly plains, to spatter in remembrance of the corporeal manifestation of a One who, despite all misguided circumstance, had been granted life, so to walk and exist, as potentially perfect and ultimately flawed as anyone before Him had ever been, would ever be, might never be.

Time had come, for the wailing of the angels to descend as howling winds, and for their cries to bind with the raging flurries, to carve by way of destructive intent their memorials, so that bit by bit, piece by piece, house by home, man and woman could be made whole again by their penance – all upon the back of one innocent child, one innocent child. . .

Time had come, for the whispering fronds that could span oceans, touch suns, warm even the smallest of hummingbirds' nests, to fall, and fall. . .

And as they fall, and crack in the cold as they do, they will crystalize, as even the most brilliant ideas of Man are wont to do, so they take with them on their journey every beautiful thought, and deed, and every last damn brickle of love that might ever have been felt. This is why, within their structures they hold the Eternal Unique, just as any soul might have held it, had it ever been given that chance. . .

For the few snowflakes that make it as far as the hearth, drawn in by the waning heat of the embers, they return to their original state. As the feathers strike the coals, they spark momentarily, then curl up, and turn to ash. As the three in their bed drift off, the Grandmother, eyes closed, fancies she can smell the faint odor of burning hair.

The dying fire in the hearth is soon wholly extinguished, and the small clock on the mantel winds down before it can herald the next hour. The chimney stones, even the benches begin to sparkle with frost. Skeletal fingers of ice creep in from under the threshold, make their way up the door. Glittering threads trail off, marking their stealthy paths along the planks of the floor. The candle flame begins to flicker haphazardly and grows smaller, smaller. . .

The Grandmother now sleeps, as do the children, whilst the obliterating snow continues to fall into its own quiet and killing repose. All those fragmented wings, with no longer any iota of feeling left in them, they bury the little house at the edge of the Uhrwald long before the midnight hour is never tolled.

As they would say, my little ones, Whenever a bell rings. . .

. . . an angel gets its wings? The two chime in, hopeful, eager to please, their words hovering within the tiny frozen clouds formed by their warm puffs of breath.

No, no, my dears, she softly admonishes, a sadness in her voice, *. . . an angel SHEDS its wings. . .*

†††††

At One With Mere Ashes

I cannot feel but rather sense the energies of the flames, their erratic dance, as candles are placed around me on the bier and one by one slowly, ceremoniously lit.

The room in which I have been laid to temporary rest is vast. And draughty. It has never a warm space, no matter how fiercely the fires in the massive hearth might gambol and whip about the charred grate, the rusted andirons. Tonight, it is a season's sweeping breeze which wafts about, winding up and around and over my body, stirring the fabric, flicking at the tongues of light. Borne on the soft exhalations of decaying armies of times long passed, be it silenced commands or cries of terror whose echoes have faded away, the cold air that sifts up from the catacombs far below us is ripe with struggle and suffering. It suffuses the space, sours it, and it seeks me out with intention, beckoning to me and to my living counterparts, *Join us. . .*

I cannot see what it is directly beneath me but can more or less discern the tufted velvet pallet upon which my corpse has been placed. Despite the bandages in which I am swathed, each little hill – horsehair stuffed and with a button stitched to anchor it – renders the *suggestion* of a cradling sensation over the entirety of my body. It is as if I were being held aloft, but by no means as one to be comfortably, safely reposed. No idle sojourn is this.

Serendipitous, that I had lain there, on the floor of my very own bedroom, undiscovered for nigh two full turns of the sun before my sisters had at last come to call, on that day when they finally found me. Their unintended negligence – for I had been failing and was in need of their ministrations – would now serve to benefit me, for my eyes had been left frozen, wide open, by the shock of my fall. By the time the women arrived, my eyeballs had been exposed long enough to the dry air for my eyelids to have been rendered stiff as parchment, impossible to close. Funny, the youngest one amongst them had tried repeatedly to ease my lids down, draw the curtains, so to speak. But my gaze remained affixed into the voids. It was by then quite firmly set.

I do like having them open. All the better to see.

Later, as my sisters anointed my limbs and wrapped them in what felt to me like miles and miles of coarsely woven bandages, I had listened with some concern to their chatter. A few of them had wanted to place gold coins over my eyes in some token, proprietary gesture, one taken straight from the playbooks of the mundane. But no; majority prevailed, and my sisters in their collective wisdom decided to leave my glazed-over deathwatch unencumbered.

†††

In this moment, I am looking much by way of memory at the thousands of hand-painted stars and moons which dot the arched ceiling over my head. The fretwork of stone which supports this expanse is intentionally rough-hewn. It evokes the bark of a tree, reminiscent of the ancient oaks under which I and my kind welcomed our solstices, our equinoxes, beckoned forth the sun, bid adieu to the moon. This nave of carved stone contains our ceremonial chambers; it shields them from the daylit upper reaches where the everyman treads.

Barely illuminated by the candles, the vast room fades quickly into deep shadow, appearing quite endless, as if the floor might go on forever and into the voids, to eventually merge with the shallows of the Underworld. This is a place of mystical confluence, homebase to a fellowship to which I have belonged for as long as I can remember.

I can hear my sisters' singing. Their words are muffled, the melody is distant. It is as if I were afloat underwater, with them standing above and nearby, as if at some pier's end. They are sending invocations into the reaches below, to me where I lie submerged in this journey of mine, and farther beyond that as well.

Farther beyond the here, beyond the now. We have always reached to the deepest depths, be it heaven *or* hell bound, be they opposing destinations, or one and the same. And I know every word they sing. I did, after all, compose some of the verses myself. I sing along in my heart, asking, willing my spirit to heed the prayer, to please, take wing, take final flight. *Go!*

We sing to my afterlife awakening. We sing to incite my post-mortem spirit to sever itself from the sinewy and aged vessel to which it was assigned in life. We sing to ask of Mother Earth and her shadowed siblings that they may lift the renewed, truer me up, off and out of what had once been in life, the woman, the witch, the temporally housed human being.

l, more than ever before, am aware of the fluidly conscious entity I am becoming. I understand that I am about to take leave of my erstwhile self, and that I am about to commence on an everlasting journey which will intersect, perhaps even link, the myriad plains of our most beauteous nook in this universe. I understand that I am on the cusp of manifesting something so magnificent, it is beyond anything I could ever have imagined in life, let alone called forth in any of my sisters who had preceded me in death.

And it is from these other dimensions not yet revealed to me, that *I will come back.*

I am about to become She who they will call forth.

It will be for me to heed the call of spells cast at midnight, to emerge from magical portals. It will be for me to pass through vapors teeming from the mouths of steaming cauldrons, and to rise up and out of fissures where reality leaves off and the real magic begins, where histories and imagination mix and are confused, where facts and hallucinations merge to become a riotous one, where the intoxicating and primordial soup of immeasurable potentials hold the power to transport – and even consume – every participant who invites me into their presence, who is willing to behold the newly resurrected and oh, so ancient Me.

I can hardly wait. It is the culmination of a lifetime of devotion to the craft; the closest thing to immortality I could hope to achieve.

Wait!

I think. . . yes. I do believe. . .

It is happening!

Gossamer filaments loosen. They pull long, thinning out like strands of spun sugar, like the threads of a spider's web when caught up in the purposeful claws of a cutting November breeze. . .

I am pulling free; I am undoing the knitting. . .

My field of vision regenerates and broadens incrementally, sliver by sliver. New eyes, new sight.

I see luminous fingertips pulling free from languid sleeves. They draw back and ease out, as if extracting themselves from the gloves of a reclining mannequin. The smallest of forms, like fireflies, these whisper-small appendages begin to stretch beyond the wizened, calloused knuckles and fingers they were in life, the work-weary hands of an old hag. Reaching furtively, the ghostly digits stretch longer, longer; they waver like the dancing candleflames close by. . .

I feel an urge to contract my core. *To push.* I start to try and lift my head. *But wait. . .*

What's this?

A disturbance in the distance?

It is a harsh breaking sound, that of a fracturing. It disrupts the soothing veil of the requiem, whose melodies my sisters and I had crafted to conjure my sentient exit from the hollowed housing in which the emerging Me, which as of this moment, still resides.

My spirit recoils. The luminous fingertips vaporize and disappear. They are gone.

No. No!

Only moments ago, as the crescendo of the song was about to peak, the faintest sense of separation was beginning to manifest itself! I know what I felt! We were *so* close! I was, I am *so* close! The frustration is almost erotically charged. My entire being hovers painfully on the brink of something so new, so wonderful, so, so. . .

And now *this?*

What in bloody Hades is happening?

My sisters' singing has stopped. An abrupt and pregnant silence takes over the space. I too am struck hard by the suffocating weight of the forced pause.

I realize, I can smell my sisters' fear. It is a stench, freshly perceived.

Recollection, recognition leave a bitter tang in my parched mouth.

I feel my sisters' terror; it swells and grows. They stand motionless in a coagulated cloud of confusion, anger, and despair. Cornered like pups, they have nowhere to go. There was only ever that one, damnably narrow door which led into this underground chamber. . .

Sisters! We have come this far! Rally! Fight! I am with you!

Out of my periphery, I can sense the women are coming to, shaking off that first, cold shock of fear. And they are readying themselves for the assault. A few of them have run to the door, thrown the bolt. They are now leaning with the full weight of their bodies against it, although it is a paltry, stop-gap deterrent. Their own lives they place at vast, immediate risk for the rest of us. But that is what we do for each other, what we have always done for each other.

I hear the tools from the hearth being lifted off their hooks. My sisters will no doubt wield these as weapons. Primitive, yes, but plied with the vehemence of a jealously protective Fury, simple, forged fireside implements can become objects of *keen* destructive potential. . .

My sisters whisper but a few words – most can read each other's minds. Hissed commands fly from the farthest corners of the room, from behind support columns, from behind the altar. Breaths are held; all are still as statues. They are ready for the onslaught. I can almost hear what they are thinking as they listen, listen. . .

We have been thusly hunted, so horrifically persecuted for so terribly long, over so many generations, that, if we jump to conclusions, we have earned that right. If we leap to violent resolution, we are merely giving back.

It has to be *them*, or some similar attack party from the next village. Again.

Boots sound on the stone pavers of the stairs and come to a stop. Shouts echo, as do indiscernible commands. I hear metal scraping, I hear the *shing* of blades unsheathing. And then, with a bang like a thunderclap, the door bursts open. The locks, the bolt, my sisters' determined postures are rendered futile in one explosive, split second.

They have come for us. Again.

My spirit winces, shrinks back into the hull that of my emptied breast. It cowers, beholden to the dead weight of long-held, painful memories, dragged down by all the fears I fought against throughout my life.

The screams of my sisters – of old, dear friends, of novices I barely knew – are blood curdling. Their voices are just as quickly infested with a garbling, as one by one they are forced to choke on their own blood.

And I? I cannot make a sound. I lie here like an idiot effigy. I, who for decades led these women in thought, intent, and in deed, do not move, *cannot* move. And I am the very reason why they are here now, and under attack. And I cannot do a damn thing to help them.

I should have known. News of my passing had spread unusually quickly, for gossip grows legs viciously fast and long. I realize, I have unwittingly but utterly and completely betrayed my sisters. I may as well have led the mob to this room myself, as their very own Delilah.

I can only lie here and idly witness the attack as it plays out around me. The candles are immediately knocked to the ground. Some flames sputter and drown in their own wax. But some flames – for I can very nearly smell the scorching of fibers – grab at the draped fabric of my bier and set it afire. There is a rushing sound as the flames stretch insidious, angry fingers, clawing at the benches, the altar, the hems of my sisters' robes. Old, loam-encrusted velvet is indeed rank as it incinerates. Thick smoke fills the room. Everyone who as yet draws a living breath is now coughing, gasping, seeking air.

Not I.

Screams dissipate, and then, more horrifically, silence follows. I can tell, the chamber is awash in a toxic fog. Acrid, putrid, it singes the lungs of the few who are yet alive, who are still fighting – ever more failingly – for their own lives. The predators who dared journey out to the ruins to breach our secret quarters with full intention to eradicate us are now likewise ensnared. They, we, are *all* trapped.

Before the last of the attackers succumbs, he grabs at the necklace around my neck. Silly fool, greedy to the last. My dear, lost sisters, dead and unrevivable corpses, litter the floor around me. Neither he nor they will have any use for those gemstones. The rubies, they fall loose to the floor. Some bounce and scatter; some stick where they fall, like bugs afloat in a crimson amber, for the pools of blood have grown thick as tar in the intense heat. The rubies may as well be gravel.

Perhaps, someday, this site will be discovered, and then excavated. Perhaps, someday, these bejeweled remnants will delight their finder, and be taken to some jeweler to be fabricated into something wearable, something to adorn the slender throat of an ignorant, willow-necked other, where they will hang and sparkle beautifully, benignly. It is almost nice to imagine that. . .

But right now, they are merely talisman of the bloodshed of this night. One faceted droplet representing each fallen member of our coven, a coven which has been effectively eradicated. For now.

And I? I will soon join the newly deceased. There is nowhere left for me to go. I must resign myself to dying the ordinary death of an ordinary human. I am fading. Annihilation unbound, they won. This time.

The force of the necklace being ripped from my neck nearly pulled me off the bier. My head, arms and torso hang inverted; my splayed arms brace my body like the spindling legs of a painter's easel. My lower half still spans the upholstered bed, although now it does so in a most unceremonious, hideously awkward fashion. To think, minutes ago, I was on the cusp of a momentous ethereal shift, about cleave, fully sentient, from the mummified remains on this bed. My elegant, sad corpse. . .

But now, as I lie ungracefully askew, and with my inverted view across the floor, I can see there are no options. There is no way out. I have met with a truly dead end. Riotously lit in a fiery dervish of oranges, blues, yellows and black, our demise flails about the ceremonial chamber like some maniac fire dancer, hired to slit our throats and then torch us, one and all. This place has become nothing more than a subterranean crematorium.

One young woman, the last initiate welcomed into our fold no less, crawls towards me, calls my name with what is left of her voice, as if there were something I could yet do for her, for us.

In that moment, the constellation bedecked timber in the ceiling coffers bursts into flames. The ceiling collapses from the heat, burying the young woman whose outstretched hand almost touches mine.

My silken sheathing is next. It ignites, becomes a kindling cocoon. It curls at the edges, which sparkle momentarily. And then, all of a sudden, I too burst into flames. As I am by the elements consumed, the last things I see are the feathering whisps of light as they seep from the bandages at my wrists. They are the dregs of a spirit making a one last, futile attempt to disengage itself from the burning remains of an old woman who still does not want to let go.

Soon, I am nothing more than at one with mere ashes. Before my mourning can even begin, it's over.

†††††

Joined With the Seas

When the sun breaks the plain of the ocean, I must die.

He gave me only one choice: Walk the plank or be hanged.

I, in my ridiculous fancy, have chosen to walk, for it will be of my own volition, and once joined with the seas, what happens next, whilst the outcome is likely, remains to be seen.

Which means, there is a chance.

The rhythmic push of the waves against the boat keeps time, the clang of the ropes against masts keeps time; the thud of the sails, thrust forward, sucked back as the winds inhale, exhale, keeps time. Every limb of this vessel, her wrists, her arms, her ankles, her knees, creaks, and bends with the coax of the tidal pulse. Every sound, each gentle lurch keeps time. . .

The captain's own clock, a wondrous ebony contraption, commands us from its mantle perch. How ironic, whilst the elite lounge in their berths, raise their glasses again and again, they are but an arm's reach from their designated damned, we who languish beneath the very boards upon which they stumble and dance. . .

My hands, long numb from the iron bands. . . My skin, it's just gone. I wear bracelets embedded so deep in my flesh, the muscle, and tendons, dried and bloodless, have curled up around the metal, as if to engulf them – such deviously symbiont replacement joints. So little else is left of the corporeal me. I feel, my spirit barely fills this jaundiced satchel, under which bone and viscera lie asleep, suspended, dead weighted. Weakly tethered to my torn body, I know a part of me is ready to let go of the silver strings which, ever more failingly, bind me to it. I hang in limbo, a sad puppet. To be executed seems almost redundant.

Food? No food. And when did my lips last know the kiss of a blessed drop of water?

There it is! The captain's clock chimes: One, two, three, four, five times. The bell reverberates, lonesome in its somber pitch and tone. In minutes, I know, the first hint of sunrise will announce the day and this final night will be ended.

I sit, and I sit.

The rhythmic push of the waves against the boat keeps time, the clang of the ropes against the masts keeps time; the thud of the sails, thrust forward, sucked back, keeps time. . .

I sit, and I sit.

And there! The captain's clock chimes one, two, three, four times. The bell reverberates, lonesome in its somber pitch and tone. . .

But this makes no sense. Am I imagining the count? Had I imagined that of the previous hour?

One hour ago, my execution was imminent. One hour ago, the sun hovered in the wings, ready to take the stage as luminous, useless bystander. But now? Everyone around me still sleeps. There are no witnesses, no one to ask, no one to count, as I do. . .

I will stay quiet.

The rhythmic push of the waves against the boat keeps time, the clang of the ropes against masts keeps time, the thud of the sails keeps time, thrust forward, sucked back. The winds ebb and flow, echo their sibling tides. . .

I sit, and I sit.

And there! The captain's clock chimes once, twice, three times. The bell reverberates, lonesome in its somber pitch and tone.

Oh, God, what is happening here? Why now is it three in the morning when a few minutes ago I know the clock chimed its pre-dawn last?

Mother in heaven, answer me! Has time come to a standstill? Has she reversed herself?

I look down at my shackles. Grown enormous, they are the size of small iron wheels. I lower my arms, hold my hands slack, and the rings slip off, fall to the floor. I step out of cruel bands that have ground at my ankles for weeks. I can barely stand upright. I have not stood on my own for days. I venture a step to the left. . .

The rhythmic push of the waves against the boat keeps time, the clang of the ropes against masts keeps time, the thud of the sails, thrust forward, sucked back, keeps time. Time. . .

Time?

I look all around me. There is nowhere to go but up. The ladder. Try the hatch. . .

And there! The captain's clock chimes once, twice. . . And stops. The bell reverberates, wanes. . .

Something has turned the tides, is afoot, and I alone bear witness to it, aware of some metaphysical reversal that offers up no explanation. . .

The skies. I can now see them above me, beckoning through jagged splits between the hatch's cover.

Dear Savior, guide me now through this spell of unyielding lunacy. What am I to do? There are no waking souls. This galleon, the deck, are devoid of humanity. The only signs of life are that of the ship's as she responds to the prompts from the waters, the winds. . .

The boat keeps time. . .

I wander stealthily amongst coiled ropes, barrels, salt-encrusted rigging. As far as I can see, no land in sight. Only endless, sleeping seas surround this ship, surround me. . .

And there! The captain's clock chimes once. One time only. The bell reverberates. . .

Do I stand here a free woman? Alive?

Lord, am I still alive?

Or am I already dead, taking my first steps towards eternity? Will a light reveal itself to me to show me where to tread?

Am I a ghost, the others momentarily suspended, my walk across this deck lasting but a handful of seconds in the time-space of mortals? Where there still resides a sun that will indeed rise above the distant cusp of the ocean? Where the captain and his crew will awaken, and their guards will descend into the cargo hold for me and find nothing but my stiffening corpse, a ragged urchin trussed in their bracelets, blood encrusted, foul edges curled with decay, soiled scraps, nit paved, open sores matted?

Yes! Let it be me as I now stand, a spirit making her way to God's heaven, and pray, some light arrives to illuminate my way, perhaps lent by the Christ child itself, to aid this wayward pilgrim's progress to the next realm.

But where do I go from here?

Aha! A small light flickers on the gangway before me, its skipping cadence catching my eye. It bids me, Follow. Is it real? Such a beautiful insanity! No, I will not question this now. No explanation, proof, or courage are needed. I have nothing to lose. . .

Nothing. . .

Sky-borne trinket, wait for me! Yes, I will follow you! You are a bearer of hope, a lantern for my soul, dear firefly. Take me from this tortured captivity!

Slow down, my angel! I come!

I can barely walk, but I grab what I can, pull my broken form forward. You, silently shimmering, my molten and glowing guide – I will grab you and hold you to my breast. I am yours; are you mine?

No! The captain's clock now chimes the hour that heralds the day's turn! One, two, three, four, five and six! Seven, eight and nine. Ten, yes, and eleven and then twelve; all as present and predictable as they are stalwart, duly counted, oddly accounted. Have we been hurled backwards to yesterday, or thrown forward to tomorrow?

The bell reverberates, its somber pitch and tone wavers, fades. . .

And yet, here I stand as all others remain cradled within its hypnotic, somnambulant call.

Yes, I am alive! My Lord, I am still alive!

Beloved lumiere, I take these last steps to reach you, my fingertips but a whisper of a wish distant from your pulsating, playing, flickering, laughing self. . .

You laugh!

You laugh.

You laugh?

And look. . . I have taken one step too many.

I fall.

The seas engulf me, the weight of my skeleton too much for the wasted and threadbare casing that barely keeps these limbs contained, one frail piece linked to another.

I sink beneath the surface, the stars by churning water are quickly erased. Your light remains, however, atop the foam of my stolen, last breath.

That laugh. . .

I remember now.

They warned me about you, but from the chaos, amidst the fog of my decrepit state and all their drunken, slipshod, and violent preening, I forgot about you.

Oh yes, they warned me. Behind that sugarplum façade, you, tiny demon, are more truly colored, by shades of a deadly jealousy that has so far evaded all capture, all correction.

Reptilian and humanoid monsters are but kept creatures, oversize henchmen who do your dirty work. I get it.

So, as one would expect, before I am a full fathom submerged, teeth the size of carving knives pierce my thigh. The soft flesh of a hot tongue tastes of me, presses against skin so freshly shredded, it flutters like strips of fabric. My left leg is twisted and pulled off in the way a licorice whip is rent. Blood – mine – warms the water around me as it bursts forth, pulse by pulse by withering pulse, a sash of red meandering skyward to the underside of the ocean's looking glass table. In the liquified moonlight, it is a stain quickly dissipated. The suspended diamond of you is recast a soft rose, like that of a conch, likewise torn from its once perfect, porcelain housing.

Hovering, sparkling, callous, indifferent you.

Tick. . . Tick. . .

I less hear that infernal metronome as now feel it, my right leg pulled into the beast's belly as it swallows and I am drawn down, and in. My foot brushes against a small, hard form. It strikes at me, keeping time, tap-tap-tapping against me. Insistent, Insidious. The rest of me arrives.

Damn you.

†††††

With gratitude to J.M. Barre, for the doors he flung open wide by way of all the lore and symbolism he pulled together in the crafting of Peter Pan.

Second star to the right, straight until morning, indeed. . .

Penchants of the Prize

How is it they call it?

"Belle of the ball" . . .

. . . oh yes, indeed. She is that. . .

Just look at her. *My* handiwork. Resplendent – plucked plumb from the jewel caskets of Aphrodite herself. What was once *merely* a set of deep blue and winsome eyes are now soulful, inviting lagoons, positively a-shimmer with *all* the crystalline watercolors of a paradisiacal cove. Her mesmerizing gaze holds one and all – most especially him – in her thrall. Cerulean, azure, cornflower blue, as if with diamonds besprinkled, lashes fluttering like beckoning butterflies. One look from her is all one – especially he – will need to want most desperately to know her. Better, deeper, longer. . .

Are they not the welcoming windows to the soul? Then, to what secret chambers might they usher one in? There is no rose window in any cathedral that could compete! So vibrantly full of promise, luminous in their clarity, aglow with a suggestiveness fathoms deep. . .

I knew what I was doing.

Enwrapped in all things benign, cloaked in fabrications wreaking of good intent, I wrought as *I* ultimately desired. Three wishes, you pretty fool; dreams come true, hocus pocus, and so on. . .

And lo! I see her now, my work at work, tapping *her* enchantments, much as any thirsty servant girl ought, merging her freshly gifted, corporal delights with that ever-present sense of duty of hers, all that bountiful virtue in which she is steeped like a fizzling Christmas pudding. All that goodness, that kindness, all that stalwart steadfastness, so tidily housed in one persona, noble and yet diminutive, with that sweetness, which positively drips from her fingertips, so naturally and so easily embodied from little girl on. . .

It makes the one retch just to dwell upon such as that. . .

Oh, I remember. Too well. And what a thorn in *some* sides that always proved to be. How easy it was to envy, and to take that envy and warp it, re-wrap it into a wellspring of hatred, to allow for spiteful manipulations to be fomented, and then to let them ferment into the stuff of truly poisonous ideation. . .

How easy it became to take joy in inverting all she represented, all she did for them, for us, for me. It was nothing to destroy the finely stitched embroideries, to tear all those buttons and hooks from their meticulously threaded housings, to topple baskets of sorted grains, track mud and offal and worse yet from the barnyard onto laboriously scrubbed marble hallways and countless, carpeted stairs. To torment the vermin she for some pathetic reason saw fit to care for. . .

How horrid must someone be, for pity's sake, to keep trying to break those threads of deeds done so stupidly well and with such good intention?

But no. Ramrod straight she would maintain her petite self as she persevered, holding up so bravely and back those slender shoulders of hers, keeping that winsome chin aloft, and her forehead as smooth and untroubled as a dove's egg, nestled beneath the breast of its equally innocent parent. . .

So admirable, it would make the worst of *them* want to vomit. Crumpets and cookies and clotted cream all over everything. Anything to disrupt the delicately divine palatability she fundamentally personified. Indeed, soil the dressing gowns and ruin every ironed tablecloth in retaliatory disgust over her even more disgusting perfection. . . That was the base mortal's method of retaliation. *My* method.

But look at her now! Revenge is her sweet sauce, gently served. For the moment, it is bestowed upon others with a warm panache and *so terribly much* grace. She is now the trussed swan which I yes, I helped put out in all her glorious potential, divinely manifested as part of something too dark for her to see for what it truly is. For, I am not merely her subordinate, some adjunct family member; *I* am the sly silversmith, the godmotherly enchantress who carved out for her the very pulpit of seduction from which she can now preach her own, peculiar, little gospel.

Behold – her innate majesty verily spirits her through the labyrinthian galleries, without any iota of fear or hesitation, and down the massive flights of steps as if upon wings transported, with only the crisp rustle of a just-conjured gown to remind anyone in earshot, she is yet but a kitchen wench in disguise, a mere mortal but unsullied as maiden, now dressed and coiffed in ridiculous fashion for the very first time in her life.

Delighted gasps and even reluctant sighs of admiration are triggered by her descent into the gilded and mirrored arena where the rest of the guests now, in comparison, appear no more comely or refined than the very cattle and sheep she fed in the barn a few, short hours ago. . .

This is an angel among women, here to join in – albeit temporarily, until the stroke of midnight – with the rabble, the rest of *them*, me, us, who were called upon as revelers in this performance of merriment, what the invitation simply called "The Prince's Ball," which we all know, was intended as nothing more than a means by which to lure from their country manors, their townhouses, and cottages, the "best" the kingdom had to offer for *him*. For his pleasure, his taking. *The* Prince.

For the princely One to choose another as one would the finest apple in a bushel; the ripest, juiciest, sweetest one of all, a plump and blushing something or other into which his teeth could be sunk. With gusto. A bride. His bride. Queen, someday, I suppose. And once bitten, partaken of, *all* his. His! Possessed until death or some such thing might them part. . .

And look at him, already smitten! He sees no other! The bewitchment not only works, it explodes like fireworks over all our heads, so powerful is the emotional combustion. Magical showers of sparks burst forth from the aura that envelopes them. For those of us who can *see*, it is as if the chandeliers themselves are shattering and raining brilliant shards down upon them. Rainbowed phoenixes small as sparrows dart and twirl, fall to the floor around them, land upon the folds of her tiered skirts, are caught in the wayward curls of her hair as she is spun about like a top, a ballerina marionette. She. . . she is positively *awash* in a pulsating nimbus of her own! Seekers of another kind might think she were the Madonna herself, come to bless us with her hallowed presence. But no. She's just a girl. Who might well be deluded into *thinking* herself one of the fortunate ones.

Oh, goodness, look at him. He has fallen to his knees in front of the entire crowd.

To *her*. . .

His legs have actually given way, so moved is he, so struck is he by the tsunami-like force of his new-found passion. His face he unashamedly buries in her skirt. Is it love, or already her True North pulling him into her divinity until he suffocates and is absorbed, wholly assimilated by her?

Dear me, it almost seems as if he is genuflecting at her feet. . .

Thankfully, she helps him up, the mere glance of her fingertips on his epaulet causing him to rise, as if foisted to his feet by a contingency of invisible cherubs. What strings does *she* maneuver with the feminine power of promise she so obviously holds over him?

They are already enraptured. The room, to them, is now otherwise empty.

No one else matters. The orchestra, up there in the balcony, sits in silence, observing, witnessing, their collective breath held. . .

At last, the concert master comes to, shakes himself from his reverie. He lifts his violin to his trembling chin, fingertips a-quiver with the shared emotion of all those captivated ones. He strikes his bow upon the strings. A thread of melody begins to wend its way down to the dance floor, like a serpentine ribbon falling earthward, swaying to the metronome of a thousand hearts beating as one. It weaves amongst the throngs, seeks out the pair, wraps itself lightly around the two, around their clasped hands, their waists, and then proceeds to unwind – slowly, gently turning, unraveling them, discombobulating the couple. The faceless, irrelevant humanity in the ballroom gravitate back and away from the couple, as if swept to the side by some cosmic broom held by none other than Amore's manservant, Eros himself.

Give the lovers room. It is an interlude and permitted. Part of the plan.

Languidly, the scenario eases back to life. Couples dance around the Prince and his fresh-fallen angel. The berm of space they are afforded has the aural gravitas of a sun; it renders of all the nobles, merchants, and their wives and daughters cloddish pebbles fit only to skip across some endless lake before they sink to oblivion. Like the planets, they circle back to their suns. They cannot help it. Subordinate humanity held captive by pristine twin stars at the center of a very small, very intimate universe.

Far too soon, far too soon, the old clock in its tower strikes the hour.

That hour.

And off she dashes.

And off he goes in pursuit of his pretty, little beloved.

†††

Oh, I suspect you know the rest of the story:

Toes were wrapped until the bones cracked, the Golden Lotus being but a starting point.

Heels were far more efficiently carved off, some with the very butcher knives *she* had so diligently kept honed to a razor-sharpness.

But still, nothing fit that damn shoe.

But for her small foot. That impossibly dainty and slender and perfect fairy foot of hers.

And when he finally found her, as they, we, I watched the Prince gather his ethereal quarry back into his arms for a welcome home my dearest darling kiss which all but melted the very buckles off his soldiers' cracked leather boots, we, they, I stepped back in obeisance and utter humility in the face of a reunion so momentous, we knew – even as the scene played out – it was most assuredly one for the ages.

The Prince, as you also well know, *did* find his immaculate bride. And when lost to him but for a brief and tortuous space in time, he searched as one obsessed until he found her again. His purposeful intent paid off. His purposeful and dark and decrepit intent paid off.

As did mine.

So then, I in my conjurious capacity, and with all heretofore feminine trappings cast to the winds, set out to follow the two (though in hideous and secret form enshrouded), as the royal carriage whisked them off to their proverbial heaven, his mountain-crested castle in the clouds. And I? I perched on the balcony railing long past dusk, a most patient bird of prey, cloaked by the rolling, wet fog, until he at long, long, and endless last took his newly wedded, beloved best to his – now their – vast and splendid marital bed.

. . . until he lay her supine onto its blanketed expanse, there in that tower abode, with its broad canopy two-stories high, thickly curtained and tassel-festooned, upon a dais as grand as any opera house stage, with fires roaring nearby like a pride of lions howling from the depths of the ancient stone hearth, with what had to be a hundred candles quivering in anticipation of what was to come. . .

Black candles.

And the coverlet? A richly brocaded one, of scarlet. No, not the cheery red of a sun-ripened tomato; more that of an old wine stain, or a guillotine's sad spillage. Nor were there any carved smiles cast down from above, but bared fangs that leered from lurid, little faces carved into the four mahogany bedposts, each one as ponderous as the pillar of an ancient, pagan temple portico.

†††

The bear's pelt, draped across the foot of the bed onto which he has just thrown her, is still pliant. It is blood-stained, putridly aromatic of rotting foliage from a recently endured hunt, of an efficiently handed, fear-imbued death. She – oh my, yes, look at her now! – she is sprawled upon a playing field ripe with the stench of murderous folly, of last and fatal battles, futilely fought. . .

The angelic bride gasps as the Prince grabs her wrists. Her whimpering cries, they drift off into nothing, into the shadowed recesses of the tower room, the pithy yowls of a cornered critter. If even heard by her husband, they are wholly unheeded – I would venture, if anything, they strike heat in his loins, like flints against the stone-carved groin of some ancient statue. Her wails trickle off to silence, settle with the dust, add to the froth of matted cobwebs which frame the scene that unfolds as I hold my breath in anticipation of what comes next.

Preening child – I spit on you!

I watch as the Prince deftly binds her arms and legs – hard and fast – and splays her like some long-legged rodent. The hoary rope he uses, crude and cutting, is excessively thick. It could ensnare a raging bull. . .

And when her eyes, those azure and cornflower blue windows to that disgustingly immaculate soul of hers, are torn open wide with terror when she spies the whip, and then the branding iron in his other hand. . .

. . . then I know my work is done. My deed is accomplished.

Pretty bitch. Damn her, and damn all that ridiculous loveliness she possesses, which always and unfailingly has so sweetly charmed and enticed. What always "*wins.*"

'twas my good fortune, you see, to know the princely penchants of "the Prize," for I myself have tarried in a bedchamber or two like that. . .

I flex my leather-clad wings and leap from the windowsill. I cannot wait to get back home to tell my sister.

†††††

Postmortem Symbiosis

There they are again, with their hateful, little faces pressed against the windows, eyes set aglow by the light of what were once lanterns, later on flashlights, more recently cellphones. They with their piggish, glass-flattened noses, flared nostrils turned up at me in grotesque distortion as they try their best to peer past the mold, the filth, past dust-laden cobwebs thick as yarn, daring themselves to cross the threshold yet again to invade this innocent edifice, this house, the only home I have ever known. Beasts one and all, they are driven by morbid curiosity and their horrible, ritualistic intentions, and to prove to their cohorts, this place truly is, as has been said, *haunted.*

They are here to take a little more from what is left of me, to plunder yet another scrap to stoke their stupid superstitions and power ideations, further scratch the surface of some rudimentary paranormalism they in their ignorance presume they can harvest for their own use.

†††

I wander, adrift in the stilled pools that are the rooms of a once grand estate to which I am consigned, supernaturally decreed like the countless other, lost souls who remain statically glued to the places where they were violently separated from their earthly housings, though few can lay claim to the brutality I was made to endure – a dubious honor, to say the least. You see, what was torn from me became the intricate, plasmic fretwork that holds me here, holds me "together." My body, he tossed like refuse into its cellar crypt, my spirit already having been broken into a thousand pieces. The floors, the walls, the staircases that link every last room of this house are now connected to me, just as I am connected to them. A skeletal scaffolding, it is all I require. Ours is a postmortem symbiosis. And, while it is not any sort of a heaven, it is neither a hell – and that is good enough for me.

I did, after all, let him in, conspire with him; yes, kill with him.

Oh, I fell for him, fell for what he said, how he said it. His voice, the way he touched me, how he held me close when he whispered his diatribes late into the night, indoctrinating me into his mindset – words so callous, which yet played like warm silk against my flushed neck. Such caustic, little kisses. He planted sordid strategies with such ease – 'twas a damning desire that bonded us. How I let myself become entrenched with his wicked inclinations, was, in retrospect, quite telling as to my own, living predilection for rot. What I at first mistook for enigmatic, I later recognized as a seductive potion to which I was addicted even before his first, dulcet *hello*.

Thusly empowered, I readily espoused the audacity to presume I alone had sole right to everything – the money, the house, the legacies of comfort my ancestors had carved out of their hard-won existences. When, on that final night, we buried the last of them in the field out back, and, once back inside, I naively assumed his impassioned embrace was in celebration, to mark a new beginning for just the two of us, how fooled was I!

He? Ah, well, turns out, his fate was as easily sealed as was mine, for I had already spawned my own plan.

I watched my ruse play out, albeit through thick, bloodied veils of my own agony, from the withering plains onto which he had just then violently thrown me. I watched, albeit through bitter, crimson tears, as he dashed the last of the poisoned wine I had poured for him mere hours ago. I watched as he choked, sputtered, foamed at the mouth, cried out in agony. I saw him collapse to the floor, writhing as if one possessed. I then saw, could practically hear, the slithering shades seep out from between the floorboards, up from beneath the foundations of the house itself, as they surrounded him like a nest of enraged vipers, set upon revenge for a dormant slumber so disturbed. I watched as his still-warm carcass was torn to ribbons, remained passive and observant as the rats were next called forth to consume what was left of him, bloodied bits and pieces macerating in their own sludge. The prurient mass rendered from my evil beloved was gone in a matter of minutes.

I then watched as his soul was sucked into the very mouth of the devil himself.

That tongue. Those teeth.

But I, as both unwitting victim and malevolent accomplice, found myself simply left behind, in the dead-calm aftermath of his hell-bent demise. As marginally relevant in death as I had been in life, I had already known the hurt of being sidelined. At first, it had been by a cadre of uncaring relatives I had dutifully persisted in calling my family; later on, it was by the hand of a killer who had duped me into an assumption of deep connectivity by cunningly posturing as my suitor. Now, as I lay there dying myself, I was even ignored by the very entities sent to assess and dispose of the evil that had so recently lurked and thrived. As they swept through the house in search of any remaining, sin-ridden detritus, they saw fit, evidently, to leave what little was left of me behind.

As neither demons nor angels wished me into their company, I could do little else but wander this house. It was and remains is my first circle. I reside in limbo, entrapped in a lethargic subsistence relegated to the most woefully, stagnantly deceased. Sometimes, I try to pretend I am a deep-sea diver, and that these lifeless rooms are the chambers of some sunken ship, with me on the brink of some kind of discovery; but the fantasy is quickly squelched by the utter and absolute familiarity which greets me at every turn. Dull repetition is the manifestation of my purgatory. My misfortunes, and a comatose imagination; they are my inheritance.

There is the deep closet off the vestibule, where disembodied coats and top hats still reside. There is the parlor, dressed in threadbare velvets and lengths of matted fringe. There is the vast kitchen and its adjoining pantry, its cupboards bare, shelves lined with a smattering of trash. There is the small room just off the upstairs landing, where a dilapidated box that was once a doll's house is carpeted with a mortar of splinters and rat excrement, and old mouse traps rusted to pieces, which even the vermin see fit to avoid. Down the hall, that was my bedroom in life. Oh, the longing with which I regard that collapsed canopy, those stained mattresses!

Enfiladed rooms, hallways, and odd, shadowed crannies are my avenues, the decaying and evermore barren markers along my compulsory path. There is no place for repose. Back downstairs, I traverse the dining room, with stained-glass windows so beleaguered with dirt and dried tangles of vines, their bejeweled panels barely manage a peppering of browns and dirty greens upon the cracked marble floor. I retrace my route, room to room to room, slow passageways which like vining tendrils wind up and around, trailing here, trailing there, circling back around, leaving me no choice but to do it all over again. . .

Most days there is nothing but the rustle of the insect populations, with whom discourse is not of words, but barely discernable patterns of sound, understandable by no one and nothing. We exist parallel, like toddlers at play, who have yet to expand their ken to the next ones over. They do their lives; I did mine. I do this now, too.

†††

But there they are – again! Their hideous countenances rise up from the windowsills as invasive as were they a gang of trolls, clambering up a riverbank, fueled by primitive malintent. How can it have come to this day again? My sensibilities are already so warped, the interminable nights seem only to overlap with what seem to be endlessly overcast days. I find myself with a decade having passed as were it a fortnight; for here, this next batch stands, again, just outside my world, enticed by the same heartless greed of their forebears. They exude an acrid bravado – lamentably familiar – a terror-imbued obstinance which seeps from every pore.

Once again, it has come to this moment, where the only way to make them all go away is this:

I listen for the lock being struck down from its housing. The doorknob creaks and turns as the heavy front door is eased open. They enter in silence, stinking of fear. It is now for me to lead this loathsome passel of intruders to my own, vile plundering. I pace myself, wending my way around the corner, bidding them on with the slightest wavering of energies – little more than, say, the reluctant flame of a small candle, furtively lit. Their dirty boots land heavy, sending shockwaves across the floors, through me. Could the house but feel, it would protest the nauseating disturbance of yet another batch of cloddish humanity, much as how what was once my gut would recoil.

I come to a tight turn in the back hall. It is here, where he first struck me with his hammer. The flash of its forged head coming at me still explodes across my mind whenever I cross this particular patch of space in time. It casts forth an image, carried within a cold puff of air that hits each one of them back there in the chest. They gasp but speak not a single word. One chokes, coughs self-consciously. Hard gazes, the motley assemblage exchanges furtively, assuming I cannot see behind me. They are perversely relishing the notion of having just witnessed one of the horrors I endured.

Through the locked door to the basement, I pass with ease. They, however, must fight the next, heftier latch, and a door whose swollen panels are ever more tightly wrenched into a doorframe that is more warped with each passing year. For me, this process of filtering passage is a little easier than is the re-visiting of my memory-laden, final hour, which lies as yet before me. I can already hear the echoing gong in my head when the hammer split my skull, taste the acid tang of the blood that coursed down the back of my throat. I am accursed to relive all this as part of their dark quest. Damn them, for desiring this, "needing" this.

They, in turn, "see" my re-envisioning in the form of a ball of emotion, projected like some tangled, abstracted event into their awareness. They serve as witness – what a lecherous audience – as have others, to my execution at the top of the steps. This is no haunting of a house, per se, but the aural half-life of my demise, triggered by their presence, playing itself out, for them. I marvel each time at their willingness to undergo the process. Lucky ones, indeed, are they who in their spiritual journeys are only visited by radiant and benevolent Madonnas. For many others – aye, for this group – the vision is more like this, provided the impact of the impression manifests fully to their minds' eyes: what apparition they will behold is that of a bludgeoned maiden, begging for mercy, drenched in her own blood.

The steps leading to the cellar are spotted. A slightly randomized path of thick, crusted droplets, black as India ink, guides us all downstairs. This obscenely obvious trail of crumbs leads the entourage through the brick-and-mortar labyrinth in which I was forced to find final purchase. I turn once, for effect, to glance back. They follow, hesitant but tight in my wake.

The pavers on the south wall were but a makeshift stone curtain, a marginal attempt he made to disguise the alcove in which he buried me on that night when I had so foolishly presumed, we *together* had prevailed. The walls reverberate still with the slowing cadence of my heart, are dampened by my dwindling sobs, chilled by my wilting breath. And they – they can still hear me, see me, die in this space.

They know what to do. The barricade is easily dismantled, the stones are stacked.

And there I lie. Already bereft of my left hand, my two feet. A withered and blackened, mummified corpse, my hair a shock of greyed netting.

They set about their task; I even pull aside the cobwebs as best as I can, mustering all the ectoplasmic materialization my being can rustle up from the endlessly deadened universe in which I remain so forlornly afloat. I wince as one of them takes out a small saw and sets about to sever the one remaining hand my parched form can yet claim as its own. If I could cry, I suppose I would. But I can't, so I don't. This incapacity for expression is a void as profound as is the inability to feel pain. It is, to me, the organic essence of death.

Charred threads, ligaments, and a slender bone snap and shed dust as they are rent from their armature. The hand drops to the ground. A fingernail breaks free, skips to a stop.

I then lift and carry with every ounce of my spectral sentience my defilement, my offering, back up the staircase. To their eyes, the hand floats slowly up, up, towards the wane light emanating from the doorway at the first-floor landing. The hand looks rather like a mud-stiffened, small glove, tied to an invisible string, hobbling, suspended. Lamentable relic.

The small group hurries past my shadow, cowers in the vestibule. They are both overwhelmed and intoxicated with a sour mix that is equal parts fear and fascination. It is a singular sensation, one of both loss and empowerment for having endured the emergence of an apparition, for having called it forth in the first place.

I drop the hand. It falls at their feet. The thumb breaks off at the joint, lies there in pieces.

The tall one, he retrieves the hand with the aid of a handkerchief he has extracted from the back pocket of his trousers. Yes, shield your unsullied selves, lest you infect yourselves with my dregs. He next retrieves the thumb, wraps the pieces into a square of crumpled wax paper he has brought with him for this express purpose.

They now have what they came for.

This happens but once in a generation.

I don't know what they think they are keeping at bay, what they imagine their hocus pocus with my effigial remains puts to bed, stills, or appeases. But I don't care. If I could feel anything at all, it would hint at a semblance of relief. I know from unfortunate experience, that for the next fifteen, perhaps twenty years, I will be able to travel this place unencumbered and undisturbed. In other words, in what the ignorant call "eternal" peace.

The group exits the house. I see to it that the front door slams shut behind them. It is not that difficult to ignore their hateful little faces at the windows as they peer back inside for one last look, hoping to watch me disappear, see me as I retreat to the much welcomed and oh, so familiar edge of my very own tenebrous horizon. As I fade from their view, I can feel myself sinking. It is a slow and comforting spiral. I swim towards the uninhabited dark matter from which I can take the closest thing to comfort I am permitted. If I had yet a heart, it would be warmed.

The house goes dark. They go home.

†††††

Book of Lucombe

2 And it came to pass in those days, that there was born a child onto the immortal Thetarus, Lord of the Uhrwald, and his consort, the Dryad Kherass
2 (And this daughter came upon the anguished passing of her brothers before her)
3 And all went forth in time was decreed by custom and the terrestrial turning of the years.
4 And the god and his wife and the maiden child were made to journey to the Ghaalyan temples to worship and make payment of sacrifice onto the ancestral Lords of the Uhrwaldian Deep in the great city Ghaalynopranthis (because he was of the house and lineage of Ghaalya)
5 To be counted amongst the forebears of the Uhr and in turn to worship and serve.
6 And so it was, the virgin daughter Daphnae was consigned to the temple to reside until her time in chaste servitude in convenance to those who had come before her.
7 And it so happened, born of ethereal countenance and lyrical form did the maiden Daphnae capture the eye and thereupon the heart and mind of the Captain of the Pranthian Army, who laid immediate and predatory claim to the vestal daughter by both decree and broad threat to any living soul, immortal or no, who dare pry self or sword betwixt the Captain and his virginal intended.
8 And there were in the same hills and dells countless armies of silent laurels lindens and maples whose foliage widespread granted shadowed crevice and shrouded hollow in which the maiden Daphnae could in secret assign both body and spirit into their safe harbour to be spared from the beastious intentions of the unscrupulous Captain.

9 And, lo, the Captain in his command bade his own men to the task, to track every footstep and to map each path upon which the fair maiden did travel, for to render escape futile in all measure, there to make instead from her flight that which did naught but guide the Captain with great ease into her midst: and she was sore afraid.
10 And the leaves of the forests unfurled in chorus and spoke unto her, Fear not: for, behold, we bring you enigmatic resolution from unrelenting pursuit, which shall be for all time.
11 For unto you is bequeathed this day a gift of heavenly commutation onto you, arisen from the divinely rooted forebears which subsist beneath all feet of Man which shall transform and fulfill you as has been foretold in the languages of the trees. A metamorphosis shall be bestowed to render within thine own self your ultimate salvation.
12 And this shall be a sign unto you; Ye shall find a solitary Quercus in the heart of our realm, standing in length and breadth above all others.
13 And suddenly there was amidst the forests a multitude of heavenly stars fallen from the skies and held aloft amidst ten thousand bracing limbs and the sky was at one with the woods and the voices sang in unison,
14 Glory to you, dearest goddess, look not towards yon strident pursuer but to the steadfast reign of the Quercus.
15 And it came to pass, as the celestine chorus was again receded into their distant constellations, and the fair Daphnae proclaimed, Let me now go unto the temple, and suffer the will of my destiny, which the gods hath made known unto me, until all is fulfilled.
16 And she went without fear and bade her mother and father farewell.
17 And when they had seen their daughter afire with quest dearly held, they made known abroad the tidings which were told them concerning this child.
18 And all who had heard of the Captain's lustful campaign wondered at those things which might yet come to pass.
19 But Daphnae kept all these things and pondered them in her heart.
20 Lo the Captain and his men once returned from their battles victorious and awash in the blood and the spoils of the ancient gods of war, heavy with conquered souls, and laden with plunder, as was beholden unto them.
21 And when eight days were accomplished for the Captain to divest himself of his station 'twas then decreed of his self same intent to pursue now a campaign of seduction, for to conquer the beauteous Daphnae, to break then to mold from the maiden a sole and forced possession.
22 And when the days of her purification according to the laws of Pranthesis were accomplished, he sought to bring her to the chambers of his own temple, to plunder now the maiden to render from her a sheath for his sword in convenance and dominion over her spirit;

23 (As it is written in the law of the gods, every male that renders the maiden asunder shall be called wholly in and of the lords of the thieves that are Man)
24 And to offer in sacrifice according to that which is said in the laws of the lords, the maidenhead safe guarded by her own gardens, or of her spirit willed, as held in her firmament.
25 And, behold, there was a spirit resided within the Quercus in the Uhrwaldian Deep, whose name was Lucombe; being of devout nature, having kept resolute vigil for the hours in which the maiden would return and come to rest upon the scaffolding of his breast.
26 And it was revealed unto him when she slept, ensconced upon his limbs and enwrapped within the harbour of his shadow, that he should see not her in mere human form and breadth, but in spiritualized manifestation, kindred kindled, soul blessed.
27 And he beheld in a vision sent by the spirits into the temple: and when the Captain sought to strike the fair Daphnae full force of broad hand, Lucombe raged where he stood, impotent rooted of place whilst the maiden was forced to solitary combat,
28 Then Lucombe held up in his thousands of arms, beseeching the gods, and he said,
29 Lords, now let now thine servant gather of conjuring thrust, according to thy words:
30 For mine eyes have seen her damnation,
31 in the face of the grave lust of one purely depraved;
32 Her light to suffer his conquest forbid, hold in its stead her sanctity intact and protected from him.
33 And the beings of light and of dark heeded well his prayers; for they as he were born of the seed, and of the stars consecrated, and they marveled at those things which were spoken by him.
34 And Lucombe was blessed by them, and when the maiden had once more fled into his embrace, he said onto Daphnae, Behold, you are set for desperate and violent downfall. Heed the signs, which shall be wrought against you;
35 (Yea, a sword shall pierce through mine own soul,) that the evil of the Captain may yet be revealed.
36 And there from the roughened tines of the bark came the form of the Lover whose branches became limbs, from whose trunk rose virile with eros intent that which in sweet agonies took from the virgin her maidenhood, thusly consecrated by act of bonded union, tendrilled intertwined, and in solace replete there encircled within the verdant embrace of what was now become man and his woman, joined and known both by pilgrim and supplicant in absolute consummation;

37 And with the dawn birthed fresh light upon the mossy floor to there reveal as rested the supine maiden newly born of woman as one satiated replete and bride of the Uhrwaldian Deep.
38 And she in that instant gave thanks likewise unto him above all lords, and spake to all of allegiance evermore for whom she now held out as of her heart and body, at one with Lucombe.
39 And when the lovers bade farewell, they performed all things according to the laws of the Lords of the Uhrwald, she returning into Ghaalinopranthis, once more to the Ghaalian temple.
40 And the demands of the Captain grew violent, and when he attempted to take for his own the espoused Daphnae, the smoldering fires of all damnation rose to fill his soul, for the knowledge that the maiden was by another divested brought in him a blackened descent which would seek to implode for whom had to his ken been untrue onto him who yet hath no claim upon her but for that in which his rage dwelt.
41 Now his fury commanded he take the fair Daphnae far from any company of sympathy and witness.
42 And into the Deep Woods the Captain with his captive did return, she dragged as quarry over fields and parched riverbeds with tines of thorn and rock to tear at her skin until with blood and debris she was matted and pocked and her robe and hair flowed frayed as beaten flax.
43 And when he had executed his vengeance, he looked down upon the woman who was not to be his and, behold, he bound the woman with chains to the standing great Quercus, verily to the tree god Lucombe, who dwelt within and there to the barrel of the trunk, splayed legged to suffer, the Captain affixed her hands and her feet, heeding not the cries of his thwarted bride and declared it Good. And lo, he returned to the city to celebrate her retribution for to then return the next day, as was his intention to next cleave the head of the woman from its torso and to leave her to rot as detritus ripe fodder for the vermin of the Forest Deep.
44 But he, Lucombe once alone with his chained bride, called forth all the Verdurian forces into his command.
45 And when they answered his call, the heavenly powers set forth and bound the lovers as had been foretold and so did the metamorphosis commence to craft from the two a single corporeal convergence.
46 And it came to pass, that bark and skin broke and bled and as it bled it did meld and fuse and thus their limbs were now welded, one into the other, breasts and belly to towering trunk, limbs wrapped, arms and hands shackled now as in enveloping embrace until both were held fast by the wandering tendrils, as vine and branch took root interweaving interceding lacing stitching merging enfolding. And behold, her face and warm cheek thusly brandished and awash with the brine of one hundred tears as wax did melt and merge with the host as ten thousand spiders were called

forth into service to knit her hair and stitch her scalp and neck to his grith and then with gentlest force the whole of her face was consumed into its depths. When three more nights had passed the Captain awakened from an unbidden and formless stupor that had passed into him unknowing.
47 And he made haste as he could to dispatch of this failed bride but once arrived, all that he found shackled to the great oak Lucombe were but the shadowed remains of a womanly form so enfolded in bark as to be one with the tree and crowned but for the budding of young leaves which flourished upon her. And in keeping his vengeful promise the Captain sought to behead what was left of the maiden with his axe.
48 And in fury dealt he ten blows to the frail column that had been her neck. And ten times over he hacked until the tree was severed from its rooted foothold: and the Captain said bitterly unto them, My bride, why hast thou forced me to deal with you in this fashion? Behold, you have left me only sorrowing.
49 And he said unto them, How is it that ye sought me not? Wist ye not that I must be about my husbandly business?
50 And yea there was no living thing to understand that which he spake unto them.
51 And the Captain laid down his axe and took leave of the Uhrwald and returned to Ghaalinopranthis, and thereon dwelt amidst embittered loss: though yet he had wielded his sword all with the fatal fervor of one utterly scorned.
52 And the fair Daphnae and her Lucombe though no more of the earthen Woods but in stature and favour of all the gods rose to their eternal place amidst the constellations and from the fathomless heavens they cast their countless stars forevermore in union as one in peaceful hearkening and enduring light.

†††††

All the Peace and Quiet

Solitude beckons like an old, favorite song, lyrics very nearly forgotten but still there, right at the back edge of my memory where the melody yet lingers, where perhaps ghosts or spirits from past lives or relationships lurk, await acknowledgement, remembrance. Vague words, words, and more words are calling to me, tantalizing me. Time alone – ah, what a wonderful prospect – invites me to a meditative, creative deep dive to which no one else is permitted.

No one. Please, for once, no one.

For the space of at least a day, plus a few hours on top of that, I should have the house – the entire property – all to myself. No other living soul – no guest or agent, no editor; no repairmen or friends, not even Grayson – will be around. In any direction the house faces, there will be no one but me. This patch of time must prove to me I can still delve into the recumbent depths of my imagination, stir it to productive wakefulness from its overlong dormancy. There have been too many distractions, too much of life and business to deal with. And the move; it was a stressful and exhausting endeavor, but direly needed, gladly undertaken. So, now is finally the time to set aside the labors of my, our, migration and settle in to do what brought me, us, here. Time to end this most recent, barren phase during which my writing was by necessity backseated. Life called, love called, I answered.

Time to craft a story.

I am standing outside, at the end of the roundabout, having just said good-bye to my husband, taking a moment to enjoy the brusque air, shift my state of mind. My gaze rests on the rise of land that marks the property's northern edge, where Grayson's roadster has just dropped from sight. It is colder by the moment. I wrap my shawl, a favorite old thing, higher, tighter, around my neck. I am feeling wistful, grateful. I look up. It appears as though the heavens are going to do their part and lend some writerly atmospheric assistance, set a scenario ripe for ruminations, which should help bring forth the thousands of words I must produce, which are to comprise the next novel I have been contracted to finish before year's end.

A good, hard rain would certainly help to ensure my seclusion, keep all those wandering trespassers away. So far, most have presented themselves as nature-seeking hikers, though a few openly admitted walking the property to try and catch sight of me, the newly landed lady of the house at her recently acquired country estate. A few brazen types dared breach the front terrace last week, came knocking at the windows like rude scavengers. And just a few days ago, a particularly audacious pair dared walk around to the back of the house to skulk along the French doors that open onto the balcony for a glimpse of me. A rude bit of nerve on their parts. It had frightened me, especially as there was as yet no phone service; no telephone had ever been installed. There is one in the hall now, thank goodness, which Grayson installed just yesterday. Hopefully, it will not become a necessity, to call into town for interference. The worrisome thing about that is, it would take anyone the better part of an hour to wind their way from the village to our front door, even in good weather. . .

Those horrid tabloids. They had seen fit to rag on our move from the city, though we had shared with no one what we were doing. One paper even published the real estate listing in their article. Fodder for a lawsuit to be sure, but a legal fight would be fraught with its own, invasive hazards, especially given the unwelcome visitations we have already contended with. Success comes with myriad costs, and we have both paid plenty to date. I have paid more than my share.

I hope, things will relatively quiet. I am so dying to be alone.

Oh, look! I spy distant lightning flickering beneath a bank of clouds, far to the north, announcing the approach of what looks to be a rain-bearing locomotive barreling across the land, heading straight towards me and the house. I will witness its onslaught with quiet joy, listen in anticipation for the storm front as it advances, crosses our property and makes its way towards the ocean. I will relish the storm pummeling the rooftiles as roils overhead, onward, and then down to the haggard shoreline, as it makes of the ocean a ferociously bubbling cauldron of brackish toil 'n' trouble.

Thunder rolls smoothly across the field, eventually passing through me. It shakes the ground where I stand. I count the seconds between light and sound, satisfied to note the ever-tightening intervals. Grayson's exit, in that damn roadster of his, officially marks the start of my very first solitary sojourn at the house. May it be but the first of what I hope, pray, will be many such spells. This was, after all, why I, we, transplanted ourselves to the countryside, excised these two weary city dwellers from their chaos.

I whisper a missive into the ether, a brief petition of safe travels for Grayson, for his timely return. And I add a few words of gratitude for the inclement hours to come. I also send an appeal to my Muses, something abstracted, more emotional than anything worded, that my solitude here, in this place, will prove abundantly productive.

Bring him home, safely, soundly. And please – help me peer deep into my subconscious; let me see the story, its direction, then give me the words, the phrases, to follow, watch it play out, and then lay it all down. . .

Before going inside, I scan the countryside once more. Its vast emptiness beckons as it yet pushes me backwards, back into my proper place, my house. It is a resplendent desolation indeed. Inland, an endless sea of grassy hills stretches as far as I can see. Small, stalwart blooms dance crazily upon the heather and bracken like colored fishing bobs. Behind me, behind the house, lies the ocean, grown restless as it awaits the storm. The rush of the surf mixes with the swell of the wind, making for a cacophonous interplay. All suggests to perfection the potential for a long evening awash in a wondrous gloom. I glance back to the spot where Grayson's car disappeared, and instantly envision the roadster racing instead in the opposite direction, towards the edge of the cliff. I see his car plummeting head-first towards the crenelated ridge of boulders lining the shore. I see the car crash, burst into flames; I see his face when he realizes impact is imminent. . .

I stop myself short, shake the scene from my mind.

It causes me to smile ruefully. As I always do, I forgive myself for the moribund imagery, which has just invaded my quiet observations, tainted my appreciations. These frequent inversions of thought are as unbidden as they are luridly sinister, but I am accustomed to the fanciful workings of my mind, which Grayson graciously accommodates, often jokes about. How else should any

Gothically-inclined writer worth their salt process the ordinary everyday? Things between me and Grayson are good. I do not wish his – or anyone's – death; certainly, not consciously. . .

And there I go again. . .

Yes, you could say, things are not just good. They are really good. Of this, I am quite certain. Perhaps things are even better than before; better than *ever*.

Who's to know? For, what if. . .

Oh, I just remembered. The housekeeper! When was it she was due to arrive – tomorrow? I fish around in my jacket pockets, searching for an envelope I thought I had stashed in one of them. If memory serves, I believe she is to arrive tomorrow, around five, supper time, or thereabouts. And how was it the woman referred to herself? My *Sous-chatelaine*? That had given me cause to smile; in all likelihood, sealed the hire. Oh, I do hope this one will be able to understand, how important it will be, to simply leave me alone. The needs of a writer, this writer at least, and one with deadlines looming heavy like those clouds over there, are decidedly anti-social. If she cannot handle that, then I will find someone else. It is what it is, and how it has to be. My isolation-reliant endeavors have funded many of our travels, a big percentage of the townhouse we just sold, and more recently played a requisite role in the deal that landed us on the front stoop of this place, a house known since it was built almost three hundred years ago as The Clyffes. A house, I feel, that has been waiting for me, us, all this time.

†††

Grayson, meanwhile, absorbed in his own thoughts, has rendered the hills a verdant blur by the speed with which he jettisons through the countryside, on what he hopes will be his last trip to the city for an indefinite stretch of time. Whilst set on enjoying the drive, the final loading up of his things at the office and the handing over of the keys to the agent are tasks loaded with purposeful intent. He is eager to be done with it all and back on his way to The Clyffes, the place they would from now on call Home. High time to close shop cityside and commence on this next chapter with someone whom he had fallen for over half a lifetime ago, who he had in the last year very nearly lost. It has been a hard-won reconciliation, most especially for her, but – God and the Muses willing – they are both on the same path, one which will take them forward together, on a journey all the more solidly paved for all the memories gathered to date, and no small amount of wisdom borne of circumspection, even if bittersweet.

Grayson depresses the accelerator, making of the road a slalom course, though it remains, as it has always been, far better suited for oxcarts and bicycles than any high-powered sportscar. His quiet exuberance, paired with his dedication to the cause and resulting determination to get back home as soon as possible, makes for a faster dash across the fields than what might be prudent, were not the driver and his machine as skilled and finely tuned as they each were. . .

. . . I can just see him flying down the road, can see him taking the hills and curves at top speed, can see those old oaks, growing so close in the crooks of those hairpin turns. It would take just a split-second of distraction, an errant insect, a cough, or a sneeze, to throw the car off-kilter and send it head-on into the ungiving, rock-hard pillar of an ancient tree trunk. . .

†††

The Clyffes, our new home, is a manor house set upon a handful of Bronte-esque cliff-side acres which front the broad, southern expanse of the English Channel, where it eventually merges with the Celtic Sea. It is exactly like many of the places I have featured in my novels. Goodness knows, I have roamed its imaginary halls as a bookish young girl, lived in its fabricated spaces for decades, and always longed for "one of my own," insofar as any historic house can ever belong to any one human. The house is so perfect, when we had toured it for the very first time, I had an overwhelming feeling, this was more than a serendipitous find. It was downright uncanny, how well I knew my way around inside without *physically* ever having been there before. And the way the house was so picturesquely – which is to say precariously – perched on its knoll overlooking the seas, affords me, us, views over both land and water that I swear I have described verbatim in at least a couple of my works. Then, there is the way the house is situated on its axis, with all the main rooms facing due west, so to take in the last rays of the setting sun at the end of each day. Even if for a few, brief minutes, when the sun has sunk below the oft-present veils of clouds at the horizon, the shadowed corners of the vast rooms are set afire moments before the dark fully descends. The floors themselves take on the colors of the sunset and appear as molten pools of light. And that balcony on the backside of the house, where those fans had recently come snooping? It is a veritable a fairy castle contraption, likely added at some later time. The balcony is suspended by way of a decorative fretwork of scrolled ironwork, and appears as if to float out, far beyond the ledge of the supporting rocks beneath, a feat of clever engineering for its day. Anyone standing on the balcony to gaze out over the water, in leaning into the hard embrace of the brusque winds, can imagine themselves as if airborne, like one of the thousands of sea birds that are forever flitting about, surfing the headwinds, hovering overhead, crying out to anyone in earshot. One can just imagine reaching out, and jumping, and seeing if. . .

My house. Well, our house. No. *My* house.

The Clyffes' many rooms – I have yet to tally them all – do make for a grand, yet fanciful retreat. By way of its isolated location and citadel-like fortifications, it will hopefully also serve to better guard for us, help keep away my followers, who have of late become too insistent, too adoring. *Such is the price of fame* Grayson has reminded me time and again as my proverbial star continued its climb. Had I known notoriety would be this difficult, I am not sure I would have wished it upon myself, upon us. Things long ago became quite confusing, and we both, each in our own way, took wrong turns, got lost, only to eventually circle back. I shake my head to think of the unfortunate, singular mix that is this hard-won sense of pride I do feel, for it comes with a certain amount of regret I cannot shake. The scenarios I have envisioned, especially these past few years, of his demise, or mine, or ours, for goodness' sake . . . and the reconciliation, and oh my, how it all could still so easily go awry. . .

Wisdom and experience are not necessarily enlightening in the illustrative sense. The net cast is a darkened, if broader, set of smarts.

This first night alone out here, I must admit, is daunting. To be left so completely by myself is an intimidating prospect, even under these best of circumstances. I have conflicting emotions, based now in part on fear of there being more invasive fans to contend with. And there are fears of abandonment I still try to reconcile, intellectualize. Perhaps I should get a dog. A big one? A small one? Grayson had offered to cancel his trip to the city when I confessed my latent trepidation, but I would have none of that. I won't be like that. I reassured him on all counts of my sense of security of both place and mind. And I will keep forcing my insecurities back into the recesses of my mindset and acknowledge my reactiveness as a byproduct not only of circumstance, but also of my chronically overactive imagination. That *has* to play a major role with me. It is like words to old songs that surface unbidden – irritating earworm ditties – which I would prefer to leave unremembered, to which I will hum, anyway.

. . . that is, but for when all that might prove useful as some doom-invoking literary twist or turn in my writing. I am forever grateful for the cathartic effects my writing has held for me, and as such, will allow my unconscious self to tap my predilection, if for no other reason than for its literary usefulness.

Ah, this place! Imagined since I was a little girl; it is my castle-in-the-clouds, my fortress.

And listen! May the muses' whispers rise above the din of this storm. May these wind-swept fields carry their mystical thoughts in from afar, pipe them through the keyholes, play the house, play me, so that the songs, and all those words, come to me, come flooding in. . .

I sigh with my moribund brand of bliss, content with all as it is.

There! One thousand and one, one thousand and two, one thousand. . . The skies light up again. . . and if I stay out here long enough, I will play the lightning rod. I should like to see myself lit up, from the inside out. . . What would that be like, to survive such as that? Or, how to describe a carcass flash-fried like that?

Enough of all this! Go back inside. Build a fire in the study. Make yourself a cup of tea, have a bite. Enjoy this time alone. Things are good. Things are good. Now, go inside and get some work done.

I turn my back on both my erratic musings and the terrain, and proceed down the stairs to the sunken terrace that fronts the house. It is a rather a reverse approach, but such was the practical charm of a stately dwelling burrowed into the swell of a surf-blighted, crumbling cliffside. In this spot, it is almost wind-still. From here, past either side of the house, I can see the oceanic backdrop, reaching to horizons so distant, one could fancy seeing the rounded edge of the earth herself. The waves are an iron gray, that peculiar shade which always foretells the approach of a major rainstorm. I turn the iron latch on the door. It screeches in protest, but to me, the age-old, cantankerous inclinations of the rusted hardware give it life. I wish there were a face rather than a cabbage rose on the doorknocker. . . I let myself in. The first, fat drops begin to fall, spattering wet and loud against the pavers. I pull the door shut and turn the lock, which grinds and clangs reproachfully at me.

†††

Can this prehistoric beast go any faster? But then, what is a girl to expect from a jalopy this outdated? It is a good thing, my dear, that you are as adept as you are – you could drive a slew of quarter horses with as much aplomb! Now, if that hand-eye acumen would only translate as well into the steering and shifting of gears this old thing requires. . . And with an engine that sounds like it may have been transplanted from a cotton gin? Who knows what Uncle Orrin concocted with all that tinkering of his on this clunker. . .

Come on, mon petit! Allez! Allez!

Merde!

My senses tell me – listen to them, screaming! – that my mistress needs me now. Tonight. Not tomorrow, no, no! No one will care that I will have reported to duty one small, insignificant day early. Why, I bet she will breathe a sigh of relief. She will be warmed, I say, by the force of her own gratitude towards me, for my being there, for the loyalty I bring with me from the get-go. . .

Just look at the show of devotion my early arrival represents – no storm can keep me away! My willingness, my desire to be with my lady is what will make all the difference. Why, I can sense she is needing me there already. Her panic in her abandonment – her fear is palpable – will no doubt have taken its toll on her. When she realizes, what I can heal within her (before she even knows from what it is she is so suffering), she will feel such gratitude, such devotion to me. The love – yes, love – she will have for me when the understanding presents itself to her dark and brilliant mind will bind her to me in such a way that she will never, ever, ever wish to let me go.

She may be the lady of the manor, but it is I who am going home. . .

Hold on, m'lady, hold on! I am coming!

Merde!

There it is again! The lightning – it is in pursuit of me! Ha, ha! The elements spur me on!

Lend me some life, you striking tridents! Pierce this lazy contraption and send it flying across the moors to my lady!

Merde! Merde. . .

†††

How can it be; midnight already?

I swear, I heard the clock chime eight only minutes ago!

I will go to the pantry and fill my glass once more. I have earned it.

. . . and how many pages is that for tonight? And the word count, hmmm, that would be about. . . Yes. Good. This is more than I have managed to write in ages. Ages! And oh, how good it feels!

Lost in the words, and the chimes go unheard. . . the storm unnoticed. . . To write straight through the afternoon, and into the evening. . . Wow. Lovely. My Muse, you were in rare form! You spoke loud and clear.

Now let me first go pour that drink. . .

I re-read the last few paragraphs.

Alright. Yes. It's good. It's really good. That new editor, what's-her-name? She will be pleased.

Oh! And another log for the fire. Leave it to Grayson to split the wood and fill the basket for me before he left. . . A rather rustic bit of gallantry, but I will take it, especially tonight.

How I love this peaceful, unpeopled place. My cozy room, the fire aglow in the hearth. . . A small paradise this is. Just me, my pens, my binder, this amazing claret. . . Look how the light bounces off the prisms on the lamp. . . And this massive sofa we won at auction; how exciting that was, when the hammer came down! Is there any better way to relish such an evening than by way of all this cozy contrast to the blustering storm outside?

How the wind howls! It causes the rain to strike the window in a pulsating rhythm. Silvered ribbons cascade erratically down the old panes of glass. . . unsettling yet oh, so calming. A metronome, a heartbeat. . . Hearts buried perhaps within the very walls of this house. . . Who knows? Who has died here, and under what possibly dubious circumstances? Who knows what body parts might yet lie beneath the floorboards, or rest entombed in the cellar corridors, wrapped in cloth, boxed in bejeweled caskets; mementos, reliquaries. . . The chapel. . . I must look into engaging an archeologist to dig around here a bit, find who knows what. . . I simply know, there will be secrets to unlock, unearth. . .

I know, I know. Here, tucked into this nook amidst elements so harsh, all I need do is to stay put, keep warm in the friendlier confines of this room, relish the solitude, feel grateful for my sense of safekeeping. I thank the fortress that is my home; I thank the brave fire as it burns despite the howling creep of the drafts. Would that they could slither their way into the room, pull at the fringe of this massive knit blanket, tug at my hair. . . Indeed, I have written of so many houses like this – mansions, castles, cottages – it as if they themselves are beloved characters, each possessed of their own sentience. And they, like their human inhabitants, have the capability to choose, whether to play the role of the benevolent and protective keeper, or the lecherous and insidious enemy. . .

It grows chill. Another log. . .

That's better. And the blanket, just so. . .

I believe, I could tuck myself into the cushions, stay right here, sleep until morning. . .

Ah, the wine has gone to my head. I can feel it; I am residing in a moment of tangible comfort. It's in the air, on every surface. And to celebrate, for once, I'll put my work, my reading aside and do *nothing*. I will simply let myself drift off. . . For once, no one is asking anything of me, wanting any aspect of me. . . There is no one to answer to, or talk to. . .

†††

I awaken from a nightmare. It is as if I have been struck in the head. There is no pain. I feel my forehead; it is smooth and dry. Still. . . I swear, I had just seen something coming at me.

Given the ferocity of the storm, it could have been a clap of thunder or a lightning strike, or a shutter flung open and clapping against a wall, or a windowpane. Whatever it was, the sound, or the dream of some sound, had just taken the shape of a giant shovel, flying through an undefinable space, but aimed square at my forehead. I could feel, see, the air above me split in two. . . Had I dreamt on, I know this would have sent me falling. Falling off some kind of ledge, or a cliff. . .

I emerge from my waking shock. My first lucid thought is that of there possibly being an interloper at the balcony doors again, banging against them. Then I realize, the sound is not coming from behind me, but from the front of the house.

The metallic echoing clang of the doorknocker sounds three more times. Insistent, impatiently.

Bang Bang Bang!

A pause.

Bang Bang Bang!

I am now fully roused and realize what was going on. Someone is at my front door, in the middle of the night, in this weather of all things, and knocking fiendishly at my front door.

Still too dream-befuddled for any cautionary vetting in the moment, I scuff to the entry hall as quickly as my slippers will let me. I yank the heavy door open, which swollen frame and oxidized hinges scream their customary resistance. The door is flung wider open still by a gust of wind, which sends a swatch of rainwater into the vestibule. The rain that has persisted for hours now still pelts the courtyard and infinite nightscape beyond. The raindrops strike at me, icy cold needles which prick me, shock me into a full wakeful mode. I realize belatedly, I should have first peered through the curtained sidelights.

A small woman stands at the portal, petite, mousy in a way, shabbily dressed in a snatch of vintage garments, which could easily be interpreted as some sort of attempt at costuming. She gives off no contemporaneous impression, could have wandered in from some past decade, or century, from a theatrical stage, or some time traveler's portal. . .

Instinct to give comfort overwhelm my better judgement. I quickly pull the woman indoors and out of the rain. Turns out, this my self-anointed *sous-chatelaine*, who has evidently materialized a day (or was it a couple days?) early, in the middle of a storm no less, in the midst of a midnight most deep and fabulously dreary. . .

†††

M'lady, forgive me! Allow me to clarify – you were *expecting me! However, no, not tonight but tomorrow, late afternoon or thereabouts. It just so happens, I was able to procure conveyance – yes, I can drive! – and knowing how the weather is, how it can take such drastic turns in this part of the country, I thought it wise to try and arrive ahead of the storm. I am your new housekeeper – your sous-chatelaine, as I like to call myself. And I must say, the creek just outside of town may yet breach the small bridge, and so had I waited any longer, where would you be? Stuck and without any help – no help at all! Why, I just couldn't bear the thought of you being left to wait and wonder, 'where in heaven's name is my person?'*

I am put off by the slavish familiarity this effusive stranger is using with me. She reminds me of some of my most ardent fans. Nonetheless, I put on the kettle, pour her a cup of tea. I set the tray on the side table as near her as I dare before quickly reclaiming my spot on the sofa, which is aptly situated on the opposite side of the study, given my latently descended sense of discomfort.

Yes, well, how sorry I am to have given you cause to undertake this trip out here during what will no doubt rank as among one of the worst rainstorms of the season. Honestly, as you can see, I am alright. And I am only sorry your call to duty compelled you to make a road trip out here under these circumstances. Truly, I am so sorry! Everything could have easily waited until tomorrow, or the next day. . .

Precious solitude disrupted, killed off, as it were, by some over-enthusiastic, oddly invasive employee. Just like "old times" in the city. Amidst best laid plans, as they say, my weekend to myself has already been taken off the table, disrupted no less than by a peculiarly demonstrative stranger who saw fit to invade me at a most inopportune hour. Resigned to the reality of the situation, I offer the following.

So, you are here a little earlier than we had planned. Well, we will just work around that. It is not so difficult to accommodate someone I was, um, expecting anyway. I am just sorry you put yourself through this. . . I mean the storm. And to be honest, my being rather wholly unprepared to welcome, well, anyone into the – I mean my – home at quite this moment, on what would most assuredly qualify as a quintessentially dark and stormy night, when I was simply going to bide some time by myself. . .

She counters, a little too passionately.

Truly, ma'am, I am here only to serve, as was contracted by you weeks ago. Our letters, your wishes, left no doubt as to what would be expected, and please understand, our agreement is ratified the moment I crossed your threshold. I am in now in your employment, at your service. I am here for you, Madame, at your side from this day forward. I will pick up where you leave off. I will take care of all the mundane tidbits of the day, all the requisite this n that which should not – ought not – trouble someone of your stature. You have far better things to tend to. . .

Stature?

Why, um, yes. Your um stature. . . your standing. . .

Do you mean, perhaps, professionally?

Why yes, of course!

Aha. Yes. So, you know who I am?

Why yes, of course. . . the writer who. . .

Yes. . . well. . .

A cold knot materializes in my throat when I hear my pen name spoken. Then, when she rattles off the titles of my eight novels, in order. . .

But how is it you know me by my, um, profession? My alias? In our conversations, I only ever used my married name, which hardly anyone knows, as I don't even go by that socially. I am quite anonymous in my day to day, for even my birth name, which I do use among friends, is so common. I know I never let on what I did in any of our exchanges, nor did I disclose any aspect of my professional identity in any paperwork I sent you. How is it you knew who I was? I know I was a bit befuddled when I let you in, but I do remember clearly, there was not the first inkling of surprise in your demeanor when you saw me.

I pause, then continue. I need to ask that one question.

Did you seek out this position because of me being "me," the writer?

No, no! I mean, yes, well, yes. . . I can explain. . .

Please, do. . .

It was nothing, just a coincidence, that I put two and two together, and came up with the realization that I was applying for a post with a world-renowned author. I, er, I have a friend – yes, that's it – who is the daughter of someone you went to university with. That's all. . .

All I can do is nod and smile uneasily.

I see. You will have to be sure to share your friend's contact information with me. I would love to thank them, perhaps send them a note. And, well, I don't know about 'world-renowned,' but. . .

Oh, but yes! You shine brightest amongst authors!

I beg of you. . .

Oh, the whole world knows of you! I mean. . . how else would I have also known? As for me, it was just an accident; a happy, little accident, that I happened upon a bit of dialogue you wrote yourself, that proved my connection to you was to be much more than casual happenstance. And that, I had nothing to do with, naturally. It presented itself to me, showed me how much I was already linked to you.

She pauses, lowers her voice.

You see, you were communicating to me as surely as you sit here in this lovely room, as the You who exists front and center upon the literary world's stages. . . the You who you *are to* me. . .

And just who is front and center. . . ?

Oh, madame, you. You are your words. Your stories embody you! Mais oui!

You speak French then. . .?

Oui, oui. I speak mais un very little, silly bit. . .

Aha. Alright. . .

But forgive me all this! I can only imagine how this feels like an intrusion. But all will be better soon. Things will aright themselves! In two winks it will be me serving you! Your tea, pouring you that next splash of wine. . . tending to you. . .

Ever more leery, I continue to listen to this woman's prattle, continue to try and believe all is not only as it should be. Good. Really good. And better, even despite this housekeeper's having arrived over a day ahead of schedule. This woman's sudden appearance in the middle of night should not be construed as anything other than any new employee's eagerness to take on their job. I am trying my best to acquiesce to the situation. Or. . .?

Yes, I suppose it will be all about our roles of tonight reversing themselves. For tonight, we will let things stay as they are. I am desperately due for a good night's sleep, exhausted for more reasons than I can share, certainly now. We will let that be for another time, I will see you to your room, but then I really must take my leave. . .

We have days, m'lady, years to share on everything. . .

Well, yes, I suppose we do. . .

We do! With me at your side. . .

Yes, well. . . Very well. But can I ask you something before I show you to your room? And I apologize, but I am mere dregs of myself. Sleep begs.

Yes, m'lady?

I am wondering, what exactly in my writing led you to me?

I am beginning to suspect, I am in arm's length of one obsessed. It is my plan to show this woman to a different room than originally planned, one on the third floor. And then I will lock the door to the west wing bedroom hall where my room is.

Oh, well it's this. . . eh. . .

Come on, it's alright. You can share. . .

I am strategizing. Should I try calling someone? But at this hour, who? I have as yet no directory, no phone numbers written down, and town is still, in this weather, more like two hours away by car. Would there even be an operator on call at a station? I in my dismay doubt it, given the sleepy antiquatedness of the community.

But what could I do in the morning? Grayson and I have only that one car. There is nowhere for me to go. And if the weather keeps up, there would most likely be no one passing by. And even if someone did. . .

M'lady, here. let me show you. . .

She opens her satchel, from which she extracts a worn copy of my third novel, the frayed paper cover pliant as fabric, the pages dog-eared.

Here. This. . .

My employee, I suppose I ought call her that, begins to leaf quickly through the book's pages and continues:

When I realized what I was seeing, it was like discovering a secret primer. Written to me. Truly. Here! It is a passage you composed yourself. It spoke quite literally to me, told me I was needed, and by whom. And that was you. Here, let me read this passage to you. You will understand then. . .

And this is why you applied for this position?

Yes.

Whatever could you mean by. . .?

There is no real reason why I should not hear this strange woman out, much as I wish to be done with our odd exchange. With all of it. I am so tired, and the wine's effects have not all worn off, and I am still shaken by my nightmare. It feels to me, the more I pull back, the more insistent she becomes. It is as if her words *must* be unequivocally received and accepted by me. True, I did "let her in'. . . I had responded to the flowery texts of her letters. I had hired her. This unwelcome, premature arrival of a hired hand I cannot construe as a home invasion, or harassment, regardless how oddly disconcerting this whole thing is turning out to be. I feel I have no choice but to maintain my civility alongside my guard. I cannot send her back out into the storm, could I?

Here it is. Page 323. Here; take a look!

She lays her book flat on the table. The desired page is quickly found, made clear to me by the insistent way she presses the pages flat with the palm of her hand. She then lifts the book up, brings it to just under my nose, as if she's thinking proximity will better force the text into my own, separate focus. I can smell a sour-sweet, flowery odor on the pages, must assume the paper is emitting something absorbed by way of contact with her, her belongings.

Chapter twenty-three. Do you see it? You recognize it, don't' you? Yes, good; you do.

She lays the book back down on the table, flips through a few more pages.

Am I being interrogated or tested?

Chapter twenty-three, and now page 323. Do you want to guess what day that is?

You tell me.

Her voice she reduces to a whisper; her mouth gone dry. It is that discomfiting, telltale rasp of emotionality, that parched click I have often heard when the shyest fans have introduced themselves to me.

It's my birthday, of course. March twenty-third. And get this. . .

Her fingertip taps the paragraphs as she counts the indented sentences, comes to a sudden stop.

The twenty-third paragraph. Here.

I look. I have nothing to say.

She begins to read aloud, her voice trembling with emotion. Pausing from time to time, she allows certain phrases to hover momentarily on their own. It is a passage of dialogue she is reciting for me, an exchange between lovers. By the end of the book – and this, I recall immediately – the main character will have murdered the other, and as the protagonist proclaimed it, "out of pure love."

She reads:

Come, darling – see things as they truly are, the way I see them.

Although, I know, every voice will tell you otherwise, to resist, to hold onto the status quo.

Stripped of the barriers that have held you, I promise, the clarity you gain will be a freeing thing.

Somewhat frightening, yes, perhaps; but going forward, it will be us, together.

Answer me, my sweet – find the courage to speak the words!

No one, I assure you, will need to know!

Drastic measures must be taken to protect the pact between us.

Regardless, the outcome can only be what we craft together, as has been pre-ordained for us.

All will be as it should.

I sit in silence as she reads. I watch, increasingly mortified, as the young woman next begins to delineate with her fingertip a circle over the first letter of each line. It takes only the fourth letter of the fourth sentence for me to see what is being outlined. My heart skips a beat. A wave of nausea, something borne of shock and repulsion, passes through me. I grow queasier with every meticulous, invisible circlet she wraps around each subsequent capital letter.

As her name is spelled out for me, I begin to doubt everything about myself. How did I manage to fabricate within the dialogue of one of my own narratives the full first name of the woman who is now seated in the same room with me? What sort of a subconscious nonsense – what kind of a callout *to this one, at this level* – did I message from the intensely personal and private plains of *my* own creative universe, which to this day has never before been twisted in such, such, a perversely detailed way, to come back to betray me in so outright a fashion?

Cassandra has finished with her demonstration, and now she just sits there, deceptively placid. The glint in her eyes barely masks the torrential conviction that has just spewed from deep within her, and all over me, fueled her very journey – her invasion – into my world, my house, my room, my very soul? At my bidding?

So, you see, there's nothing either one of us can do about it. I have to be here. I was meant to be here. We were meant to be together. It's our outcome. Our destiny.

I am on the verge of retching, feel light-headed. It isn't the wine, nor is it the disturbing presence of the encoded name which sickens me. It is what I had literally, literarily "made" this particular character do in this particular novel, which is making my senses reel. There was something that had warmed me to the core back when I was writing this, spiritually, erotically. This was during my solitary nights when I was living by myself during one of my separations from Grayson, our journey having had its ups and abysmal downs. This particular character, whose words had just been quoted back to me, was a seductive alter ego I had conjured up when an imaginary, personified catharsis could be indulged in with no collateral damage to anyone. A being that manifested my secret thoughts, my most intimate imaginings, embodied my most gut wrangled words. That character's desires had ultimately led to a murderous hatred, and the most violent resolution I had ever put to paper – resulting, of all things, in my most tragic but best-selling novel to date. Never before, or since, had I resorted to this tightly wound an emotional journey in a novel; but then, never before had any of my novels been written during as difficult a time. What had existed within me, to cause me to message something *back then* that would, letter for letter, summon this stranger-by-the-minute person into my presence, leave me feeling so entirely out of control at this time?

It is then that I realize, the woman has yet to touch her tea. My imagination flickers, takes off. *This is no worker reporting for duty*. This absurd scenario begs for the sorts of conclusions only someone like me, alone in a house on a cliff by the sea, in the middle of night, in the middle of a storm, could rationalize into existence.

I let out a long, slow sigh. I have crossed over and back onto myself. I am now a character in one of my stories.

This disheveled, rain-soaked woman *may have once been* some unbalanced fan who had finagled my personal information to wrangle a job offer from me with the intention to serve – at least on the surface – as my housekeeper. But this woman is no longer who – what – she had started out as. She can be nothing else than a ghostly redux of whomever she had been in life. For some reason or other, this strange stranger met with some sort of demise, and some alternate entity has arrived in her stead, leaving this representation of my employee to manifest to me by sheer force of some obsessive drive, some personal agenda, which had originally fueled her, evidently, for years.

Cassandra has crossed my threshold in order to haunt me. Possess me? The only thing left to do is to take a stand, try and confront her, however illogical it may have otherwise appeared, had she come to me by light of day as a living fellow human being. As ridiculous as it seems, I must tap my memories, reach back into the recesses of my imaginings, and do, say, what any of my characters would have done in a similar situation.

Cassandra. I believe I know who – what – you are. I am so very sorry, but I must say this: you are not welcome here.

But, but. . . !

No! Cassandra, you were not invited in as you are now. You made your way into my room here by deception, and as such, I am compelled to reject you. I reject our contract. It – all this – is null and void. You must go!

I cannot help myself and launch into platitudes.

I am so, so sorry. . .

Very nearly beside myself, I remember to hold my ground. I summon the ludicrous wherewithal to tap the entirety of my writer's realm, draw from everything I have ever written, or even read, to confront this entity. What would Shirley Jackson have penned to resolve this scene? Poe? I will think, believe, remain convinced, this feminine apparition has materialized by way of the very ingredients with which I for years concocted the substance of my narratives. Why, its very demeanor suggests her own subconscious drew heavily, almost exclusively, from a repertoire of details harvested by way of repeated readings of my novels. This familiar is incredibly familiar to me. This is a being possessed of a spirit fed down to the last details by my own literary invention. I not only know her; *I exist within her.*

I have fabricated my very own ghost. And I, we, are enacting a nightmare.

But. . . but. . . It doesn't work that way! I am here, m'lady! And I am here to stay!

The poor woman wails, imploring me with an ardor that would have resounded even more pathetic in its needy emotionality, had she been alive and breathing. I must try to stand strong. Be "mean," somehow.

I don't want you here, not like this! You need to go! You cannot stay here. This is not a place for you to, er, languish. This is MY home. Mine and my husband's. I cannot let this place be some harbinger for failed pasts. I cannot not let you use these rooms as your purgatory! Please, in the name of. . .

The ghost interrupts me, mutters to herself as she looks off into the distance. It is as if she is waiting, or watching, something approach. An expression of shock transforms her face. She pales visibly, and I do believe, a transparency begins to manifest. I start to think I can see the outline of the window behind her, shining through her the crest of her shoulder. At that moment, her body levitates, leaves her hovering just above the seat cushion. She casts a shadow on the sofa beneath her. Cassandra remains motionless, her face broadcasting fear and confusion. The weightiness of her phantasmal transformation has momentarily crippled her. It is failing to keep her fully grounded, yet it falls short of lifting her heavenward.

There is an audible *pop*, which causes me to jump.

A split appears at Cassandra's hairline, grows quickly into a jagged fissure that slues its way down, across her forehead, as were a fountain pen dragged across her face by a quaking hand. Blood – or is it ink? – begins to flow from the wound. The seepage is dark, depleted of any life-giving substantiality. Her eyes likewise fill with inky fluid, becoming so bloodshot as to appear opaque. The ocular pools spill over the lids, run down cheeks that have sunken in and gone gray. She, the ghost, starts, looks with surprise at her right hand as it suddenly snaps backwards. The hand falls useless at the wrist, dangles loosely, visibly broken in several places. Her head is next wrenched backwards. It lurches forward again, striking chin to sternum. Her slender neck seems to lose its ability to hold her head up, which falls hard to one shoulder.

The ghost is reliving something catastrophic by way of this horrific enactment. What is she bearing witness to? What is happening to her?

She begins to cry, her weeping, seeping eyes affixed on me. A suffocating pressure descends upon me. I can hardly breathe. What does she want? And why from me? Is she seeking answers? Comfort? Help?

The ghost suddenly reconstitutes itself, more or less, and resumes its blubbering protestations as if nothing just happened.

M'lady, you have to take me in! You have to let me stay with you, be with you! You asked me here – you made me come all the way out here! There is nowhere else I can go! Look at me! I am, I am falling apart!

She tries to walk towards me but remains stuck where she was. I recoil, yet do not move an inch. We are both somehow frozen. Across time? Place? Her fear, which is to say the fear she was feeling at the moment of her death, which I believe she has just relived for the first time, is holding her with a force that is worse than any nightmare of futility. She cannot even take one sluggish step towards me, the one person she was determined to reach, to be with, no matter what.

The ghost, my ghost, is mired to some other-dimensional anomaly of her own circumstance. It has rendered her a tragic and broken spectral fixture. She is but a plasmic statue, stuck, neither here nor there, nor anywhere else for that matter. And her desire to be with me, the woman she had planned to glom onto by way of practical employment has served as the spiritual glue, which now neither allows her to fall into the benevolent unconsciousness of mortal suspension, nor lets her exit the plains of the living to seek out that proverbial light, find a more restful peace. I suddenly realize, my ghost's frantic need to get *here*, to this country house on the cliffs, and to me, *may have been the cause* of her death. It may now be the root cause of the psychic bog in which she is entrapped. We are entrapped.

I am both frightened and heartsick.

I slowly rise from the davenport, ease myself back into the corner of the room, as far away from my entity as is humanly possible. She should not be here, but she has nowhere else to go. The spectre's pathos is as thick as the guilt I feel over my part in her demise.

Don't you see, this is what you asked for? What you *wanted?*

The ghost rambles on, her words bubbling amidst the wet mess that still masks her face.

You spelled me out, you called me! You were the one who determined this destiny! There is nothing you can do. Nothing either one of us can do about it!

Intuition warns me, this entity would follow me if she left the study. My gut tells me this, *this thing* will follow me to whichever corner, or room, I might attempt a retreat. And I do not want to do as much as give it, her, a tour of the place. The last thing this poor being needs, is to be shown where else it might wish to slog about in the event it, she, still fancies herself entitled to get to know the place better, make it more her own. I begin to realize, I am effectively shackled to my very own supernatural symbiont. And to think, I had thought my *living* fans were sometimes too much. . .

I am afraid, to be sure, but anger smolders in me as well. I am completely sobered and on high alert. I understand, I was a part of this visitation from the start. And while this petite feminine entity is nothing to be that afraid of, the obsessive, possessive potential is frightening. The two of us attached at the hip as they say is an unbearable thought.

My mind takes a small turn. Did anyone of my characters in any of my novels ever have to rid themselves of any paranormal nuisances? Thinking farther beyond my own ken, I try to remember how other authors have penned their parapsychological denouements. I try, but sheer exhaustion stunts my capabilities. I can no longer recall a single relevant chapter, scene, or bit of dialogue in any of my novels, nor in that of others'. I too am now stuck in my own quagmire. Hers.

Why, oh, why did Grayson have to be gone on this night of all nights?

I realize with a start, the violent transformation of my visitor might involve more than what evidently brought her to The Clyffes. The grotesque transmogrification I just witnessed was clearly depicting a violent event, but something in the apparition's charade seems to suggest more than the obvious. My gaze drifts towards the French doors that open to the balcony, my thoughts wandering in the way they are wont to do when I am pondering a new twist in a story line, or fabricating some puzzling bit of circumstance to warp the predictive.

Beyond the balustrade, I had so far noted only a midnighted endlessness. The storms clouds have travelled over the sea, and now obscure most of the sky. A thin stripe of silver sparkles wanly into the distance, the moon's attempt at demarcating its path across the waters. Lightning blitzes soundlessly from far away, illuminates a ship on the horizon, making its way across the Channel. I wish desperately, I could whisk myself out of the room and over the waves to where the freighter is traversing the shipping lane – anything to get away from her, to escape this haunting. I feel completely cornered by the ghastly dregs of an afterlife interloper who hasn't even acclimated to her own demise. She is but the saddest of ghosts, emanates nothing but a soul-sucking desperation. Mine.

I dare turn my eyes back to Cassandra, who has somehow managed to clean herself up. She looks as she did before that, that *thing* happened her.

Cassandra.

Is even the use of her name a mistake? I speak it anyway.

Look, Cassandra; we can talk about this. Calmy, please.

Cassandra, able to motate once again, walks over to the sideboard as she speaks. She is calmed, one could say collected.

I only wish I could articulate everything so you could understand. Also, so you would not see this as being my fault. None of it is, but nor is it yours. Nor is there any ill wished upon you for my being here in this. . . this, er, state. If you would only accept my presence here, everything would be so much easier. For both of us. Please, let me take care of you, like we had both planned!

Cassandra feigns a cheery energy.

Here, let me pour you a little wine. The look in your eyes tells me you could use another splash. . .

She goes to pick up the carafe, but it only wobbles where it stands. She tries to steady it, but the decanter, a Georgian beauty chased in silver, is heavy. Far too heavy, too solid, too tactile, most especially for a fledgling poltergeist. The decanter is, in all honesty, a weighty, awkward object, even for the living.

Cassandra's wavering corporeality is not enough to handle such an object, and so, rather than lifting it from its tray, she only manages to topple the carafe. It falls to the floor, spilling its contents, its base now dented, its smooth, crystal lip fractured. The wine spreads across the rug as Cassandra, mortified by her clumsiness, starts to rise up off the floor again. Once more, she begins to degenerate into the gruesome state she was mere minutes ago, this surge of emotion appearing to be a sort of trigger. Her ensuing expression of shock and dismay speaks volumes. Clearly, this transformation is something over which she has no control. She is herself mortified by its occurrence.

Oh, madame. . .

Cassandra casts a pleading look my way as her forehead cracks.

Please forgive me. I only wanted to help. . .

I turn my head. I must look away, unable to behold the apparition's grotesque, bloodied mutation.

Minutes later, Cassandra transforms once again, back to her intact self. I resolve to adapt a more aggressive, defensive demeanor with "my" spirit. Though it worries me, that it might trip yet another gory degeneration, I feel I owe it to myself – and Cassandra – to try a different approach. The fact remains, she cannot stay here. She *must* go.

Cassandra! You. . . you cannot just take up residence here and force yourself on me and my home! This is not *how things can play out. No! You have to go! Now!*

Cassandra replies with a calmer voice, her pale eyes filled with unshed tears.

I do not like this tone of voice.

Fact, my lady, would suggest things can – and ought to – be stranger than any fiction. You have said that a few times in your speeches, most recently in London. I think it was just last December. We all laughed – together – at your point.

London?

. . . yes. . . or perhaps it was St. Ives. . . I can't quite remember which book signing it was. . .

You were in the audience then? You attended a couple of my talks?

A couple? Oh my, I have attended at least a half dozen. At least! Traveled long distances to get to them. And I spoke with you every time! Why, I have a book that you signed on three different pages at three different events! You never second-guessed me, when I held my books open to you on what would have seemed odd, random pages for you to sign.

Cassandra sighs resignedly, resoundingly, as if there were a hint of suggestive insistence embedded in her nostalgia.

But, being that you never recognized me, never remembered me from one time to the next, I pretended each time it was the very first time I was meeting you. Seemed a bit easier, looking back, to not have to hold back on my enthusiasm! Every time was like the first!

There is something so very *sticky* about the one-sided, unrequited, passion of an ardent fan whose adoration oversteps the bounds of basic admiration, where inklings of emotional dependency also subsist. How to reason with someone, *something* like this, from within a purgatorial sentence having just been meted out to one so pitiable, so desperate?

I am sorry, Cassandra, truly! But I will not waver. You cannot be here. You cannot stay! Go! Please go and leave me alone! This house is no place for you. You must listen to me and accept this. I cannot be punished by your punishing yourself. Move on, move on!

A new approach presents itself to me.

Look. I can pray for you. Is that what you want? If I say a prayer for you would that help? What is it you need to find your peace, to go wherever it is you must go? What can I say to you, or for you to. . .

Cassandra opens her mouth, ready to protest, but she is stopped short, distracted by something. I watch as her eyes grew wide with terror, as if she were facing something monstrous, coming right at her. An ear-shattering howl bursts forth from her. She reaches for a chairback, appears to brace for impact.

No sooner does the feral cry escape her, as does the now familiar, disgusting little popping sound occur. A fresh fissure appears, makes its way across Cassandra's forehead again, breaks the skin anew from her temple to her jawline.

Blood so dark it appears black drips from her face and onto her collar, her dress, all over her crimping and snapping wrists and hands.

The insidious, violent scene is repeating itself, again.

I cannot help but look away – again – when Cassandra's eyes burst. The library in which we are trapped has become a far too intimate theatre of the macabre, with me held hostage, made to play audience of one to a looping enactment of utter carnage.

It appears as though she is being struck, head on. Not by any one being, or a hand, or weapon. Her reflexes, and the damage, are too broadly cast over her entire being. I suddenly remember the dream I had, from which I was jarred awake to the sound of the knocking at my front door.

I feel the hairs on the back of my neck prickle.

A random and unexpected bolt of lightning flashes directly over the house. The electricity goes out. The few bulb-bearing fixtures in the house are snuffed out, leaving only the fire in the hearth to broadcast the weakening flicker of a fire about to be snuffed out as well. In the more complete dark, I can now see Cassandra emanating the faintest glow, a feeble luminescence, barely discernable, but there beyond any shadow of a doubt.

Cassandra has morphed back to herself again. Rather quickly, I would say. She lifts her shoulders, extending her hands in a gesture of abject apology to demonstrate to me, she understands. This isn't working. This was never going to work.

Perhaps, madame, I can make myself useful to you as, er, a sort of sentry. I can keep watch! Over you, over the house. . .

I can do nothing but look away. Cassandra's beggarly attempts at rationalizing her afterlife compulsions are so heart-wrenching as to make them as difficult to stomach as her blood-soaked transformations.

Cassandra, please!

I am no longer above begging. Nor is she.

I promise you; it could work! Please, please say you will let me stay here. . . anywhere. . .

No, Cassandra. . .

What next step to take is an absolute mystery, for either one of us.

Cassandra has projected herself through sheer force of will into my presence by way of a final, living burst of energy at the moment she passed over. Her obsessive desire to get to me, the author whom she had worshipped for years, who had never bothered to notice, let alone remember or acknowledge her at any the book talks and signings she had attended. I am now as trapped by her as she is trapped by her own desire to be here.

What a pair we. . .

No! I will not go *there.*

Cassandra doesn't want to leave because she can't. The longing of her living soul is preventing her from exiting the perimeter of this place, my presence. Given her way, not only would she continue to haunt me at The Clyffes, but she would not even possess the ability to venture outside the immediate sphere of my own aura, my living energy. I would *never* be alone again. I would go forward on Cassandra's post-mortem leash, never more than arm's length from her, day, or night.

Good Lord, would she also infest my dreams?

I want to crumple to the ground, struck with the horrific realization, I may never have a moment of solitude ever again. Cassandra would subsist as my metaphysical leech.

†††

As it is, compatriots of the spirit world possess the capacity to understand the hierarchical ranges in which hauntings can be conducted, whether by way of a malevolent and accursed harassment, or as some kind of blessed presence, in which protections, guidance, or even rescue are part of some far happier magic. The ghostly cadres that wander the plains of the Neither, who manage to breech its abstract hold to invade the spheres of living, possess amongst themselves rank and file, with capabilities and authority over each other.

As such, it would be left to another to come to the aid of a dearly beloved other, not to grace her with his presence, but to ensure a state of peace and quiet she had with all her heart and soul been seeking *for years*. A final gift of love would be the spectral cleansing of one grand manor house on the cliffs, newly haunted but for the space of a few hours.

†††

Something shifted. Katherine sensed she and Cassandra were no longer alone.

An invisible hand, or a puff of air, stirred the lace curtains. It was as if the panels of glass had become porous, allowing for the winds to waft through the walls, the doors. There was something – someone – a new a presence, outside, on the balcony, illuminated as well, but unlike Cassandra, by way of some moonlit reflection, captured, and integrated.

The dawn, though no longer too far off, was still distant enough to leave the scene – indoors, outdoors – as of yet in full, dead-of-night dark, the moon so small and distant, it was but a weak bulb hung in the arc of the towering clouds. The newly arrived entity stood motionless, right outside the door nearest to where Katherine still cowered, cornered and recoiling from the second, unwelcome occupant of the room. Katherine in her corner was backed on one side by the snug junction of the walls and braced on the other by a sturdy walnut bookcase, another one of Grayson's auction coups. Katherine realized, she had kept one hand upon its smooth surface much as she had done on the day they had resolved to try and win the bid for it, at which time they had both came to a tacit agreement, this acquisition would be for a new home in the country they would undertake to find together. It had been this bookcase that had solidified their recommitment to each other.

Katherine further realized, she had been supporting herself, taking refuge behind something that held a direct connection to Grayson, and what they had decided together. Its solid form was now serving as a barrier against a blighted spectre by way of both its meaningfulness and its tangibly solid construction. The bookcase felt real because it *was* real.

Katherine, alerted by the caress of moving air against her arm, felt the ends of her hair rise. She began searching the dark beyond the door, to see what – who – was out there, standing on the balcony, looking into the room, at her, at them.

She gasped, then cried out.

No. . . Nooooo!

All other words failed as full realization hit. Katherine swayed visibly, as if she too had been hit head-on. Struck head on by an oncoming storm, or a locomotive, or a truck, or a roadster. . .

Grayson, his car, him at the wheel. In an ice-cold flash, Katherine saw it all: Cassandra, racing across the fields to a place of employment she had wrangled under less than honourable pretenses. Grayson, in that little sports car of his, and the way he had emphasized, how he would hurry as best as he could, to get back to her, to their new old house, back to The Clyffes, to their freshly promised life together.

New chapters to craft together. And all those books Katherine yet wanted to write. . .

They had been there for less than a month – twenty-three days to be exact. For a precious handful of days, Katherine and Grayson had resided in their Garden.

And now, here she was, and there *she* was, and there – there he was now, as well. Katherine understood. She could barely breathe. And she knew this too: That she in her study in that house lay at dead center of a crossroads that had come together for all three of them, two of whom would have no choice – no choice whatsoever – but to continue to pass on through, and then onward, to some kind of Beyond. For one woman, it would be to her relief; for the other, it would be to the fractured breaking of her heart.

A latch clicked, and the French doors sailed open. Cool, damp air swelled into the room, filled every nook, every crevice. The coals in the fireplace inhaled, quickened, and were extinguished.

Grayson, afloat and aglow, cast a long look of tragic apology to his wife. His pain, his regret, was a palpable fountain of otherworldly effusion.

I am so, so sorry. My love. . .

The words wrapped themselves around Katherine like a comforter. No, a shroud.

I am so, so sorry. . . he repeated, caressing her with all the directional energy he could muster.

Katherine's entire being quaked with the rage of one cosmically forsaken.

My love, my love! Why, why? God help me, I would kill you all over again with my own hands if I could! How could you do this to me? To us? How could you leave me like this?

†††

Grayson, his gaze affixed upon the face of his beloved, sails across the room with a smooth elegance that is eerie, otherworldly. His expression casts volumes of thoughts, impressions, sorrow, and longing. He imbues Katherine with all he the emotion he can yet send her way, all the thoughts he can yet form, to try and explain, leave something of him, his heart, with her, some slice of his soul she can use to survive it all.

Reluctantly, he turns his attention away from his beloved to lift an arm towards Cassandra, his reach stretching preternaturally. He grabs the woman by the wrist, for he is there to take her. It is the least he can do. It is the last thing he can do. It is out of the question, to be there to selfishly manifest to Katherine specifically, and heaven forbid, to try and lure her to depart this world with him. No, he will have to settle with the taking of the unwanted, deceased eccentric, who had no business being in this house in the first place, dead or alive.

As for Katherine, she will remain where she is standing. She will witness in silence the last act of this little melodrama. She knows, is wired to understand despite her pain, there is too much life yet to be lived. She has books to write, stories to tell, a legacy to finish building. She has readers to inspire, kindred spirits to touch; yes, especially those most intensely adoring amongst her fans out there. Words, phrases, narratives, meaning and intent of this nightmare, will remain buried beneath her sentences, stay hidden inside the negative spaces between each and every character she will eventually put to paper, for it is in the silence that underlies every written work, where the soul of the writer has always forever lurked.

Grayson is there solely to grant his beloved all the peace and quiet she has ever wanted. Not in the way either one of them would have wished, but this being no longer any kind of option, it is the least he can do.

And he owes this other being, this woman named Cassandra, an apology – and an exit. What she owes him, does not matter.

Katherine watches as Grayson draws Cassandra from her presence. She sees the fleeting acknowledgement in the woman's face, senses a calming that could be nothing else but acceptance, foregiveness.

Katherine in her corner falls into a deep quiet, as if some self-preservational attempt is being exerted to carry her through this bizarre and tragic final scene, something that will keep her going, however difficult it will undoubtedly be. Onwards, and of her own accord.

The entities move together towards the open doors. Katherine watches as they pass soundlessly through the curtains, cross the threshold, as they glide like swans on still water across the balcony, and then as they pass effortlessly through the stone railing. Katherine sees them recede, not just into the distance, but into some kind of liquid void, a place from which neither one of them will ever return. It is a veiled passage that speaks of rest, and is beyond all pain, all disfigurement, all confusion.

As for Katherine, the agony she can see coming at her is like new stormfront. It barrels over the lawn, through the rooms of the house, blows through one wall after another, a bank of rippling elements dead-set on a head-on collision with her. Its predecessor had been an event that had rendered the narrow roads too slick and dangerous as to be fatally so for her husband – and that woman. Ultimately, ironically, whilst Katherine is now spared from the confusingly coerced invasion of a delusional, obsessed stranger, she has been likewise robbed of the one person she only now has come to realize, she did indeed love best in the world.

The agony in recognizing the horrific duality reminds Katherine, she is the one in this *débâcle a trois* who has survived, is more or less still alive. And so she will remain this, despite the pain in the present moment, despite her fevered imagination suggesting otherwise, that she too could hurry up and join her husband, hurl herself over the railings and down onto the rocks, into the churning turbulence below, which the unrelenting shore would wash clean in minutes.

Katherine will have all the peace and quiet she could ever, ever wish for, thanks but no thanks to the man she has loved for so long. Still does.

The phone in the hall rings; its chime hammers out a tinny dirge that shatters the silence. Katherine knows what the caller has to tell her.

But she is already distracted.

Katherine is composing a story in her head, only in this narrative, the heroine will descend with her home when the cliff collapses and tumbles into the ocean. *She* will fall *with* the house in an avalanche of split trusses, broken stone, splintered beams, and shattered glass. The heroine's crushed remains, they will be cradled within a flurry of debris, and taken swiftly, brutally, to the ravenous waters, past the breakers, out and then onward, far beyond the horizon, and then finally into the everlasting embrace of her deceased beloved, who will have been waiting patiently, so patiently, for her.

†††††

I have dreamt in my life, dreams that have stayed with me ever after, and changed my ideas; they have gone through and through me, like wine through water, and altered the color of my mind.

Emily Brontë, *Wuthering Heights,1847*

For the inimitable songstress, who has also sought peace and quiet in a grand, old house perched on a crumbling cliff, overlooking the sea.

None Are Sold Before Their Time

Here. Have another slice.

Very well. A sliver. How about this one? But, surely, a dollop of whipped cream to top it, yes? Life's simplest pleasures, as they say. And this particular torte is only made available this one month, when the last of the plums are brought in. Very seasonal. It positively *tastes* of a late summer's day, does it not?

Ha! I understand. Always just a smidge. . .

You were asking?

No; none are sold before their time.

How long, you ask? You mean, for the plinth to be fully developed?

The average duration stands right now at just under twenty years. Each plinth is considered "complete" only when the *Ostesces* naturally expire, which generally occurs at the point when the larynx is fully collapsed – of its own accord, naturally – and the host can no longer breathe. Interestingly, hosts can survive every other osteal bend and break, but for this one. It is generally their swan song, the final transmogrification to occur. To be sure, the sequence of transformation and the shapes each host ultimately takes is never repeated. Wholly organic, really, and as unique as is every individual so blessed with the ability to absorb the suffering and be physically molded by it. Each and every resulting plinth is therefore utterly unique, and positively imbued with. . . ah. . . how should I say it? *Tangible affliction.* They are shaped – literally – by the transference of all negative sensory experiences of our people. This renders the plinths quite mystical. Quite priceless. Wouldn't you agree?

By today's value standards, the price is practically a bargain, compared to what our ministers were able to ask of the nobles and later on the merchants who were granted privilege of purchase. There are fascinating entries in our ledgers as to what over time has all been made in payment: gold, jewels, spices, even mining rights, as I recall. But, given the history, the rarity, and the magical powers these plinths are rumored to possess – legends abound, trust me – it is a small price we ask for an *œuvre d'art* of such, hmm, let's call it *magnitude*.

And I have heard, this one will be especially lovely. An exemplar. I congratulate you pre-emptively!

Sure. I'll take a little more coffee.

Thank you, no.

Now, a little more of the backstory. Forgive me, do, if I repeat what you have already been told, or read. Presently, only twenty-two plinths are known to exist – still exist, to be more precise. All secreted away by their owners, kept out of the public eye. Plinths that pre-exist our system of documentation have for the most part gone by the wayside, lost to history, to the elements. Violent circumstance, fire, degenerative collapse, willful destruction, much as any antiquity has ever met its demise. Likewise, it cannot be helped, that while the initial procurement of a plinth was always a carefully culled transaction between the committee and those who qualified to make the purchases, the sorry realities of subsequent ownership no doubt levelled and turned to dust not a few of these plinths in their varied, shadowed enclosures the world over. From impoverished and unappreciative heirs to the ruinous wake of local skirmishes, wartime conflict, housefires, and other, random destruction based on negligence or deliberate sabotage, all take their toll.

So, if you would allow me to tell you a story about what we call a jewel of a very special kind? There is an opalized length of vertebrae housed in our archives, the only one known of to date, here or elsewhere. It consists of seven small bones, fitted together like jigsaw puzzle pieces. The center bone itself has been bent, and at such a tight angle, as to be at a perfect ninety-degrees. It is a gem of such beauty, I can get choked up just thinking about it. Imagine the depths of exquisite suffering its host must have internalized, to have manifested *this* level of osteal transmogrification. . . The opalized specimen, our researchers have dubbed it the *Spina Aurorae*. If it is what we think it is, it suggests that Ostesces may have been among the god-like beings purported to have lived on this planet eons ago, in some of evolutionary cycle pre-dating our own, so-called origins of life, a theory generally relegated to tall tales of gargantuan Promethean forefathers and star seekers who travelled here from distant constellations, to scatter the seeds of life on this planet, perhaps live out an entire existence. . .

Yes, indeed! A rather darkly romantic theory.

What was that? Yes! I love it. Romantically dark. I *knew* you two would be perfect. Sir, my I offer you a cigar?

Anyway, where speculation stops short as to the opal's origins, is the specific question, as to whether or not the jack-knifed vertebra was formed that way, or externally broken and neatly healed, or if – as we prefer to believe it – it was transformed by way of a sort of empathetic osteal response. No other such specimen, opalized or fossilized, has ever been found. Given the grandeur of the one specimen that we do have, our scholars believe other such artifacts were likely sought out, excavated, and either hidden or placed with ancient collectors, scientists, what have you, ages and ages ago. Perhaps the gems were spirited off this planet by celestial travelers, descended from the originators. As for us and our eras of existence as we all know them, scattered mentions in ancient writings suggest the osteal phenomenon was carried forward into our cycles over time, but kept secret to safeguard its continuation. Man has had always been possessed of a discomfiting propensity to erase the extraordinary, would you not agree? Only at the tail end of the Middle Ages, did our forebears begin to officially document the 'gift,' and their incremental occurrences. From the mid-1500's onward, we kept detailed hand-written notes, on vellum parchments and later in bound ledgers, to record the evidence and track the presence of this condition, as well as the residual legacies of our gifted ones, their resulting plinths. What our researchers eventually dubbed *Hyper-osteomalacia* was implemented as our separatist, societal cornerstone. It is where the history of my people fully merged to identify with the phenomenon and its host carriers, who we with great reverence named *Ostesces*, after the old French word for "hostess." This is what separates us from, well, any other society we know of.

Um, yes. . .

No. I am not sure I know what you are asking. . .

They are *all* women. Young women, generally in the early bloom of adulthood.

Eighteenish, thereabouts. Nineteen, mostly. One was twenty-one when she was brought in, that would be back when I was just a child. I remember her.

Onset of, er, a novitiate's monthly, um, days as you might call it often triggers the empathetic events, but it can take several years before a host is identified and confirmed, for one, because the signs are so hard to detect at first; and later on, because most are kept hidden away by well-meaning but ignorant family members, loved ones who struggle to adjust to their situation, which is their obligation to hand over their gifted youngster. *Ostesces* have – thankfully – generally been located, verified, and confirmed in time to immediately replace their predecessors, thus keeping the, er, transferences of communal pain more or less unbroken.

What do you mean? Oh, I get it. You mean, were there ever periods of time with no host in place? Where *we* hurt?

We have only ever experienced two such gaps, but they were exceedingly brief. It is too critically important to have an *Ostesce* installed in the Sanctuary at all times, and the few instances we had to scramble to find one, the ministers have always had small armies of volunteers (ardent supporters ready to hand over their very own daughters were they so blessed), to locate the next one. Our people understand the import of the situation.

The absolute absence of trauma evolved us and solidified our culture quite organically. Once our forefathers recognized the capabilities of the *Ostesce*, and once they learned to more quickly identify the carriers of this ability, the parameters of our society were quickly laid. Next, was to formulate our social structure, to best implement all the good that could be done for the many by the one. We sealed our cultural identity by establishing ourselves as a closed society, for though the phenomenon by which we live could conceivably benefit everyone the world over, our academicians, who studied this at length, who even met in secret with peers from other nations, concluded over two centuries ago, it was decidedly *not* for everyone.

Yes, you could say it is – up to a point – a belief system. But it does, to be honest, affect *every* aspect of our society. This 'thing' rules us; it guides us.

True. I have heard it summarized that way by others. But where our people evolved let's call it differently, is by way of our core psychological makeup, for having lived in absolute and unbroken comfort and harmony for many hundreds of years, thanks be to our vestal and blessed *Ostesces*. Our collective state of being has been in place so long, we are leagues from even considering doing things any other way.

One gets used to it, is the simple man's way of putting it.

Now, we have only made the plinths available to outsiders since the late 16th century. 1588 to be precise, which is the year of the first recorded such transaction. Was to a Romanian Prince. That one, and the next half-dozen or so I believe, were acquired by highly select members of foreign nobility we could trust, *bon vivants* who had an adequate level of appreciation and open-mindedness, who could be sworn to secrecy, who also had the means to purchase them. Those plinths have resided in opulent shadow for centuries, housed in secret rooms and offsides niches of remote summer palaces, secluded hunting lodges, even a few houses of worship. Not a one was ever on display in any room to which the so-called general public had access, a stipulation we have always mandated in writing, even enforced by way of agents whose only job it is, to track the locations and general accessibility of the plinths. I do know of a good number of plinths which were gilded or silvered, a popular, old-world embellishment with which we have no complaint. It does, in fact, help preserve the artifacts, them being made of bone, much in the same way a saint's relics might be chased in silver or gold for purposes of display for veneration. I do know of two – or is it three? – plinths which serve as the actual altar bases in private chapels, one of which was entirely encrusted with jewels. What a breathtaking *objet d'art* that must surely be!

Yes, it might seem rather ironic at the outset, but we venerate the *Ostesces* to a level that, to us as with their subsequent owners, such embellishment, such use, seem only fitting.

You see, it invariably came about, commerce being king, that it became a necessary evil to offer the plinths for sale to elite collectors outside of our communities. Foreigners, like yourselves. The Elders concluded this to be a way to infuse our Lilliputian economy with much-needed foreign capital, to replenish our province's proverbial coffers, so to speak. The plinths, since the beginning, have been consigned for sale in sums equivalent to many millions of pounds, or yen, or dollars as it were – whatever you choose as a fiscal reference – so they have served our general estate wonderfully well for a very long time, in addition to the living service their hosts have bestowed upon our citizenry.

Everyone wins, yes?

Well, everyone wins depending on how you look at it, I suppose. *It is how we choose to look at it.* It is how we ask *you* to look at it, as our next investor.

Yours will only be the eighteenth officially consigned plinth – and the first one to cross the Atlantic! A rather exciting prospect for us it is, to know that one of our plinths will – provided all goes smoothly today – find a home upon the *terra firma* of a North American continent. I suppose, you could say, we are branching out, yes?

I might add, we were quite impressed with your application. Thrilled, actually, that you will be the owners of this next one. The levels we perceive you both to exist at, both fiscally and let's call it esoterically, are essential in our having singled you out.

Oh, I wouldn't say so.

Correct. Everything is going quite according to schedule. With this one, we are at year nineteen, just shy of what appears to be the average duration of a host. Based on what I observed last week, I am thinking yours is almost ripe, as we like to call it. In other words, due to expire within the year. Then, it is only a few months' time wherein we cure the remains. At that point, as soon as payment is rendered in full, the plinth will be on its way to you. It is a relatively simple process, considering the amount of money that changes hands, and considering the significance of the artifact itself.

You could say, as in keeping with our way of life, it is a completely painless a transaction, a white glove delivery all around. I read in your application; you intend to have yours situated with an alabaster tabletop? Beautiful. A simply brilliant idea! It will take the functionality – the aesthetics being such a glorious given, yes? – of our plinths to new, dare I say modern, heights. They call that design a "coffee table," if I am not mistaken, yes?

Aha! You see, I know a thing or two. Ha!

Now, I could talk for hours on the plinths, but our time is limited. You did say, your driver will be picking you up right after breakfast tomorrow, yes?

Of course. It is a good two hours to the harbour from town center, and the last thing we would want on our conscience is to have made you miss your boat! Time is always of the essence. Just as it is in the formation of the plinths. *Your* plinth. Hence, your having to travel here at this particular moment to finalize details and to take this tour, and our having to complete everything before nightfall. Your understanding – and full acceptance – of the backstory, which is to say, what the *Ostesces* do, and do for us, is a key component in the acquisition process. One of the last hurdles to surmount, if you don't mind my saying so. No one who doesn't understand fully the significance, the singular beauty, of the plinths is permitted to own one, let alone be made privy to the details related to their creation. We estimate, ninety-nine percent plus of all human beings whose eyes ever happen upon one of these plinths never know what exactly it is they have seen. And we prefer to keep it that way, for obvious reasons. *N'est-ce pas*?

Your plinth, it will possess in its very fibers everything that you will witness and experience today, directly and as proxy, both peace wrought by the absence of all suffering as well as the internalized chaos of constant suffering. A full spectrum, epic in breadth. Your uttermost appreciation as a collector is imperative for the cementing of your commitment to ownership. These wondrous things must be adequately housed, with vigilant guard kept close.

Now, when the next *Ostesce* comes into residence in the Sanctuary. . .

The next one? Oh, yes. We have already identified our next host, although I cannot say too much about its, or rather, her identity. We are still in the final stages of confirming the markers, as the ministers call them.

The marker specifically, you ask? Sure. That much, I can share. There was – I believe it was back in June – the occurrence of a slight breakage of a finger on the left hand of a maiden, a niece of the governess to the mayor's children, whilst in the presence of a toddler who injured herself at play, of all things. I've been told, the child was romping about in the courtyard when she fell from her wooden pony, just as a group of councilmen were leaving the mayor's residence. The poor lass fell flat on her face, popping two brand-new front teeth out of her cherub's mouth. I heard, it was quite the bloody spectacle, with those pearly white buttons skittering across the walk like a pair of knucklebone jacks tossed to the ground for play! It so happened, when the child began to laugh at the sight of her teeth bouncing across the pavers, that the caregiver's niece (who was helping her Auntie that day and standing close by) suddenly cried out. According to my good friend, one of the councilmembers, the young lady held up her hand, pale and slender as a dove's wing, and as all watched, the tip of her index finger bent itself backwards mid joint, and fractured clean in two. All knew then and there, the very next *Ostesce* was very possibly standing right there, in their midst. You can imagine, how quickly she was ushered away from the scene! Her empathic transmogrification was so instantaneous and obvious, and so on par with the pain the toddler *did not* experience; well, we knew we had a good one there. More than a mere, next prospect.

You got that right. We are all quite certain, we have our next "The One."

Most rare, to have an initial empathic manifestation occur in public like this, where willing witnesses – which is to say no protective, possibly uncooperative family members – are present. Were that not the case, one can generally rely on telltale relatives and friends (money always fuels the willingness) to lead us to our next *Ostesce* before its predecessor has expired, continuity being critically important. Some transferences are drama-laden processes. Happily, very few play out like that. With this most recent incident, we had an instantaneous identification of a transmogrification, leaving no one to question (or deny, as it were) the occurrence. I might add, the girl's parents were immediately paid off to ensure their compliance. We require both familial silence *and* support in the procurement of any host.

And let me tell you of the collective sigh of relief making waves throughout our communities. Parents and most especially daughters everywhere are feeling quite confidant in *their* comfortable status quo, knowing they were spared the honour of a confinement in the Sanctuary. No one denies the hard work involved of any host. Any day now, we should get final word on this next *Ostesce,* and the timing will be perfect. As I said earlier, the current *Ostesce* does not appear long for this world. She is nearly replete with all the transmogrifications over these last few years, which, to your benefit, will render her quite wonderfully complete before too long.

This is an acquisition process that requires patience, wouldn't you say?

Indeed!

So, come then. Let us commence with our tour. Did you get enough coffee? And was not our luncheon a delight?

Yes. I will be sure to pass your compliments on to the chef!

This way, please. We have a few stops to make this afternoon and need to be done and out of the compound by ten. Bedtime is strictly adhered to, for, even such an *Ostesce* – most especially she – needs her rest.

Shall we?

†††

Come, come. Now, lend me your ears. Listen carefully.

Aha. So, you don't hear a thing, do you?

This is precisely what we were talking about earlier, at the dentistry atelier. Yes. Quiet. Only softly spoken, genteel conversation, room by room. Instructions, timed breathing, coaching by the midwives and their apprentices, and of course, the conversations of their loved ones. Here and there, you might encounter a physician in attendance. You see, we have centered the event of giving birth in this facility, where community and assistance are immediately and ongoingly available to our citizens. Efficient and forward-thinking, is it not? Yes, we love this concept and see it as an advancement – no doubt you are also seeing more of this where you live. And why the casual camaraderie present in our facility? As you might discern, aside from the occasional, generally insignificant biological realities, where a practiced helping hand or medical acumen is required, the act of giving birth has developed in our society as a time of serene, celebratory gathering, of welcoming. The key being, of course, the absence of pain.

No pain. None at all. No pain to fight against; no moans or cries, no sound to distress anyone in attendance, no verbalized negativity, no fear of any kind. And heaven forbid, no profanity. We long ago drew that line. The absolute non-violence which exists as a bedrock foundation of our society, simply does not warrant the aggressive use of foul language. There is no need for any outburst of any kind amongst a people bereft of *all* residual elements of suffering, at every level. Terribly *nice*, isn't it?

Aha, so you noticed the quiet the moment you entered? There you go. No sound, really, but for the music playing in the grand hall. You can hear that too, yes? Wonderful, isn't it, how the acoustics work around here? Brilliant architectural design, *intended* to carry sound. There is nothing to squelch or stifle. Only music to break the stillness of the place. Blissful mother, blissful baby, blissful everyone.

Here, we can take a peek inside. They've agreed beforehand – it's an agreement of disclosure we offer our patients where they allow us to engage with them for a bit – with discretion of course – when we are working with a prospective collector. The proof this offers you is in the moment. In the act of giving birth, as you can see, all is taking place in absolute quietude and calm, in an environment of zero pain, no discomfort but for the natural effort of a little core strength, tapped – with assistance, of course – to deliver an infant.

This is itself the embodiment of *Stille Nacht*, is it not?

She? Yes, hmmm. Let me take a look. This young lady is nearly ready to deliver. The last notes are but from a couple minutes ago. Won't be long, and these lovely people will be welcoming their little one into this world.

Ah – I see. . . Reading this here. . . Yes, your first! How wonderful.

And how are you all doing on this miraculous day? How momentous! Congratulations to you, young man. I am addressing the Father, yes? Lovely. All my best to you.

And you my dear. Well, well! You are looking positively radiant! Feeling good, I hope? Wonderful.

You see? She is feeling 'wonderful.'

I take it, your pregnancy has been a blessedly pleasant and uneventful one? Good, good! It shows. Truly! Your happiness, your health, have you looking as they say radiant. These most beautiful aspects, all reflected in your face. And to think, it won't be long, and you will have your child in your arms, and introducing everyone here to your newest family member!

Thank you ever so much for sharing, for permitting this visit.

A son you say? How lovely! Congratulations to you all. Our very best to you.

Yes, time flies.

And speaking of which, our time is on wings as well. We wish you all the very best.

Good. Good. Let us move on.

Next up, I would like to show you the surgery theatre. There are hmmm let's see two procedures scheduled for today, and I am quite certain at least one of the patients is signed on as a tour stop for us. Being that our patients are all fully awake and aware during their surgeries, there is no undue invasion of their privacy. Most are happy to have us stop in to chat a bit. I might add, even our recovery statistics are exemplars of our way of practicing the art of medicine, the catch of course being, we cannot divulge anything about this to outside communities or professionals. This is something we, unfortunately for the rest of the world, must withhold. You understand, yes? Wait until you see this – a patient lying on the table, reading from a book whilst they are being operated on. It is almost comical!

Et voilà, one's time in the operating room becomes a simple opportunity to catch up on one's reading, spend a lovely set of hours at rest, after which, in a happy and calm state, recovery is undertaken with restful ease, allowing for the healing to commence that much more quickly.

Here we go. We have arrived.

Now, before we can be admitted into the surgical theater, we do ask that all admittants don these robes. It is just a little cleanliness measure, for although there is no pain, no iota of discomfort, there will be blood. Are you alright with the sight of blood? Good. Very well. Here you go. This one is for you. . . and this one is for you. Just for this part of the tour. I apologize in advance for the somewhat unfortunate fashion challenge this presents, but we will wear these for only a few minutes, only during this part of the tour.

There you go. Yes. Good. Your humble cooperation is so appreciated! Take your time. We are, I am happy to note, a few minutes ahead of schedule.

Oh? Why, sure. We can sit a moment. . .

Better? Good. Let us proceed.

Hello Doctors, good afternoon to you! Nurse, hello to you too and thank you for allowing us to spend a few minutes with you.

Yes, yes. That is correct.

Why hello there! And how are we doing today? Oh, wonderful! And what are we reading on this special day?

Fabulous! I just love that book! Although don't remember it all that well; it has been a while. . .

Of course. And might I ask, what is the procedure being done today? Aha.

Why, thank you ever so much.

Indeed – drawn and quartered? Well, not so much. . . You do have a decided sense of humor, good sir! Wonderful! No, we need not look too long. This is not for everyone, madame.

Doctor? Where are we in the procedure? If you don't mind elucidating the steps you are taking for the benefit of my guests?

And sir, do you in fact feel any pain? Any at all? No? Any discomfort? None?

Splendid! Truly!

And so, my friends, as you can see, the chest is split wide open at this point and the pins are. . .

Oh, dear! Here! Please, take this chair.

There, there. . .

My apologies. Come. We can catch our breath over here. And here you go. A sip of water. There, there.

Another look? Why of course!

Yes, there is a curve, one could say, a brief period of let's call it acclimation.

Wonderful. Yes, as you can see the heart is beating, good and strong. Quite the miracle, is it not? We see this here, as we saw in there, the practice of humane science. No distracting, damaging throes of agony, neither here nor there, against which any other human must instinctively fight. No one in *our* world struggles against pain.

No pain. Right.

Yes, well, it is a little like magic.

We see it as dignity in a sea of calm. Like Grace. Every citizen is granted this. It, our way, has the capacity to elevate every last one of us. Patients, physicians, alike.

And Ma'am; you said you had a question for our patient? Go right ahead.

Yes, Doctor? Of course. Thank you most kindly. This has been a wonderful visit. Enlightening, and, well, beautiful in its own way. To see the cheeriness of a fellow citizen as we, good sir, see in you, to chat so pleasantly, so nonchalantly whilst a surgery is being performed upon your person, makes it all worth it.

Wouldn't you agree?

Splendid! I for one, could not agree more!

Oh, this? I will explain later. I would rather do it in context.

After all, there is still the portion of our tour during which we – as it has always been done – present in full, which is to say in context, how all this is borne by our *Ostesces.*

We have learned over the years that it is an imperative to first and fully illustrate the peace, the calm, the gentility that reigns, the absence of all negative energies and emotions as so miraculously lived and experienced by our people in order to bring home to such as yourselves, what this is really all about. How beautiful it all is.

It is key, we have further found, to imprint you with the beauteous nature of painlessness, to ensure you have ample illustrative opportunities to witness first-hand the vast, the, um, colossal capacities held in what we do, and with whom, and why. It is part of the absolute grace we live with as a result of our reality.

Yes. Correct. As a result of our ongoing partnership. I prefer to view it as a communion of souls with our most venerated *Ostesces*, each one of them a star in our Pantheon, may they stand long and proud where they find final rest. We live longer, better, healthier, and fuller lives for it.

Happier, peaceful lives.

That heart, that splayed chest. It is the stuff of paintings, is it not? A veritable landscape of the Human. The humane, dissected, resurrected. Bravo all around!

And if I wax a bit poetic when I conduct these tours, I cannot help it! When I revisit the contextual activities of which my role as your guide consists, I am profoundly moved each and every time! And I must warn you, I am a bit of a mush in the presence of an *Ostesce*. I have never built-up resistance to their, um, beauty. Oh, and thank you again for your willingness to don these robes. It is the least we can do when in the presence of a split ribcage, wouldn't you say?

Here. I'll take those back now. Thank you. And thank you!

Come, this way!

Feel free to peer in through any open doors as we make our way down the hall.

Let us go this way. Allow me.

Now, I propose a cup of tea before we head on to our next destination. A bit of fortification, let's call it, before we go to the Sanctuary. Our carriage awaits us.

Yes, that is where we will see her. Our brilliant and suffering hostess.

†††

So, we have just an hour before the Sanctuary is turned down for the night. By that, we mean the candles are extinguished, the incense burners are put out, and the *Ostesce* is fed her daily ration. Whether she actually sleeps, no one quite knows. There are strong indications of reduced activity and diminished responsiveness, which suggest some form of rest, some level of recuperative non-activity – non-absorption, as it were – in response to whatever might be occurring during the overnight hours. We discovered centuries ago that a twenty-four-hour watch – the constant witnessing and gauging of a host's condition – resulted in an increased pantophobia in them, which diminished their capacity to absorb our citizens' pain experiences, to internalize and then manifest them, that empathetic hyper-osteomalacia I was talking of earlier. To that end, about the turn of the 18th century, we set about to create a night of sorts in the Sanctuary, despite there being no indicators of night or day in the room. It is as you will see a windowless enclave in the lower cellar, at the very center of the temple footprint. While the night, so to speak, is only about five hours long, it keeps our *Ostesces* at full capacity, *et voilà* it keeps our people pain-free. We can only enjoy the gifts of the *Ostesce* so long as it, I mean she, is fully functional.

The ration, you ask? That consists of the host. A piece of consecrated, dry bread, and a sip – about a soup spoon's worth – of holy water. The host and the water are blessed right here, in the nave, by the senior Goodfather.

No. nothing else. It has little if nothing to do with actual nutrition. There has never been an *Ostesce* who has required food, which is to say, to eat, or digest. . . I rather cringe at the potential *outcomes*, so to speak of that. . . 'twould seem rather *unpure*.

No. Far as I know, few have ever *asked* for anything.

Trust me, we would know. The ministers charged with their care keep watch and log every detail, every action, including any word they might utter, so long as they can still speak. Often, speech ceases sometime during the third year.

Teeth tend to fuse, yes top to bottom, and tongues get bitten off when the jaws do their spontaneous thing. One never knows what exactly will happen, or in what order. Suffice it to say, the transmogrifications tend to commence with the largest joints first.

Yes, it can be a bit messy at first. But our ministers are fastidious housekeepers. Or should I say nursemaids? You understand, yes? We really do need you to be clear on this before I take you downstairs to see her.

Yes, of course. Take a seat, right here in the pew. We can take a minute to catch our breath. Would you like a bonbon? I have a bag of humbugs. Look. Right here. Take one. It'll soothe the tummy.

Let me advise you both, it is quite recommended – or might I venture to say it is rather an imperative – that you are both able to maintain a calm state of mind as we proceed on this last portion of our tour, even now. You see, the *Ostesce* is but a few feet below us, right here where we stand, in the nave. We will access the Sanctuary by way of the stairs over there, through that arched doorway. But while you are in this close proximity to her – and part of our little universe, as it were – she will be compulsed by the nature of her gift, to home in on your distress if you are feeling anything, and to internalize it.

Yes, and to manifest it.

Yes! Even newcomers such as yourselves!

Try and think of it this way: the more calm you can maintain during what is, yes, far more a personal revelation than any basic sharing of information, the better for us all. It is not always easy for the prospective collector. A last hurdle, you could say. A bit of a test. The negative vapors you might be emitting, she will be picking up from you, which might only make the first sight of her that much more difficult for you, if indeed she is in active degeneration thanks to your very own emotionality. The birthing halls and surgeries today will have made this a busy enough day for her already, notwithstanding all the other random, little incidents constantly at play in the lives of our citizenry, all no doubt resulting in some marked transmogrifications in her today, even this close to let's call it her bedtime. Let us not add to the host's distress in our moment of introduction. Agreed?

Good. Thank you.

Indeed, sir. I understand. Of course. It happens.

Yes, I can wait. But we cannot wait too long. We have – let me see what my watch says – about fifty minutes left in her day. When the attendants close shop for the night, the Sanctuary doors are locked, and they too are windowless. No latent glimpses, no surreptitious peeks. Either we go in and you meet your *Ostesce* face to face or we will have to consider, um, let's call it other options. . .

No. Yes. Good. You are feeling better now? Good. And you are both still committed to this acquisition, yes? Good. I can tell you are, sir. I am trying to accommodate your wife, here. It happens. Empathy is an emotion you in your world still contend with, being that suffering is still elemental to your existence. Try to imagine you are visiting on some distant planet. Tap some cathartic imagery to set aside what all you are trying to digest. You are being made witness to something not of your world, so that you can ultimately take a little portion of what we have, *what we are*, into your world. This has been from the outset the goal. Agreed?

Indeed. Otherworldly is a good word for it. Brava, madame, for your circumspection. Would you like another humbug?

No? Very well. Let us go downstairs to meet *la Ostesce*. . .

Come my dear, allow me. . . Take my arm. . .

†††

Yes, of course, you can speak.

What was that?

Yes, she can hear us.

No. That she cannot do. In this one, the mandible split a few years ago, and the two halves have now fused themselves to her collarbones. Makes for a dramatic orifice, does it not? Almost like something you'd find on the masthead of a pirate's ship!

Oh, sure. Yes, the attendants just need to administer the host with a little more finesse. Nothing a large pair of tweezers or a long-handled spoon can't accomplish.

No. Like I said, there is no hunger. This one has never once asked for food.

No worries. Your eyes will continue to adjust.

That is correct. No sunlight, or moonlight. Ever. Just these candles.

Oh, dear.

Madame, here. . .

No. I, ah. . .

Sir, sir. This will not do! If your wife cannot help her tears, we will have to exit the premises. Please, madame, I beg of you. . . Come on now, I know you can do this. You are both high level, prime collector applicants. And just think, when this *Ostesce* is expired – and it'll be just a couple months more – you will have your very own plinth. Why, just look at her! Look at the rotation of her right leg, with her foot hooked over her shoulder like that! Colossal. Truly, what wizened apple tree is as eloquently gnarled? What grapevine is this poetically twisted?

Correct, sir. Well. . .

Ma'am, look with me, let us talk about it. . . Talk it through. . .

Let us not be distracted with negativities as you might be inclined to perceive them. That is not what this is about. Think. . . Think, um. . . magical mysticism. . . think living sculpture. . . Here! If you look right here, you can see movement. No doubt it is the remainders of today's events manifesting in the host. There! did you catch that? Look right there, at the shin bone.

No, on the left leg. Do you see the angle of the bend there? Watch. . . It's almost imperceptible but it's visible. It is bending farther as we speak. Can you see it? Minute breaks now. . . a small, sequential splintering. . .

Oh, I know. Well, the sparse illumination I have always found somewhat romantic. . .

There! There it is again! Did you hear it?

Good, that was a bit more obvious. Yes, the skin is now breaking too. Part of the process. How else can the bones come into contact to fuse? Osteal fusion has always only occurred by way of bone melding directly to bone.

Yes. As I mentioned, the attendants keep things cleaned up in here. Some days are a bit let's say messier than others.

Ma'am. . . Ma'am! Please!

Sir, can I ask you to try and calm your wife down?

If that doesn't just. . . Now, look what we have done! The *Ostesce* was dozing when we entered.

Probably too much commotion. Too much *emotion*. She is wide awake now. Well, so be it. You will probably soon become audience to her moans, and this one's is not a terribly mellifluous song. I should warn you: To bear witness to audial lamentations can get in the way of aesthetic appreciation, on which we must all remain steadfast. Right my dear? And brave. Remember, the host is only doing what she was always set out to do, what all the *Ostesce* before her have done. And no one here – no one in our world – would have it any other way. You do understand, don't you?

Please remember, you both were thoroughly vetted and, unless you were a bit less than one hundred percent forthcoming with your applications, what was presented to us on paper – but for this unfortunate display of emotion on the part of your lovely wife here – showed you two as being more than suitably conditioned for the honour of acquiring one of our plinths.

Yes, of course. My condolences. Would that you might have seen fit to disclose it.

Oh. I see.

No, this is not the first time. You – I mean we – are only human. And the suffering you are witnessing I promise you, will only serve to heighten your appreciation of the plinth once it is in your possession, for the serenity it will embody in its final, deboned state.

Oh! Excuse me. Rasmus? You might want to see this. Bring rags and a basin. There is a sizable break happening in the left shinbone, right above the ankle. Getting pretty, er, muddled over here. . .

Thank you, my friend. . .

Yes, a hazard of the process.

There. that's better. . .

Oh dear.

Sir. . . oh my goodness! Your wife!

Here you go! Let me help. Oh my. I hope she didn't hit her head too hard when she fell. Oh deary, oh me-oh my-oh! This does not look like it's going to work.

Yes, yes. I know *you* are good to go. But what about her?

Indeed. But here is the problem. This all needs to be alright with *the both* of you. It won't work to divide you as a couple this late in the process. Had that been the case from the get-go, it would have been better for you to apply solo, just yourself. You could perhaps have managed to house the plinth in such a way that your lovely wife would never have wondered two wits about it; perhaps kept it secreted from her altogether in a second residence or something. But we don't generally stand on deceptive, or divisive, collecting practices. Things get complicated, and the fallout is often not worth the trouble, certainly not the cost.

Oh, I know.

I am sorry but. . .

Pardon me, could you repeat that? It is a bit difficult to hear over the din.

Yes, of course. The pain *she* feels is as real as any pain ever felt to anyone. Probably worse. No, definitely worse. That's part of the splendor in all this. There is no experiential middle ground inside these ancient walls. The Sanctuary is deep underground for good reason.

Yes. Nineteen years and counting on this one. . .

What was that again?

I know, I know. Oh my. The noise is disconcerting. Fracturing is especially let's call it dramatic. When she settles down from this, um, episode, I am certain she will doze off again. It *is* late. . .

Um, no.

I am sorry, but no.

Oh. I see.

Very well then.

No. That is fine. The deposit *is* non-refundable. But you knew that, yes? It doesn't, however, alter the unfortunate fact that you two now know too much. . .

No. We have never done that. It *is* about the money, of course, to a notable extent. But there is far more at play here. . .

Oh, dear. Well, this *is* a problem.

Rasmus. . .?

Yes, it *is* a problem, to back out this late in the process. Once you have laid eyes on a living host, you can neither unsee it nor forget any other sensory impression gathered in these chambers: the sight, the sound, even the. . . the, um, stench. . . It is something of an imprinting, pain recorded and molded into a tangible, measurable, flesh-and-blood incarnation. Therefore, the risk factor of your *spilling* on all this exists in droves. Huge problem. Unwanted disclosures. . . Risky, risky, risky! Trust me, we have been there a couple times. Not a pretty thing. No good outcomes.

I know. That is what they all say.

Look; at least you do not have the dubious honour as being the first ones to fall off at this point. Would that I could say it'd be the last, but that would be an inordinately great expectation of you all, no matter your standing, no matter how agreeably you presented yourselves to the vetting committee.

I truly am so sorry as well. Now, look here, if you would allow me. . .

Rasmus! Thank you, well done. Oh, you are quick!

Well, yes, if you've got him good and tight, go right ahead.

My dear sir. It'll hurt for only a moment or two. And your wife will never know what happened. She hit her head pretty hard, poor thing. Did a real number on herself, all by her lonesome.

Yes, Rasmus. . .

You see, we have perfected our methods, for, the last thing we would want, is to put the final sufferings of a couple of wishy-washy foreigners upon our busy little hostess here. *La Ostecse* is almost ripe. I mean, look at her! She could prove to be one of the most divinely formulated specimens we will have produced in some time – in my lifetime at least. And so, the quicker we dispense of you two, the sooner we can have our driver bring over the next candidate, who, if you must know, is staying at the same inn where you two are booked, in the suite one floor right above yours. How about that? We will be able to pick right up with him where, I am afraid, we must now leave off with you.

Oh my. . .

My most sincere condolences, dear sir, that this didn't work out between us. But as I said, time is of the essence. This one has been doubled over onto herself coming up on twelve years, and the parallel sections of her spinal column are commencing to fuse into each other as we speak. We simply cannot jeopardize any minute she has left to accomplish this. A two-tiered spinal column on a plinth is beyond rare. A special sort of origami, you could say; rare and highly decorative. It renders them a tad compact, I suppose, but. . .

Oh, do shut up. There is nothing you can do.

Rasmus? On my mark. . .

Come to think of it, we may even raise the price on this one, given the fact that we have not yet finalized the paperwork with the next candidate, and he can well afford it. Owns his own island; arrived in port aboard his own yacht. But I digress; must sound like some common gossip. . . Shame on me!

What do you think, Rasmus? I'd bet the ministers would latch on to the revisions in a. . .

Now!

†††††

"Everything was beautiful, and nothing hurt."
Kurt Vonnegut, Slaughterhouse Five, 1969

Santa Domnia II: *Hellscape Wrought*

Santa Domnia – no, no!
Santa, stay where you are!
Let me worship you from my spot on the floor!
No, no, Santa Domnia – do not take my limbs!
This I sought not – I must plead, I implore!
No, please, not the spikes!
No, not my left hand!
I beg you, dear Santa, leave my right hand alone!
Inglorious Santa,
You were not called forth to crucify ME –
I had foolishly thought you had simply come home!

And thus, our passionate upstart cuts short his mortal sojourn on this, our beautiful earth, in his misguided quest, to resurrect the darkest deity among saints, la Santa Domnia.

Granted re-entry from the eternal twilight, to rejoin the plains of the living, She shall once more roam freely about and feed as She desires, much as any lividly famished, freshly re-animated entity must. La Santa Domnia has finally returned to reclaim Her rightful place amongst Man and Monster, on the very same terral plains across which all are swept, whether finely strung like marionettes or lashed together as beasts of burden. She walks among us, so together we will be made to slog through the pain in which *all* must partake. Agonies were wrought for Eve on our behalf, so that god or ruffian, we may be delivered to Mankind by way of our universal suffering, which still defines us as the starkest of Truths.

Abandoning Her hapless gatekeeper, pinned to the walls of his study a desperately skittering, insectuous specimen performing his last and dying dance on a barren stage of his own, meticulous making, La Santa lumbers off. The *rigor mortis* of Her cryptic tenure as yet renders Her memory rather spotty, Her mottled limbs less agile than might be desired for one of such hallowed and exquisitely base origins. Verily, with every footfall, our Santa limbers up, gains incrementally a purposefulness in Her stride. Trust me when I tell you this: She grows surer with each step taken. She knows just where to go.

Into the wintry night la Domnia vanishes, taking rapid leave of the writer in his study, his house, his corner of the city. Swallowed whole in the misting flurries of a December storm, oblivious to the cold, the night, the hour, our Santa commences on a junket most purposeful. Dust-laden memories hatch like flies' eggs in the curdled slurry that stirs, quickens, seeks to function as Her brain. A ravenous hunger is sparked; demand for sustenance pierces Her consciousness. First up, is to fill Her cavernous belly; after that, Her bottomless soul.

La Santa has carelessly left wide open Her conjurer's door. It yawls in submissive welcome to the avenue and elements, for practical tasks like this are beneath Her stunted consideration. Listen! The alley dogs bay offsides, having smelt the tang of the dying writer's panic, and his malodorous excretions, which stripe his garments wet and dark, grow the steaming puddle on the floor. No sooner does our immortal One turn down the allée, as do the hounds rush up the front steps, working their jowls and snapping at each other, in pursuit of their putrescent quarry, who calls to them with fetid promise, hangs in waiting for them in his posh, little chamber at the top of the stairs.

Do you, my sweets, dare believe a one like this desires to be so roused from so heavy a slumber?

How is one to know? How, children, how? Very well, then, I shall now tell you the Tale of la Santa Domnia!

Here we have a Being as profane as may ever have been by the constellations rendered, whose resurrection was accomplished upon such a nexus of nightmares, the sleepless themselves would nigh pride themselves of their insomnia. This is One birthed to heed desperation's every call, for whom prayers were never anything but limpid nursery songs and hymns the weakest of lullabies. Even if at the bedside of innocents, when whispered or dared sung bare above a furtive hush, unwitting postulants might try and keep one such as She at bay. But no. Rather, they invite la Santa in!

Not every child seeks to dream of sweetmeats and confections, longs to hear of princesses and cheerful, "happy" endings. Do you?

And so, She makes Her way down the street. Oh, yes, my dears. She will come!

Our everted deity of the underworld hears everything. If wrung from that residual nook wherein honest fear dwells, neither momentarily shaken off nor ever fully vanquished, She exists as a fear-filled call's requisite response, within the tickling nape of a neck brushed by an uncanny cold. She is in that spine feathering, cautionary flicker of unfortunate realization, the gut grown queasy with some nameless recognition. Santa Domnia resides within the infinitesimal falters of a tremblant whisper, the reluctantly uttered word as it falls off short, right there, at mid-gasp.

These are but the coarse vespers as delivered by la Santa's postulates, lauding Her, luring Her. These are the missives penned by Her iniquitous minstrels, who play to Her swollen, black heart, much as the poet once wrote of Isafrel, his angel, whose heartstrings were like a lute. Hers, we all know, are far darker, more wicked.

Who then, among us, seated upon the shoulders of wingèd beings, seeks to be carried aloft in this manner?

If that, my dears, be you, look not to the saccharin clouds above.

If that, my dears, be you, look into the shadowed corners below.

There is no need to reach for the soft, the benign, the forgettable if you seek the embrace of la Santa Domnia. Lean instead into obscurities, deep into the hubris of Man, where soot and flesh co-mingle and degenerate into the decrepit soup from whence all are born – and some re-born. There is indeed an incorruptible persistence amidst decay re-animated, and la Santa is your proof.

Come at last is She who has slumbered in a static suspension we humans euphemize as the deepest of sleeps. From that cold place, She has been made to rise. Slow, woefully stiff as the brittle linens which enwrap criminals and Saviors alike, la Santa presses ahead, against the hardened cloth that could stifle every harrowing cry until it too is drawn down to silence. There is nothing in Her hollows but a liquid, echoing quiescence. She remains oblivious to Her agonies. Any residual whimper here would be laid to waste, no matter which mouth might ever dare utter it. Nothing is heard when no one listens. Nothing ever changes. And no one will hear tonight. On Her singular foray, la Santa has no time to pay that sort of attention.

And oh, the misery She personifies! With Her own, small mouth so stuffed, any chance of a fighting fresh breath is brutally quaffed! Wretchedly gagged, slack jawed in suspended shock, Her countenance is hideously displaced. Coal ash spills from Her withered lips, brickles from the small ledge of a bone-jutted chin. Coarse gravel is a solvent offal ground to grains, an obsidian salt crystalized between two rows of ambered teeth worn down to their quicks, invoking the fundamental demise of the prehistoric doomed. Rotted remnants curl up in a tenuous grimace, but any semblance of a smile was long ago erased. For She has been fed from the ashes of the very same beams that were cast down on the square, to encircle the righteously, falsely accused, to immolate them as they stood guard against their accusers. La Santa can nigh taste the burning martyrs, who roasted like fatted beasts, gruesomely exonerated by way of their incineration, whose virtuous sisters and brethren observed in smug silence, stoking their apocalyptic passions by way of their nemeses' annihilation. They too will rise from the beds of their own ashes to serve as kindred cutthroats, in deference to our Santa – but only when the time is right.

Fascinating is it not, the ones who created and let be fed the Beast, all partake in its insatiable lust for destruction?

Oh, children, children, have you any imaginings of what pain truly can be?

Such a sweet and brutal agony as what our la Santa endures opens wide the subterranean doors, from which caskets She was extracted. Her mind is but the fleshy cradle wherein rests Evil's wizened eye, deep seated, unblinking. That eye, it cannot see as we simple humans do, but yet imagines the worst. And so, it sees *everything.*

Past, present, yet to come. . .

Every sin, every vile deed and rank wish, all base desires. . .

. . . each trifling cry of some lost babe, or the bellows of an enraged father; or the silence of a stone-hearted mother, false friend, or turncoat partner. La Santa is there at the ready and has partaken of them all – and they reside in Her.

The lacteous all-seeing eye lolls about in its cavity. Ignited by forces of all that drives our Santa, it gathers in and broadcasts back to its host: *Think! Do! Act! React! Destroy, destroy!* Blink and something might be missed. It knows this. Torn open, gawking, frozen, it shall remain on dreadful, constant watch.

All the better to see you, my dears!

And once within the husk of yon hollowed skull, whence the incantations have been re-commenced and recited upon the strikes of midnight, how quickly that skull of Hers fills itself anew! Vermin gathers in a bizarre dance, creeping, and clinging, growing, and grabbing, branching off each orifice, tail to head in a beastly chain, orally affixed coral twining and taking root as do creeping fungi spawn in their beds of sludge. Waxen matter encrusted, melding to fill the void, reaching first one eye socket and then the other, then breaching the sinuses, the mass crawls and slithers towards the mouth, wherein fanged teeth have long lain embedded, petrified within the gums. All takes root, tears at the mandible, until, agape, Her grin is laid open in an expression of wonderment, the nightmare having manifested itself as a terrified awakening. When, from this macabre hive, the collective skittering calls to Her, tickles Her hollow belly, She is at last roused in full from the stasis of Her oblivion.

Time, time, Santa Domnia, to enter into the odiousness of Man once more!

Come, Santa Domnia, come!

And the children recite:

Santa Domnia, fair maiden, thorned ringlet, brow crested!
Your forehead and scalp pierced, your curls thickly matted.
Garnet rivulets flow 'pon a dainty lace collar, so painstakingly knotted, so thoroughly spattered!

Laborious endeavor is required indeed to bring Her forth. Everything, everything must be in place. Everything must be just so. There can be nothing of kindness, nor hope. Not one iota of wisdom. Only fools and misanthropes are granted their say in Her domain, wherein the bleakest of magic can flourish. How else to knit back together the rotted parts and dried bits that will have lain fallow for eons upon folds of stained rouching and mold-imbued lace which line the sunless berth that has served as Her cradling sarcophagus? These are but the ill-made beds for sleeping harpies. From that place – where no scream, nor cricket's lament nor cry of a dying cicada could wrest its way past walls cemented with mortar made of blood scraped from the flayed backs of its victim builders, She will make Her way through the soil to announce, to beg of all wayward souls.

Here I am! Here I am! Save me!

If you could see with your own eyes the resurrection, bear witness to la Santa when next brought forth from Her burial chamber, there would be nothing at first but a layer of black silt, a few stubborn nubs, a swath of matted hair, an empty ribcage as delicate as a coop for a songbird. Ancient of days come and gone, Her reconstitution is a time to re-craft what once was undone.

With spittle and secretions, the vermin toils and spins and combs. Pinchers plying and splintered, tiny legs fabricate from the remnants a mottled ball of cranium and skeletal bone. Liquified skin seeps over the housing and hardens like wax. Cobwebbed masses writhe lividly, grow as do tendrilled hatchling snakes. They intertwine, pull long and lank their primeval forms, until proud as Medusa, la Santa can toss Her hair with the impudence of a rabid filly.

Dissolved by the very acids her dying struggles fermented – Such fear! Such panic! What a delirium! – la Santa lies awash in a bath that once boiled the very skin from Her flesh, curled it, and curdled it into a stench-imbued slop. It is now the bath in which Her corpse is stewed. Dull bone to rancid flesh, to one transparent and pallid human beast. There, at last, She is.

If you must, know this: La Santa sings own piercing requiem. Her laments ascend in pitch to a dirge of screeching metal, only to resolve in a string of guttural, spit-slurried pleas. When the air has been duly tainted and the spirits of Hades sufficiently riled, they will creep in to impart in Her a first, whistling breath. It is then, She can ascend from the infernal depths to answer, clawing Her way through fissures carved by the knives of whispering shivers. She will fight Her way from the depths to invade our homes. If you do not take care, She will breach your floorboards, and pass through you, catch hold of the underside of your scalp with Her nimble hook and then pull you out through your belly, turning you inside out, and then She will take you back to Her realm!

> Santa Domnia, fair maiden, candle crowned!
> Dripping, molten, hardening fast; ensconcing, encasing your pallid, pained countenance. Streams flowing unfettered with blood imbued wax!

Aye, it must have been a stubborn and stolid chap, to call la Santa from Her depths. His remains bear witness to all he managed, the words he spoke, the blasphemes he invoked. Hear him, She did. Heed him, She did. Visit him, She did. Haunt his home, She did. Crucify him, She did. Leave him nailed to the very wall of his study, pine branches spiked through his outstretched hands, his feet, through his breast, She did. Left his mouth stuffed with the glowering coals from his very own fire, much as had Her own mouth been packed so long ago, She did. With twin sprigs of holly threaded through each of his eyelids to pin that panicked gaze of his wide open, She left him, there to reap the rewards of his impudent conjurings. She walks off to the cadence of his weakening sobs, leaves Her suitor for dead. She has forgotten him by the time She has crossed the avenue.

> Santa Domnia, sweet maiden, fair princess!

Snow-white was your dress, now with holly impaled blooms darker, red-pocked from that gash in your breast!
Your heaving, your breathing, belabored and pained, your moth-eaten bodice most thoroughly stained!

Now, listen, my dears! Cast your sound seeking ears to the shutters I say, for 'tis none other than La Santa Domnia now coming our way!

Listen for that most peculiar of footfalls, that stumbling trip. . .

She will soon be near, and starved for the sweetmeats of you, children, here!

La Santa has set off to wander the emptied city streets. Midnight just passed, deathly cold fills the night. 'twould be no living soul about but a spectral entity such as She!

Listen for Her lumbering stealth, as yet an awkward gait. What would one expect as much of an ancient corpse, so freshly resurrected? Heavy of foot, la Santa carves a rickety path through the snow, leaves a scattered trail of detritus in Her wake, so packed are the layers of Her skirts with graveyard matter. Droplets of cold, thickened blood drip from Her fingertips, proof of endeavors of a few minutes' past, and what was made of Her host. Left him nailed to his own walls, She did, him not being to Her taste, such a soured old soul was he. Quite unfit for our queen. Santa seeks something far more delectable!

Crowned 'pon a mass of tangled webbing is now a brambling wreath of thorns, thick and wicked as a black-needled sea urchin. Spikes point to the sky, skewer drifting flakes of snow, are turned inwards as well, breaching the calcified depths of Her patchy skull. Stigmatic perversion renders sound the mockery of an agonized crowning, as good books of yore still tell. But la Santa seeks no salvation, oh no. Inverted, Her glories lie not in prophetic resolution. Ink-black liqueur slides like machinist's oil over temple and sallow cheek, dripping to Her collar, Her bosom. No bridal purity exists to preserve the sanctity of Her sordid radiance. La Santa is flower bedecked by the very brushstrokes of Her own bloodied seepage as it gathers and spreads crimson blooms and black streaks. What was once a grand burial gown is repugnantly spoilt.

Let us recall those wondrous wings with which She was blessed: Broad, leathered expanses, wilted and folded, inset at each peaked, little shoulder, each mummified appendage pleated tightly onto itself, tapering horrifically, gracefully, in both line and form. Accordioned arrays, a means of flight, clad in serrated, metallic tines. Next to the brackish muck that marks the ground with each step She takes, if you look, you will see the snow raked into tight lines, bitten by teeth, pointed like knives.

Our Santa comes now 'round to the town square, spies the wan colors of the chapel windows, its portals alit. The vicar has hung out his shingle. At least, *He* is in. Yon feeble beacon calls to all sinners, admonishing them to gather:

Midnight mass, children; save yourselves.

Santa's brain endeavors to frame a rounded, sentient thought:

Big stone house. Human, fresh. Food. For me. Inside. Go.

The pipe organ's caterwaul stops short in the frigid rush of wind and snow as the doors fling open in spirited compliance with Her desire, which is to cross the hallowed threshold, breech the sanctified air of the Lord's chapel lair. Last notes linger sadly; their echo weakens and falls to silence, the sort of audible absence Mankind like his gods has long recognized as the harbinger of tragic denouements for those who have come – they presume – to worship, who in that moment fall still as mice as the barn cat approaches. Supplicants and sinners, reduced to one and the same, equally subject in their frailty, remain stock still, eyes locked into a distance devoid of neither seraph nor redeemer.

In this space, la Santa Domnia need not plod about. Here, where magic is christened a miracle, where incantations are re-titled as canticles, She sails down the long center aisle, a Mephistophelian vestal, held aloft by all the unanswered prayers which yet languish in this hall, in supplication to the One designated as having dominion, the penultimate recipient for all the countless pleas, wishes, and invocations intended for a far finer ether than the frosty dirge She has just allowed in. Futility hovers suspended and weighted, atop the stone floors, a slurry as thick as the bogs. Here exists a wallowing swamp of stifled entreaties, wholly deflated in the face of Her uninvited imposition. La Santa by Her arrival alone has quashed each confession 'neath the soles of Her mud-encrusted, satin slippers. Upon the loft of every heaven-shunned missive, She positively floats.

Lest we forget, tales of monsters and saints are both born of Mankind. All reactions and results are of His feats, His deeds, His sins, and misdeeds. Where the universal is refracted and shot back to earth, much like the snowfall is sent when winter deepens and the year is killed off, the sublimely horrific transmogrifies and is spiced – sweetened – to become the stuff of bedtime stories, which is where the malleable mindset can still be shaped. Perhaps a few dare question or challenge; most will conform. By design. Still, all delight in the resonance of a tall tale, well told. And so, our Santa gains in stature with each word written, every recitation uttered. Dreams of la Santa are reliant on the questionable bridges built, one fallen soul, one compromised generation, at a time. In our wake, endless room for evolution is left. Story upon story, over and over again.

Santa Domnia exists, my children, because WE do.

. . .and mind, you, as She makes Her way towards the apse, our Santa reaps a transformation most magical! Bigger and bigger She grows, children, until Her thorn-crowned head reaches nigh to the arches, brushes 'gainst the carved ribs of the vault. See there, bloodied smears She has left high up there! Santa must soon crouch to fit, so quickly She seats Herself 'gainst the altar from where She can better gaze down, 'pon the cowering parishioners below.

No, no Santa, not me! the simple fools plea.

Those who can, fall hard to their knees.

Little do they know, 'tis not their sweat-salted carcasses She desires for Her feast.

No, no! La famished Santa casts a hungering eye towards the plump cherubs lined up the choir; there seated like pigeons, a passel of plump, savory boys!

With a long-armed sweep of Her outstretched hands, la Santa spans the distance with a motion so quick, 'tis but a blur to those stagnating at Her feet.

And with a One! and a Two! Before the first folds of a choir robe are stirred, before a blood-curdling cry is expelled from a single Cupid's bow, Santa tears Her jowls open wide and then swallows them whole!

One choir child! And then two, and then three, and then four!

Chomp, chomp, and a belch, and She eats them all whole!

With a gobble and a crunch, yon souls be swiftly wrested as their bodies squeeze down – down to the gullet they go, one, two, three, more. Such unfortunate children, so to meet with their doom.

Which you too, my dear ones, ought remember when done, whether crumpets or children our Santa devours, She will cast all others aside with Her shoe, leave them piled like refuse; for want, nothing more.

Thus, our Santa departs the hellscape just wrought, and now I will bet She is coming for you!

So, rush, rush to your coffins, you little minxes, you two!

Enough of tall tales for the morning now looms.

You must now quick a-bed, lest the sun strike your heads, bake you both like fresh bread, leave me with no choice but to eat you instead!

†††††

We Thalassophiles

There is none so quaint as a seaside village, with its board-and-battened cottages, postage stamp lawns, picket fences strung with fishing buoys more colorful 'n Easter eggs. Where porches are curtained off with driftwood-laced lengths of twine, and conch shells blossom in window boxes like caramelized mushrooms. Where narrow garden walkways are lined with cockleshells on parade, and paths are strewn with the tumbled shards of bleached oysters. All these rusticated grottos and ocean-invoking avenues might best befit a slew of vacationing North Atlantic Mer-kings and their queens, but they are more simply the familiar trappings of the small town we two-legged, air-breathing ocean lovers call Home.

Be that as it may, there is none ever so much *more* quaint as a seaside village when, at long and summer-dragging last, the last of the human tourists have finally high-tailed it back to the city. Lugging their overstuffed valises and carrying those stupid, broad-brimmed hats made to catch even the smallest of breezes and go flying off into the water or smack dab into muddied eddies, away they all go, tanned and better fed than what's good for them, into their waiting trains and auto caravans, onto the ferry as is warranted, leaving our oceanside domiciles massively disheveled, but nothing that can't be fixed – or erased.

Main Street's shutters are quickly shucked of their cobwebs, eased shut and slatted into place. Front porch wicker is draped or stashed away in offsides sheds. And all that foreign-made kitsch in the shopwindows? Those baskets of *imported* seashells? Everything is gathered up pronto and packed into waiting storage trunks, put to bed until next year's Memorial Day weekend, when it's all brought out again for the next round of dry-land-dwelling city folk.

Oh indeedy; once *they* are good and gone, our season begins. We *Thalassophiles* have much to do.

The shore has over the last three months by way of all the sweaty and stinking humanity been nicely chummed. Pungent beach lovers, the best lures, cast themselves into the water for weeks on end at highest cost, many of them willing to pay triple and more for the small rooms we let out to them, in all those gingerbread rentals that line our avenues. Spotters – the very same lifeguards who bronzed their tawny hides during the long hours of open public beach time – kept, as they had been trained to do, one eye on the swimmers and their safety, another on all the aquatic activity just past the buoys. It was those massive, slinking shadows, flitting in and out of view over the course of the summer, for which we were all keenly keeping watch. We knew – but we would never dare say anything – about those sea beasts. They were, more or less, just checking things out – sensing, smelling, contemplating all those flailing arms and legs. Waiting, waiting, and waiting. . .

Oh, and how the city folk loved to visit what we called our Aquatic Refuge! Just like the rooms they let, they'd pay twice and more the regular price to walk amongst the ponds and the huge, saltwater lake my very own grandpa and great uncles helped dig by hand. There is a huge, circular pool, which over the last several summers now has housed our two dolphins. The dolphins, hand-raised by our keepers, are reliant on us, but none of us could help that. The dolphins spend the summer performing for their handlers and the simpering audiences; they seem content with what they know to be their lot. Upon departure of the tourists, Mary and Pickford always get transferred to the lake at the back end of the grounds, where they can romp more freely in the murkier waters, which much more closely resemble the oceans. They, the sea turtles, and the random fish we have collected over time all get along famously. And I tell you, there is nothing like sitting poolside with a cup o' coffee or a root beer come and gone Labor Day, to just hang out and watch the critters cruise the water, break the surface here and there, show off for us a little, happily re-settled in their off-season confines.

Once the last of the tourists are gone, and once our ocean creatures are situated back in their pools, it is time to prepare the main tank for bigger fish. More specifically, a single, much bigger fish.

You see, we had suffered a most unfortunate rise in, well let's just call it infiltrations, and there were a few choice candidates who needing dealing with.

To that end, the lifeguards had reported on activity beyond the swim zones, and their counts had been noted with a whole lot o' glee. A particularly massive specimen had been spotted cruising the outer edges of the ledge, right where the shallows fall off into the gray-blue trench, which frames the ocean proper. A Great

White has this lovely way of, well, we call it shadow playing, against the drop cloth of the Atlantic's chillier depths. Easily spotted from a well-placed perch, they were easily missed at ground level, which suited us just fine.

Aye, they told us this one, this year's target, was a real beaut'.

Our town angler – yep, his post was an official one – with his wizened face all mapped with sun and life as it had befallen him, had perfected the process of capturing our Great Whites. The big fellas were brought in quite nicely intact, never more than a tad scuffed up, that being thanks to their ever-lovin' propensity for a good fight. The sharks would be delivered to the Aquatic Center under cover of night, with only those of us charged with the task, the Milky Way, and a distant moon present to play witness, do the deed, cast light upon our delivery. The Refuge staffers had long ago honed their timing and skills to keep calm our catch, so all could be quietly transferred to the crystal-clear waters of the central tank, what we called the Pool. Once come to, boatloads of fish and rank, leftover innards from the butcher's made for one heck of an all-you-can-eat buffet for the hungry beast, after which they were left to their quiet devices, so to build up a next, good, solid appetite for things to come.

Twitch, so the angler called himself due to some nerve-triggered tick above his eye, had promised us, this year's candidate was looking to be the biggest and best one to date. The lifeguards' notes had suggested our quarry had been long at hand, loitering in our waters' peripheries most all summer long, which they said seemed to 'indicate a marked preference for our specific area.' He was practically waiting for us, Twitch had noted as he'd stuff his kerchief under his cap like he always did. Twitch only surfaced once a year, come early September, when time came to bring in the given year's catch, but he'd stayed on from one year to the next by way of a stipend that consisted of room and board in the ramshackle lighthouse on the island at the mouth of the bay. No power, no running water out there; nothing, as Twitch would say, 'but the blue of the seas and skies and a block of rubble for to rest me tuckus.'

This year's Great White arrived by light of the Full Corn Moon, which thanks to the maritime gods we all know are out there, had been perfectly timed. A bunch of us had gathered, as we always did, to haul the beast on over to the Pool. The moon's light bounced off the Great's pitted flanks as he hung there over the pier, awash in Neptune's candle glow, nearly a-snooze in those slings like some enormous sea monster baby. We all took turns looking; the bastard had so many rows of teeth, their total could only be guessed at. What had this fella grown? Four rows? Five? Judd Coolidge poked about with his walking stick to try and get a count, but the sheriff, a big fella himself, scolded Judd just like he had over the summer, whenever he'd catch a pack o' brats punching a beached jelly.

At any rate, our catch was a big one. Biggest one ever, far as we could tell. And from the looks of his rough skin, an old booger to boot. Many a skirmish of the deep had left its mark; perhaps not a few of the scars he bore were from encounters with unsuccessful fishermen long come before us. Evidence to be sure, of a long and illustrious career as killer-of-the-sea. And his tail; why, it was as big as pair o' kites! It took extra help that night, thanks be to Moe Tutweiler's trusty backhoe, to extract the Great White from the boat, and to cut away some natty, old netting he had twisted about himself, who knows when. Twitch said this catch had been a particularly ferocious one. But how could we hold that against such a fella? I'd be furious too, if I were ripped from my saltwater heavens, and plunked into a concrete pond.

How it is as obvious as it is, I cannot say, but when a shark is truly enraged, you can see it in their eyes. This was especially evident with this one. A silent, primitive fury lit those black marble eyes. And he never blinked. It was like he preferred to just stare at us, size us up. Once in his tank, the Great White circled and circled with a clip many of us figured, was an attempt to stay good and fully pissed off with every last one of us.

You bet; he would do wonderfully well! He was a dandy in the worst way. The Great inhaled everything up we tossed to him that night. Good-sized tuna may as well have been krill. And there was no iota of pleasure in his consumption – it was a quick-as-a-flash fast track from mouth to belly with a "so there" that could only be taken as disdain for us creaky-limbed subordinates. So obvious was his spite, that a few of us began to dare whisper, we might better not harvest him after the proceedings, as we had been doing for centuries, for our annual Village Fish Fry. Dorian Tellman even broached the notion, he might be worth holding onto all the way into the next year, for the next round, come Fall. Nah, we nixed that pretty quickly – our tourists were too reliant on all things quaint and friendly and nice about us and our village. Heck, the town had been christened "Sweethome" back in 1728, and with our street names all in keeping with the preciousness of the place – Harmony Lane, Pleasant Drive, and so on – how could we present anything of a less sugar-coated nature? This Great was way too kranky for the likes of our city-folk, and so he would be harvested like it had always been done, for our Fish Fry.

Fine. The White would go by the way of his forebears.

One week before the Fish Fry, we were to gather at the Refuge to witness the annual Reconciliation of the incarcerated folk that had been kept in the town's underground holding cells for this very event. And so, we did.

The Great White hadn't been fed in more than a week. Could he have snarled at us as he circled the tank, he would have. Just the other day, when the mayor had stopped by to take a look at him, that old shark did nothing less than but to butt his logger head up against the side of the pool, to where the mayor out of total shock very nearly fell headfirst into the water! Would that have made for a spectacle or what?

As we had been doing for pretty much ever, we all arrived near sunset and took our seats. The air was heavy with a harsh nip, a southwesterly drift carrying the dregs of a Canadian chill onto our town and over our shorelines, the Atlantic long since answering in kind, with her own slew of bitterly cold breezes. Cloud cover, trapped on either side by the sparring winds, had painted the skies thick in shades of gray and blue, which resulting cold we townsfolk did our best to stave off with our plaid woolens, our hand-knit mufflers, and our flannel-lined, rubberized boots. Most of us had brought thermos bottles and flasks with us, filled with everything from Irish coffees and buttered brandies to cocoas or hot ciders – whatever anyone fancied.

It was, for us, a happy time, the start of our holiday season. Right after our Festival of Thanks and our Fish Fry, Halloween would be upon us, followed by Thanksgiving, and so on. The Reconciliation, which launched the festivities, was for us a spectator-driven event much like any football homecoming would be, where warm clothing and a ready supply of hot beverages would make for a far more enjoyable experience. We were a ready audience, there to cheer things on, though it never was much of a contest, so to speak.

A band, well, a quartet to be exact, played our town's anthem, an old, old ditty that pre-dated the Star-Spangled Banner, upon which conclusion the mayor, with a gingerly disposition in keeping with what had just about happened to him the other day, took center spot on the service platform. He recited the customary greeting and instructional, all while our Great White circled below him. Some of us fancied the shark was actually slowing down for the brief space in which he passed immediately in front of the platform where the mayor, the sheriff, and his deputies were standing. The Great White managed to convey this glowering rage, which we figured he was directing at all of us, but oh yes, most especially at that flat-footed mayor of ours. That dead eye of his never blinked; it stayed affixed crossways and up at the platform. I think the beast would have enjoyed taking us *all* on.

What a prize our catch was. One of the best ever, and 'brutally emotive,' as Doc Darwimple put it.

Upon conclusion of the mayor's reading, which most of us knew by heart anyway, he nodded to the sheriff, who in turn gestured to his deputies. Petrus and Vic, brothers, stepped off the platform and exited the small arena by way of a heavy door, which led to a staircase that took them straight down a passageway connected to the holding cells in the cellar of the sheriff's headquarters. All this stood about a solid stone's throw from where we were seated, just on the other side of the fence.

The deputies were not long gone, when the door squealed and opened once more, this time to let them back in, along with a trio of chained and shackled men.

These men – I suppose one could call them prisoners – had been bound and gagged, which phased no one, them not being one of us, not really. Their wide, eyes betrayed – what was it we all saw – anger? Fear? Were they scanning the area for escape ideas? No one, me included, bothered much to try and interpret what their panicked stares were conveying. For one, we were still held far more captive by the Great White's skyward-leaning eye, and for another, whatever any one of those three men was thinking was, well, of no consequence to us. Their fate had been sealed by the crimes we had been told they had perpetrated. I remember hearing Vic go on about it over beers at the bar the other night: one of them had stolen something, one had damaged something, and one had. . . well, I just don't remember. There was no preferentiality nor differentiation between the crimes, or details as to who had committed what. Per our ways, it was all punishable by death.

Punishable, that is, by death per the whims of the Great White, with whom all three would soon be swimming as the rest of us watched. If the White chose to kill, and maybe even eat any one of them, or part of them, well then that would be his sentence having been carried out. Any survivor, should the shark decide to leave him to live, would then likewise be considered as having had his sentence carried out. He could even go free, provided his condition allowed it. Any physical damage met with along the way, say, a loss of limb or whatever, would also be considered as punishment having been naturally meted out, and case closed.

Now, were there injuries to contend with, our town's lone physician, who also happened to be our dentist, would tend to the wounds to whatever extent he could. From thereon out, however, it would be up to the now-former prisoner to move on as best as he could manage. To date, we had never experienced a former prisoner surviving. As such, we had never been confronted with any issues of disclosure of our, er, methods. That basically meant, there was no leaking to outsiders any details of our annual Reconciliation by way of our Great Whites. Nor would we ever have to explain to anyone about how delicious a clear water-cleaned, human-fed batch of shark meat tasted to anyone outside of our community. I'll tell you, it is a meat so rich, and so rich in meaning, as to be regarded by us all as being as close to seafood ambrosia as anything could ever be. My mouth positively waters as I relay this to you. There is nothing like a thick-cut, fatty shark steak from a Great White which has been housed in clean brine for the better part of a month, and fed to bursting with living human flesh and fresh blood.

I and a few of my friends had actually voiced our reservations, as to how this old codger would taste, for the Great had to be one of the oldest sharks we had ever caught. He'd most likely require some slow-food recipe tapping, but as my grandmother used to say, there was nothin' a cast iron Dutch oven couldn't cook to kingdom come, given a little heat and enough hours. Why not a nice, thick shark stew this year?

So, there we sat, with our blankets and our mugs, as the men, still bound and gagged, were unhooked from their line, and for all the ceremonious import of the occasion, rather unceremoniously pushed off the platform and into the waters of the tank. At that moment, the Great White had just circled past the far point of the pool. When the three hit the water in a single, fat splash, the shark cut a hair-pin turn and zipped across the pool with what was quite the geometrically precise beeline, straight to the floundering trio at the mayor's feet.

Breaths were held in anticipation. We made no sound as we balanced our cooling drinks on our knees and as one leaned forward, craning our warm-wrapped necks to get a better look.

The Great collided head on with the man in the center, as if to test the density of this newly chummed mass. Finding a compactible torso with a bouncy, little ribcage, the Great was instantly able to discern what his sense of smell had already indicated, here was a trio of good-sized, long-limbed edibles which had just been deposited into the water for his dining pleasure.

The Great backed off by way of another tight spin, which permitted him a second go at the central creature, this time with his eyelids sealed for impact and his jaws split open as far as they could go. The son of a gun simply bit that first man's head off and swallowed it whole, like a bonbon, or a jellybean, popped past the toothless grin of a six-year-old. The Great made it look that easy.

Instantly, the tank was dyed a soft pink. There was not enough blood to turn the water a true crimson, the effect being more like a seltzer having been transformed into, say, a nice, French rosé. A spiraling thread of red wended its way to the surface from the stump of the man's neck. It swirled about and dissipated as the waning heartbeat of the headless prisoner shot out less and less of his blood.

The frantic splashing of water of the other two panicked prisoners broke into our collective reverie. Had the remaining prisoners strategized this next move? It was almost clever, the way each one of them paddled off in opposite directions, as best as they could, given that their wrists were still braceleted together, which only allowed for an awkward scooping against the water. One of the men kept sinking below the water's surface. Not much of a swimmer, we all suspected as we watched him flounder time and again. Oh my, his sputtering alone would get the better of him, we feared. Whispered bets began making the rounds between those of us who enjoyed that sort of thing.

For myself, the spectacle has always been more a study of the shark itself. Several decades now of witnessing the Reconciliation has lent itself to my ken, making me, if I do say so myself, a bit of an expert on shark personality. Quite fitting, I think, me being the town librarian and something of an intellectual. My personal affinity for in-depth observation only served to underscore my belief, that here, with this one, we had found ourselves a singularly supreme specimen, regent among killer kings of the open seas. Moreover, I had never before fancied *emotion* in a Great White shark; but with this one, I came to think differently. He not only emanated this kind of energy towards us, which could only be interpreted as hatred, he also radiated what I could only call a god-like disdain for his quarry. He thought himself *above* us – and he may have been spot on. The Great may as well have been filtering plankton as he was separating humans from their lives and limbs.

One down so far. Two to go.

The Great turned his attention to the poorer of the swimmers. For all the man's wild gesticulations, which were clearly attempts to stay afloat, they only broadcast through the water, *Here I am! Eat me!* One arm flailed in the air as if he were waving to us in our chairs, asking for help. The other arm, being submerged, made for easy pickings for the shark. As the Great lunged past the flounder, he simply ripped off the left arm and took it with him. Shock and loss of an appendage rendered the swimmer quite helpless to say the least, and he began to sink again, this time with a look on his ashen face which suggested he was ready to surrender, just let the shark take the whole, darn rest of him. One quick turn and the Great was upon his one-armed catch, this time to bury his teeth into the man's chest, and to pull him down to the floor of the tank, granting it better leverage so that the beast was able to bite the prisoner clean in two. The water was still clear enough for us to see everything. We were awe struck. Few sharks go back a second time, once they have identified their quarry to be human. We must taste pretty bad, eh? At any rate, we watched as two shackle-weighted legs dragged the rest of number two to the bottom, where they all stayed. The pool *now* glowed a soft cherry amber, for it was also reflecting the sunset skies, where lavender and orange still sat upon the clouds' western-facing crests. Soon, all would dissolve to the monochrome of night.

Our fella needed to keep up the pace. We all wanted to see.

The shark skimmed the perimeter of the pool with the man's right shoulder and lifeless, yowling face bobbing above the choppy surface of the water. His corpse mask looked just like those clay wine jugs Gracie Nesmith sold at her dry goods shop, down to its dark-rimmed eyes and puckered fish lips, with their frozen, jack-o-lantern smile gawking humorlessly at the crowd as he was made to circle the pool, as if on display for our purposes, which, golly, I would have to say he was. With every whip of the tail, did the shark work its jaws farther over the man's chest – what was left of it – until at last the shark succeeded, and the head floated off on its own, and then sank as well, and prisoner number two was sent down, into the gullet, to join his predecessor. By now, the water had gone full-on to the rich red of, say, a merlot, which happens to be my favorite wine. In the growing gloom, the effect was pretty darn dramatic. No wonder we had no crime to speak of. Who would want to be reconciled with their transgressions in this dramatic a fashion?

Now, number two had been a member of our community. One could say, his was largely a token inclusion, to help keep alive what the elders had always called the "unequivocal absolutism" of our system of justice. The other two had been out of towners, a pair of those worst-of-the-worst tourists we all loved to hate, a couple of slavish ocean-loving, big city-types who had been announcing all summer long to anyone in earshot, how they had "fallen utterly in love with the place," and who had started to inquire as to available real estate, going so far as to even leave nauseatingly sweet but oh, so pushy letters in the mailboxes of many of the houses on Dulcet Square. It had been an easy matter to get this pair of chatty poetry-pushers to compose letters to their loved ones and their employers, to inform all as to their rather abrupt decisions to relocate to the coast, and that they would in due time send updates, likely by way a post office box number, but that it might be a while, them being as busy as they were. The fools thought they were writing their way out of their confinements, to say nothing of their sentences.

What we have always wondered: how dare outsiders presume they can just stay on after Labor Day, keep on infiltrating our community with their arrogant, ignorant, sea glass-collecting, lobster guzzling, outsider ways?

You surely have known someone like that – the dry-land Johnny-come-lately who purports to fall so in love the ocean and the notion of living by the sea, who becomes, often in the span of one puny little vacation, ready to put everything and everyone behind them in favor for a new life in a community as idyllic, as tightly knit, as ours. Become "one of us." But they can never be one of us. They are shark fodder. And eventually, so long as we have our way, they will serve best as the human-spice secret ingredient for prime double-AA shark meat for our yearly dining pleasure, in celebration of what we believe, and believe ourselves to be, and what we will always protect.

To our surprise, the Great did not turn to the third man in the tank, who just ran out of gas and allowed himself to be pulled down on like a weighted crab cage. He, like others who had pooped out during their reconciliations, the staff would later unceremoniously fish out and eventually feed to the shark anyway, once he got good, swollen and nastily pungent.

Here, however, is what the Great White *did* do. He pretty much repeated his deed of some days ago, leaving me to wonder if the old coot possessed not only memory but also planning capabilities based on earlier impressions. As if he could *strategize*. With the speed of a motorcar, the shark hurled himself up and out of the water and against the platform upon which the mayor was still standing, right there, front and center, in what he assumed was *safety*. We witnessed, again in awestruck silence, as the sheriff and his deputies fell backwards onto the sidewalk behind the platform. Then we watched as our mayor, Bruce Winesap the Insufferable (as many of us had long called him), was catapulted forward, into the water and straight into the hundred-toothed meat grinder of that shark's mouth. Headfirst the mayor did sail, past all those serrated teeth, his head and his arms disappearing in a flash, but with his legs left sticking up, skywards and out, which commenced on a wild, flailing jig, a jumping jack's dance of death.

Old Mayor Bruce's limbs jiggled about as the shark recommenced on his circular stroll. Why, the sassy Great kept that gray boulder of his head above the water's surface for the longest time, showing off to us bystanders what he was hauling about with him, a horrifically floppy and unctuous, two-legged dinner. The mayor's legs lurched about for what seemed like forever. We all wondered, what that old bastard Winesap was thinking, stuck inside the hot, wet, smelly sleeve of a Great White's esophagus, as the life was slowly being squeezed out of him.

I believed then as I do now, that toothy son-of-a-gun had been waiting for just this moment to re-up his attack on the not-so-beloved leader of our village, so to rip him apart and consume him, much like how our penultimate first mate, our dear Lord and Savior, was once executed alongside His two criminal companions. Like an old roman soldier, the Great did his deed without compunction, zero remorse. Perhaps, this unexpected turn was meant to be. Many of us sitting in the bleachers found ourselves genuflecting the sign of the cross in cautionary reverence, just in case. Man, that shark – what a perfect denizen of Hell. Or, was this just brutal "Nature" doing its thing, as city-folk often say? Poor old Mayor Winesap, a few amongst us thought. Most of us surmised, that tongue-eating louse of a Mayor finally got what he had coming to him.

†††

It was decided, after some debate, we could not consume, in effect, our very own, late, duly elected leader. But nor could we kill off such a fine and rabid specimen of *Carcharodon carcharias.*

Instead, it was decided we would set the Great White, along with Mayor Bruce, free after all. Yes, we were actually taking to calling our shark Bruce, in deference to the recently departed blatherskite it had pretty much fin-picked and swallowed whole, all of its own, primitive accord. This beast, who in the end had killed and consumed darn hefty portions of three adult men in one short session, was far too great a predator, far too perfect a water-borne killing machine, to harvest for his flesh. This fellow needed to live on, carry his line forward, produce more like himself. This year, our Festival would be re-tooled into a funerary observance for the Mayor; the Fish Fry would simply consist of cod. We were fine with that. There would also have to be an emergency election to organize and carry out before year's end. Our town needed its structure intact and held together by another official who would fully understand – and fulfill – their duties, as had been done for centuries. One of us.

So, in the dead of night, early in Spring, our team brought Mayor Bruce back to the bay, and we lowered his massive carcass into the shallows, nice and slow and gentle, thanks to the slings that only Moe's backhoe could've managed with such a gargantuan load. We waited like a bunch of anxious parents until the tranquilizers wore off. When that big, old tail began to do like good ol' Twitch always did, with a *heave* and a *ho* for good, seafaring measure, we foisted the shark back into the waters of the Atlantic. And like a passel of sad, sentimental dads, we watched him disappear. Bruce was gone in a flash, as if *he* had been swallowed whole by its mucky depths.

Emotional farewells aside, we were awash with pride, the kind only true ocean lovers like us Thalassophiles can ever understand. We didn't just hope, we *knew* beyond any shadow of a doubt, that we – more specifically, our descendants – would someday have the great privilege of – yep, if truth be told – aiding and

†††††

Farther Up That Hill

I imagine I am pushing, pushing, pushing. . .
Farther up that hill. . .
Almost, almost. . .
. . . and Wheeeeee!

The crest of the hill upends itself as I breech the steep incline. I grab at the momentum, hurl myself downward. There is no stilling of pace, no easing up.

Although I see trees soldier past me in an ever-increasing whir, and the sporadic farmhouses – so quaint, with their carved shutters and thatched roofs – become little more than bright, stucco-walled blips as I fly past them, I keep keen focus on the narrow road ahead of me. . .

There!
There it is!

But for this being what I imagined it to be, have always known it to be, my mile marker is small and innocuous, a mere fragment of reality situated into a riotously beautiful landscape, over which I gain repeated dominion as my speed increases. I pedal my bicycle, urged forward in desperate determination. I surge onward, straight as an arrow, never to slow, never to slow. . .

I glance overhead. The light above me is bright and steadfast. My sun, seated like a crippled chariot in the sky, remains stuck at noon, noon, noon. . .

All the time in the world I have, to make this journey.

My mile marker is a bit closer now. I begin to see its faint glow, which sets it apart from verdant fields so daintily pockmarked with crimson blossoms, whose small faces grin back at me, fringed as it were with delicate petals, which to others might look like wildflowers, which to me, make for Lilliputian countenances, here to bear witness to my travels, my mission, to cheer me on. . .

The marker lures me onward, both by way of the warmth of its steadfast symbolism, and by the metronome so close to it, which keeps time as it beats one, two, three, four. . .

Again, and again, and again. . .

I am hurling myself forward, feeling the terrain level off, relishing the momentum as fueled by my roller coaster decline. The road has now evened itself out and pulls long over a vast plain that is now so abstracted, it could be two miles there, out in front of me, or it could be a hundred.

So far to go!

And yet, I see my prize. I know I can make it, grab it, take from that win whatever strength I will need to keep on – for keep on, I must!

My legs pump, numb with exhaustion, machine-like; they are now mere appendages to a dedication in the holy name of a task that could rival the sacrifices of the best of wannabe saints.

But I am no saint. I am nothing but one who has lived, and loved, who in the name of that love must continue to labor on its behalf.

The beautiful lands that stretch out before me keep building onto themselves, over and over, as the distances are reeled into a point at which they fold over and re-form anew, like an old cartoon background. As soon as I make it to the next post, I know the next, infinite expanse will appear like magic before me.

What should it be this next time?

An ocean scape to my right? A gentle surf, pulsing away upon the shores to help clock the rhythmic depressions I must maintain unbroken?

The field whizzes by as I contemplate my next vision. I think I spy a traveling carnival off towards the horizon; there, on the left. If I squint against the unrelenting, shadowless glare, I can even make out a small carousel. It, like the wheels of my bicycle, goes round and round and round and round. . .

And lo, I make my final approach and behold the marker, a beating, brilliant valentine that hovers almost at reach and allows me so close to it, that I may acknowledge it, briefly, and then pass it by, so I can move onto the next one.

This is but a vision of my beloved's spirited core as I perceive it, who in reality lies just over there, a few feet away from me, on a filthy, makeshift surgical gurney, his chest split wide open, his beating heart exposed to the dank air, stuck like a pincushion with colorful wires, a Frankensteinian ball of wet, convulsing muscle so crudely excavated from its surrounding cavity, infection has already set it, begun to rot the organ, its anguished housing. My beloved is not spared a thing; he is fully aware, knows exactly where he is, where I am, what I am doing. There is torture in his wakeful agony; he has no means to dream, to disassociate, to exit *this* picture – or to cast blame anywhere else but upon the one person he thought he could trust.

I can *feel* his gaze beseeching me, screaming: *LOOK AT ME!*

I can tell, but only by way of my peripheral awareness, that he is convulsing. It's from the pain he feels every time a fresh shock of electrical current is discharged, by which each heartbeat is now artificially induced. By design, each jolt surges painfully over the rest of his body – all thanks to me and to *my* efforts, *my* decision. *I* was the fool who insisted, we accept the stranger's invitation.

I dare not look upon my beloved, for the pain in his eyes will be more than I can bear, and I cannot let *anything* disrupt my focus. *Nothing* can rip me from the wondrous, fantastical world I have created, through which I will – must – travel as I pedal the stationary bicycle that our kidnapper, the depraved surgeon, commanded me to *Ride, motherfucker, ride!* in order to keep the machine running, which is keeping my beloved alive.

I understand fully what the doctor told me. If I stop, my beloved will die, and *I* will be the one who will have killed him.

†††††

Rectified

"Sugarplum! Love – are you alright?"

"Wha. . . what happened? Whit, what happened?"

"Oh, Love, you blacked out for a minute. Well, more like a few seconds. Still. . ."

"My head. . ."

"Shush now. Here, have a drink of water. It's got to be the heat. The humidity. Air is like soup. . ."

"I . . . I don't know. . ."

"And you've got to be hungry. You're running on empty. I've told you; you've been pushing yourself too hard. Harder than what's. . ."

"I know. Good for me. But I love my work. . . But forget about that. I'm still a bit dizzy. And my stomach. I feel like. . ."

"Okay, okay, Sugarplum. . ."

"Please, Whit, don't call me. . ."

Before I could finish, I threw up into the dampened handkerchief Whit had just used to wipe my brow. What had been in my depleted system to purge, I couldn't even think, but I somehow managed to feel better, having done so.

My husband hovered over me, practically clucking, the attentive mother hen he had always tended to be.

While my sides ached, my head tried to aright itself. I cast a reconnoitrive glance around me. Nothing seemed amiss, though there was the slightest abstracted quality to the room, in part, due to my wooziness from what I assumed was a fainting spell (the first one I had ever experienced), in part due to the sallow cast of the morning light, as filtered through the bank of low, rolling clouds coming in from the southwest. It seemed, the atmosphere, the air pressure itself, was shifting. The light-headedness was, in fact, not that unpleasant, all things considered. It lent my inner, still heedful self a veiled distancing from my immediate surroundings, which, however *nice* they were, included in that moment someone hovering over me like a doting vulture – a someone for whom, truth be told, I held *quite* minimal regard.

The setting was this: my husband and I were spending a few weeks alone at our summer house, a lakeside lodge situated a few hours from the city. The rustic, three-season room in which we found ourselves was a vast, windowed space that spanned the backside of what served now as a most comfortable second home, what Whit presumed we would eventually retire to full-time. The house was rather in the middle of nowhere, and I for one appreciated its relative isolation for my own, somewhat selfishly introspective reasons. Away from the hustle and bustle of city life, I had been able to quietly ponder all that had needed consideration, my emotional plate having been far too full for quite some time. Whit, so different from me in so many ways, had never been anything but a glib braggart about our real estate acquisition. He persisted in telling everyone of the 'campestral hinterlands' where he enjoyed "roughing it," I suppose his way to insert a modicum of false modesty into our most comfortable situation by pointing out the bucolic datedness of our second residence, which he (far too often) referred to as *his* alone. The house was, yes, an extravagance, but a solid investment. Having come into our possession furnished and "as is," most everything was original, inside and out, which lent a timelessness to the place.

Seated where I was on the floor, on a hooked rug the shape of a lily pad no less, the ceiling fans rotating overhead appeared miles away, their pace languid, their effect inconsequential. Islands of overstuffed furniture dotted the room, providing also the cushioned perch upon which Whit had lit to administer aid to his ill-taken partner. Right in front of me – I could have rested my chin on its edge –

stood a coffee table laden with stacks of books and magazines, which appeared to neither have been read nor changed out in a decade. Their faded covers aided to the sense of perenniality which pervaded the house. My nose was but a few inches from one such stack; I noted how they smelled faintly of age and lake water.

Whit, easing himself off the loveseat, positioned himself rather gallantly with one knee on the ground, his left arm wrapped proprietarily around me, although I was quite stable where I sat. He grimaced as he held the wet cloth close to my face – too close – gingerly seeking to contain its noxious contents, while yet keeping them right under my nose. His demonstrative attentiveness had brought his face barely two inches from mine, and though I would have to assume, he was feeling the same off-put way about me in my less than agreeable condition. I winced, discerning Whit's halitosis over my own sour breath. His condition – I always wondered it had something to do with all the herbal supplements Whit swore by – had plagued him from the get-go, which I had in our first years together relegated to the temporary, the 'fixable'. In this moment, he was oblivious to my wincing, wholly occupied by his mothering and muttered platitudes, which I, but for that god-awful "Sugarplum," hardly registered.

"Here, here. . ." he continued, laying the damp cloth onto the morning paper and grabbing a linen napkin from the breakfast tray.

I pushed the wad of stiff fabric away from my face, which Whit was pressing against my mouth as if in a pre-emptive, catch-all measure. I was done being sick, and he was only making it hard for me to draw a next breath.

"Love, do I need to call for someone? Should I take you into town, or go with you to the . . .?"

"No, no, Whit. I'm fine. Stop, stop, would you?"

"Alright. . ."

"Give me a second. . ."

"Very well. . ."

Give me a minute. Give me a mile. Give me a day, or a week, a month; give me a year. Give me the rest of my life, back to me. . .

A sheaf of divorce papers I had secreted away in the corner hutch, out of sight and unbeknownst to Whit. I had filed for a dissolution of marriage last week, and today was the day I had designated as being the one where I would give him the paperwork and break the news, try to talk things out with him, help guide him to some compatible place of understanding I wondered he might be heading towards as well, for all his innocent ministrations of the present moment. Today was the day for my official second step – my appointment with the lawyer and the filing having been step number one – on a reclamation of life I knew I needed to retake for my own sake, to simply be able to keep on *breathing*. I had been slowly suffocating for some time, my commitment to our waning relationship having been for years incrementally depleted. And though his affair – a stupid, brief thing following a career crisis nearly as damaging – was now a distant part of his past, our past, his subsequent overreach and apologetic dutifulness, not to mention his half-hearted displays of sexual attentiveness, were only part of an ever-growing repertoire of irritating shortcomings I could no longer put up with. They were part of a worn-out realm no world of comfort, no lake house setting, could override.

I had to make this ending happen if I was to continue to simply *live*.

Yes, it was nearly *killing* me to be with him. Pretense had worn paper thin to the point of breaking. Our wedded tapestry, you could say, had been laid bare by circumstance, and the undeniable, fundamental disconnects I could no longer ignore had made of our fabric a scrap of wet tissue, about to tear.

I was also at a point where I was ready to give up everything to make this thing happen; and so, I would be the nobler and wiser one, and take this first, crucial step for us both.

My generous filing had no stipulations whatsoever, the plan being to walk away with little more than the wardrobe I had pared down to a manageable, packable size, plus the few thousand I had saved up over the last few years, which no one – meaning Whit – had ever missed. The funds were intended to get me 'out of there,' transport me somewhere 'far away.' Though I had not yet decided where exactly my 'far away' would be, I had resolved I would go far enough to eliminate any chance of random encounters with their forced civilities, far away enough to prevent the crossing of small-world paths by way of workaday or social situations. This would, I rationalized, freely permit Whit his own fresh start, which I suspected he would launch before the pillows had even cooled off. I wanted to know nothing of his next chapters, but nor did I want him to know about mine. I did not care what would comprise Whit's new life; I only wanted desperately to be able to put our old one fully behind me and re-start mine.

In the more immediate picture, I also wanted to *not* endure another night in the same bed with Whit. I was finding myself not wanting to hear his voice anymore, either. He had this simpering, overly sweet tone he was inclined to use with me, which had come to only irritate me. Moreover, he was possessed of an ever-present vocal turn that hinted of question marks, which I suspected we both knew was borne of the half-buried, disparate realities we had each slogged through, all collecting as the hubris of our twenty-plus, long years together. First, there had been the collapse, and then the lawsuits. It had now been nine years, almost to the day, since the disclosure and our horrible fallout wrought by his betrayal; eight years since we had bought the lodge (with the thought this place would be one of healing), and seven since the ardently advised re-commitment ceremony, which had kept us on a stalwart but ever more numbing uphill climb, up and out of the trenches we had dug ourselves into. So much, too much, tugged at each one of us, each in our own way.

It was time now to end the quiet nightmare and move on. Time to reap what was left to harvest by way of this last act of sincerity, time to allow myself to come back to life and seek out who I yet hoped to become as middle age loomed. Time to to be me on my own. Me, yes, me.

With a sideways glance, I surveyed the hutch in its corner. I noted ornate the tassel, hanging as it always did, from the key in its ivory escutcheon. A faint film of dust dulled the cabinet's top surface. Like everything else in the house, the hutch appeared to have stood undisturbed for months, this being our first time out since the turn of the year. Lucky for me, I suppose, Whit was apathetic towards things not intimately related to him. I could have had a general store of forbidden sundries hidden in every pigeonhole of that hutch, which he would never even think to seek out. And were he to open any compartment of the hutch, he would not give a moment's pause to whatever he might see stored in there, including any fat, legal-sized envelope he might encounter. In Whit's peculiarly restorative world, to overlook and to ignore, was to enjoy, and to trust.

Passing out or feeling unwell would *not* deter me. I would present Whit with the papers today no matter how I felt. But later. I would do it later. I needed to re-group. I had waited interminable years for this day; I could wait a few more hours.

"Here, Love. I've poured your tea afresh. How about some toast? With butter? Honey? Jam?"

We ate breakfast in relative silence. I let Whit take my subdued demeanor as some kind of weakened state. In actuality, I was counting minutes. I was formulating introductory sentences to the explanation I still felt I owed him.

Lunchtime. I would do this by lunchtime.

†††

Near noon now. Whit and I had spent the remainder of the morning in the three-season room, him reading and clearing his throat repeatedly, like he always did – he had maintained for years, it was allergies – and me, trying to focus on a manuscript I was editing, trying hard not to be annoyed by his unconscious cacophony, which I resented for his never having pursued its medical resolution. Still on the first chapter, having repeatedly read – well, mindlessly skimmed – the first few pages, I found myself looking for a sign (ridiculous, I know, but still), some indication from the cosmos, that *now* was the time to broach the subject, allow the words to find their way into my mouth so I could launch the conversation that would help us across the chasm. It was almost like the sheer anticipation to actually create a more official division between us was holding me back. I think I feared Whit trying to pull me back – and winning. I feared his hurting, sure, but more than that, I feared him intellectualizing the fallout and then spinning it as a positive. We had both become too adept at faking our prolonged denouement, which in effect had served us both as a sort of trap.

"Whit, I need to. . ."

"What was that, Love?" His eyes lifted from the page.

"Whit, could you put your papers down a minute? We've got to. . ."

Before I could complete that critical, first sentence, my husband's gaze shifted away from me, lured away by something behind me, off in the distance, which had caused his eyes to grow wide with something – fear? While I could see the lake from where I was sitting, Whit's view, what lay behind me, was to the west of our property, a sea of pale green that stretched to the horizon's edge.

"Did you see anything in the forecast today?" Whit interrupted me, his eyes affixed on the distance.

"Uh. . . no; I. . ." I had not been paying attention to, well, anything.

"Well, Love, there's something brewing out there, and it's looking mighty angry. Look!" He pointed emphatically. I could tell, Whit was neither kidding nor trying to sidetrack me. Why would he do that, anyway? He had no idea what I was about to tell him. I was quite sure of that. . .

I turned around on the sofa; there was no denying the foreboding mass of clouds, several miles out, right about where the fields met with the quickly narrowing sliver of a yellowing sky. The front grew visibly – larger, darker, and more ominous as its rain line, a distinct curtain of gray, approached. I could see the clouds' roiling, could feel as much as hear the odd, pressurized quieting that precedes any powerful storm.

Whit had just begun to rifle through the newspaper, looking for the weather forecast for substantiation of the obvious, when from far-off the tornado sirens were deployed. Their wailing chorus soared across the land, beating the storm to further inform us of what was fast becoming evident. At that moment, the rain line crossed over the house, bringing hail with it. Ice like pea gravel struck the seamed metal roof of the sunroom with a deafening percussivity.

I could barely hear Whit as he yelled over the din.

"Honey!" he sputtered, folding the newspaper in a compulsive gesture of orderliness. "Bad weather indicated for today! Hadn't we better. . ."

The sirens cycled through, their howl pitching up and over and erasing whatever it was he was trying to say.

But I was once again deep in my ruminations, far down the familiar path of my imaginary exit, I could hardly steer my attention back into the room, or the voice of the one person I did not want to be isolated with, let alone for the duration of a dramatic natural event as this was fast proving to be.

Whatever it was Whit kept trying to say, my attention, now turned, stayed outside with the elements.

I watched as an angry swath of clouds swelled at its underside, then erupted. Caught by a vortex, a misty, gray funnel began to spiral downward, reaching long-fingered for the terrain. Pitch black the moment it hit the ground, the tornado gorged on the rich soil as it tore through the field, fueled as if with a monstrous hunger for the tidy plow lines, as if with a desire to destroy the farmers' handiwork.

I watched as the tornado intensified, grew in stature, in girth. It lost its ribbon-like elegance, took on the pedantic, triangular heft of a real beast. The storm was morbidly statuesque, and I was fascinated. I wanted to run out to meet it. I wanted to reach out and feel the force of its turbulence.

Whit's voice shattered my moribund reverie. I was surprised to see his delicate hand on the sleeve of my cardigan, those small, smooth fingers of his tugging on the knit, insisting on my attention but oddly devoid of panic.

"Sweetie! Love!" he cried, "We should get ourselves to the cellar!"

What overtook me in that next instant, I cannot justify, nor do I wish to try and explain it, but it was as if all pretense of matrimonial civility in me had been sucked out of my soul and lifted up into that storm. In that same moment, I realized, the looming tornado was my sign, my longed-for *missive*, an illustrative mandate from a most wicked Mother Nature herself, calling me to arms, to expose my absolute truth, no matter the cost.

Level it all.

"You go!" I yelled back, yanking my sleeve away, breaking off Whit's latest grab at care and concern. "You go!" I repeated, "Take care of yourself and I will take care of me! Now go on; let me stay here!"

And I meant it. I had just made my proclamation, an unexpectedly crass prologue to step number two.

Let me go!

"Darling! Come on! Don't be ridiculous! Sugarplum, let's get ourselves downstairs!"

The urgency in Whit's voice had escalated, which was understandable, given the approach of the storm, the wind's howling, the windows' rattling.

"Stop calling me 'Sugarplum'!" was my only response. "How many times do I have to tell you that?"

Whit just didn't get it. Despite all those degrees and all the money he made, I had often thought of him as oddly dense, suspected it had as much to do with a fundamental stubbornness, which to date had served him only too well. His perpetual show of being righteous *and* right had been a strategic charade, a working mensch virtue that had indeed facilitated his career climb – and not just once, but both times. For me, that aspect of Whit had long run its course, and I realized in that moment, I had almost come to hate the man I had once loved – or *had believed* I had loved. Not only that, but that I had perhaps come to this point a long time ago, but been loathe, as most any marital partner would be, to admit as much. Such is the toxicity of falsehood within the paradigms of forced devotion. It can erupt as rage.

"You go downstairs!" I cried over the bedlam. The hail had passed, but the rain pelted unrelentingly, falling nearly sideways in the onslaught. The floor at the far end of the room was already drenched, the rain having pushed through the screens of the windows neither one of us had seen fit to close in time.

I at least had enough wherewithal and practical knowledge to assess the storm's immediate path. "That tornado isn't even going to make it to our property. Look!" It was my turn to point emphatically. "It's going to follow the vale and stay on the other side of the lake! You go on downstairs if you want. Go! I want to stay up here and watch! And I'll," I huffed with exasperation, "get the windows!"

"Well, if that isn't the stupidest thing I ever. . ." Whit fussed as he crossed the room and began throwing the latches of the storm windows, his shoes squelching on the wet floor. "Well, alright. . . If you insist on witnessing the show, then I am going to stay up here with you, Sugarplum!"

And then Whit did what he undoubtedly expected me to expect of him: he planted himself on the davenport next to me and put his arms around me. What – to protect me? Comfort me? Witness Nature's spectacle with me as if it were *our* divine apparition? It was such an unwanted show of needless chivalry and unity, I wanted only to recoil, push him off of me. I longed to be free from his insufferable embraces. I wanted to run out the door, across the field, and catch up with the tornado as it took its inevitable turn along the valley. I longed to let it consume me. *Take me with you!*

The day was half over, and the one thing that needed to occur, had not yet taken place. It might now never take place. Today was to be the first day of the rest of my life. It *had* to be that!

I *would* do this by bedtime. I exhaled.

Whit stroked my hair as he held me. I remained motionless, gritting my teeth, my eyes traveling lockstep with the storm, willing it on, alternately wishing it to change course and come back to strike us where we sat, like a pair of stooges in our huge, lovely room, with the roar of the rain and the wind in our ears, encapsulating us by some kind of circumstantial default.

†††

The tornado passed on, and soon enough, it dissipated and receded back into clouds, which still hung heavy but now benignly so. Its waning had left the air imbued with that interesting calm where ions and the sudden quiet might make for any other couple caught up in such a violent visitation a memorable spell of relief, perhaps even joy.

Whit, at least, seemed elated.

Before he leapt up to launch into exclamations of wonderment laced with self-congratulatory bravado, Whit slapped upon my lips a wet kiss he no doubt fancied as passionate and spontaneous. I lifted the thick sleeve of my cardigan to wipe my mouth like a child, licking the rough fabric in a symbolic gesture of erasure, against the repulsive intrusion of his tongue. I never, ever, ever wanted to endure another kiss from him again. His kisses, never that "good" to begin with, were now downright stomach-turning.

"Sugarplum. . . Love! Oh my God, Darling!" he kept on and on, "That was amazing! Miracle of Nature! What did we just witness? Oh my gosh, oh my golly!" Whit went on and on.

Dear me. So, was this to have been some bonding event between the two of us? The cosmos hadn't been messaging *me*; the cosmos was mocking me.

Whit fell to his knees before me. He took my hands in his.

"Sugarplum! Can you believe what we just lived through? Together? I mean, what does something like this mean? For you and me?" he implored, squeezing my hands, "Yes! Here is what it means: The universe is showing us – you and me – its grand design. It is saying, you and I were meant to serve witness the storm *together*. See? The signs point to how right it is, that we have managed to come this far! And, that we now – together – must continue forward, together. We were *meant* to be together!"

Always such grand statements. Was he convincing himself by way of his own effusiveness or so mulishly infatuated in the drama of the moment as to not remember the myriad inklings of soul-baring troubles *I know* each one of us had been hinting at for years?

Was his tone-deafness just another aspect of the unfortunate constructs of our relationship? Was it wishful thinking on his part? Or was he just afraid, after having re-committed so many years ago, of losing out in the end once everything was at last said and done?

†††

We had no power. Lines were no doubt down everywhere, and the roads were most likely impassable. Whit – foolishly, if you ask me – ventured out in the car to survey the damage but returned within minutes. He could not even reach the main road due to downed trees. I could see evidence of massive damage from the windows. Our terrace and lawn were littered with all manner of debris, even parts of some sort of signage, which had ridden the storm winds who knows how far. Red and white shards pierced the groundcover, as did an angry, thorny array of splintered limbs from nearby trees. It was a mine field out there. Best to stay put, I had to admit.

The wake of the storm had left the area cooled and damp. I swear, though the days were still growing longer, it felt as if autumn had suddenly descended upon us, wiped away the summer in the space of a few seconds.

The divorce papers still lay untouched in the hutch drawer. I could think of nothing else but those papers. I could see them in my mind, there, in the dark, little space, signed and stamped and ready to go. Uselessly so.

†††

Whit built a small fire in the living room's tiled hearth as evening fell. He proposed we even sleep in there, camp out, if you will, to enjoy the light and the warmth. The furniture arrangement made that a practical decision, for we could be separated by logical placement. I could arrange my pillow and quilts on one divan, so to situate my head as far away from Whit's as was possible, to both minimize the intimacy and the snoring I would have to listen to for yet another night, alongside his dreamtime muttering and sputtering. Whit had always boasted that he slept like a rock. Lucky him, I would think to myself. For me, it had been two decades of nudging and tickling, later prodding and pushing, night after night of disrupted, intermittent spells of sleep. Whit denied vehemently any breathing issues. He would laugh out loud, become angry with me no less, when I told him he often quit breathing altogether. That was always the worst – to lie there, waiting for the choking sounds to break into snorts to announce he had resumed the intake of breath, though with no small amount of grunting and coughing. I had once broached the topic of separate bedrooms, but Whit had exploded over my proposal, accusing me of making an incremental divorce ploy, and that married couples not only should share a bed, but that if they loved each other, they would even enjoy such as these Pickwickian bouts of airless and fitful sleep – and that it was in actuality a measure of love, to keep slumbering watch over the other. In retrospect, I would concur, that the absence of loving support I came to feel after countless nights of poor sleep was indeed symptomatic of our situation. That he presumed I ought to *enjoy* his laborious snorefests perhaps epitomized his ego-infused shortsightedness.

I had come to understand, the falling out in a stunted partnership is a sum reached by way of myriad, otherwise inconsequential maths:

1,2,3. I wanted out. I wanted out. I wanted out.

However, before any blessed spell of sleep might lay its claim upon me, perhaps steal for me a dream or two that upon waking I could recall from which I could take solace, there was still an evening ahead of us and an important task at hand. Perhaps the evening would be a shorter one than usual, thanks to the premature darkness, but it would still be something of an endurance test. There was an odd endlessness in the prospect, for the way the day to this point was merging with the gloom of a long, quiet night. I could almost feel the weight of the heavens pressing down upon the house, as if we had been placed inside some sort of inverted glass bowl, a god-scaled enclosure, like a colossal snow globe, or a cheese dome a mile in diameter. I felt trapped. . .

†††

. . . I wax poetic on my ruminations. They embody the futility in which I am bogged down, about to sink fully under. It is, according to my watch, not even eight o'clock.

Whit proposes we 'make a lovely night out of this,' and has prepared a light meal of bread, cheeses, assorted dried and pickled fruits, and wine. He is in a festive mood. As if there were something to celebrate.

"Love, here. For you. To us!" he proposes a toast.

Before I can think about it, I have dutifully struck my wineglass to his, but say nothing in return. It takes a moment, but I muster and begin afresh, "Look, Whit. There was something we needed to talk about. . ."

"I know, I know, Love," he says, "there is much we need to talk about. But Sugarplum, there is something I need to tell you, too."

"Whit! Please! Would you please, for the love of. . ."

"Sorry, sorry," he continues, benevolent indulgence rendering his voice too thick, too syrupy.

The fire crackles in the hearth.

Despite the deluge of just a few hours ago, the wood Whit has brought in ignites readily. Flames dance picturesquely, set the living room aglow. Even the embers seem to spark on cue, in response to his words. When Whit pauses and I stay silent, unable to think how to respond, their crisp patter fills the momentary voids. A minute, erratic drumbeat. . .

The wine, per the label, is a good one. I taste not a thing. It may as well be colored water.

My conviction, my desire to finally state my case, takes on a tinge of desperation. Purpose is now edged with panic. How is it, that I – never one for loss of words, lack of temerity – have been unable to complete a single sentence on the one topic that needs to be broached? I am nowhere near making my self-imposed deadline. One scene progression to the next has so far only resulted in yet another stage being set for yet another awkward and forced romantic interlude. And all of it points to re-bonding, to appreciative acknowledgment, serves like emotion-evoking glue from which no soul with any iota of good conscience can seek escape.

I take another sip.

"Golly, this is good stuff. One of our very favorites, right, Sugarplum?" Whit holds the glass up, studies the garnet light-play. "Just think," he pauses, sighs. "Imagine for a moment, this is all there is, Love. You and me, and this place we have so lovingly made into a home together; a quality glass of wine, quiet time unbroken, no deadlines looming, no distractions, just you and me. . ."

I need to get the paperwork. Now.

I take one of the brass candlesticks from a grouping Whit has arranged on the table and make my way back to the three-season room. I know the space, the hutch, so well, I need little to no light to find a clear path through it, and for my hand to find the key, turn the lock, pull open the drawer.

I hold up the candle to see better inside the drawer. The paperwork is there, of course, as I expected it. Untouched, as I expected that, too. I extract the envelope, slide it into my sweater pocket.

To be compelled to inject a piece of most unfortunate reality into an evening better situated for Waldenesque poets and their romantic partners must be the cosmos now just testing me. Having fun at my expense, at my dour intent, the selfish reasoning behind my motives and my plan.

I am merely a human who was hurt, who is at one with the hurt, and the only thing I can do to exorcise the residual pain is to leave behind *all* its participants: One, he who "never meant to hurt me," and two, me, the unwilling recipient of all that incidental pain, the one who had been convinced by self and others they could shelve the whole, hideous lot and stow it in the past. Chapters like that hold insidious half-lives; their toxicity ever hovers, in at least *my* atmosphere. They fester and render the essential distorted, even deformed. All I wish now is to rescue what is left of me and go. No rewards for time served, no consolation prize for honourable adaptiveness. It is no longer a contest, as I don't care who won back then, nor who wins now.

I am calling a draw.

And so, I re-enter the living room, replace the candlestick with its mates, take my wine glass and down its non-descript contents.

Whit smiles knowingly and with satisfaction and refills my glass. He is adept with bottles of wine; pulls corks with panache, pours deftly, never spills a drop. Between the two of us, we have consumed more than our fair share, especially in more recent years, whilst in each other's ever more wearying company. Wine is an elegant numbing device. It smooths many an edge from within its proprietary loveliness. How convenient. I have always suspected, Whit, who is much taller than I, has poured more than generously over the years *with intention*. Was it to shut me down just a little, effectively sedate me? An inner voice chides me, points out how paranoid I am and shame on me. Makes me wonder, all those three a.m. spells of wakefulness, with my system trying to recalibrate itself from all those hefty pours, which would leave me lying there, wide awake and with temples throbbing, forced to listen to the incessant rattling of the undisturbed, sonorous journeys through dreamland by a calculating other. . .

Or, is he deliberately trying to screw me up only to scratch further away at my subconscious defenses by way of base irritations? Have my walls been that obvious, that easy to breach?

Have I become as intolerable to him as he has become to me?

And thus, I circle back to where I started. I am doing this for the both of us. For his sake as much as mine. That I am not in love with someone I committed to once upon a time is one thing. That I no longer see an erstwhile prince in an ordinary human is another. I too acknowledge my own deficits, my own ordinariness. But that I am on the cusp of being completely repulsed by one to whom I find myself *still* connected to at the close of this day of all days, is a different issue entirely. I fancy I can actually *see* the line I am about to cross. I cannot put this off any longer.

My heart racing, I assume an air of what I hope passes for nonchalance. I take my place on the settee, tuck my feet under me in what I hope is a disarming pose. I wish to suggest ease in the moment. I open the envelope; my hands still shake. I am readying myself to finally say what needs to be said, and I suppose the adrenaline must do its thing.

"Sugarplum," Whit interrupts my train of thought and imminent presentation. "Sugarplum, wait. There is something *I* need to tell you," he begins again.

The fire in the hearth crackles its friendly refrain.

The brie is melting – just the way I have always loved it. The butter in its crock glistens.

Whit starts in again. I stay quiet, allow his persistence to grant me a few seconds to calm myself.

"Love, we have come so far; so very, very far. You and me. We have weathered so much and learned so much. And Sugarplum, I have never loved you as much as I do now. And I thank you. I am so very, very grateful for what we have, and for you. I adore you. *You are the one.* As I have always said, we were meant to be. . ."

"... meant to be..." I echo robotically.

"... but there is something that happened. Today. This is going to sound terribly strange, but hear me out."

"What on earth, Whit?"

"Here, have a sip. Want a fig?"

"Yes. I mean, no. No, thank you. Look. *I* have something I need to speak with you about. It's not..."

"No."

"No?"

"No. *This* has to be cleared up first. Something has to be cleared up. But it's going to be okay, Sugarplum. That, I can promise you. So, stop. Hear me out."

"Whit, what are you saying? You aren't making any sense..."

As I speak, attempting an inkling of pushback, I begin to extract the paperwork from the envelope. I am balancing my wineglass on my knee as I have a habit of doing, and so the laying out of the documents is hindered. Somehow, I know I must move something, *anything* along. It must be past nine by now, and soon going on ten, but the evening doesn't really have any pacing. It might as well be an interlude in an otherwise endless chain of hours at home, alone, with him. Just him and me, alone and together, for what is starting to feel like a suggestion of forever. What a nightmarish concept. I strike the ideation from my mind just as soon as it appears on the dim horizons of my comprehension.

"Honey, this morning, you had a fainting spell..."

"Yes...?"

"You had just kind of passed out, but you came to, right? You felt alright after that? Tell me you felt okay. That you feel okay now."

"Yes, yes. I felt fine. I mean, after a bit. And yes, I feel fine now."

"And that colossal storm we witnessed today; that was amazing, wasn't it? I mean, frightening, but all things considered, it was like seeing the hand of God, wasn't it? Frightening but awe-inspiring, yes?"

I don't know how I am supposed to answer.

I had seen the storm as something unique to me and my predicament. I had seen aspects of myself in that storm. I had wanted to see myself at one with the storm, had wished it could have swept me up inside it.

I remembered what it did to that little girl from Kansas. But I was not seeking a way home. I longed for winds of change to engulf me, cast me up, out, and away. To some isolated island, or a foreign city. . . I needed to be gone. . .

But no magical, happy universe is out there, poised to assist me. I need to take my destiny in hand, and find the courage to present the documents, place them into Whit's hands, and to say the words. We are over.

"Whit, Whit!" My voice pitches, cracks. "Stop it! I can't. . . I can't. . ."

He has no idea.

I swear, it seems Whit is coming from not just another angle, but from some other dimension. His reality is not mine. We are two people who have never been so close yet so far apart, as to represent polar opposite marks on a compass that could never find True North, ever again.

"Sugarplum, it's alright!" Whit cuts in. "I promise you! What we are sharing now, in this moment, is ours forever! You and me – we need never, ever be apart again, and I will spend the rest of my – our – eternity to show you how much I love you! And, you have now all the time in the universe to really and truly understand that what we have is what is right for the *both* of us!"

"Whit!" I am now screaming back at him, confused by his inflection, his extreme phrasing, sentiments far better suited for old Hollywood, or some Wagnerian resolution. I hold out the paperwork, am shaking it in his face. "Please, just take these! Take a look! I have to do this. I am sorry, but I have to do this *now*!"

Whit finally takes the documents from me. He opens them up, reads in silence. His face falls but remains composed, unreadable.

"Well. . . ?" is all my faltering mind can come up with.

"Well, Love, I had no idea you could write like this."

An icy cold wave descends over me, lands at my feet, takes my gut with it. Nausea twists through me. It is done. At last.

When I look up again, Whit is still seated in that rocking chair of his, this creaking, oaken contraption he had insisted 'we' needed. His glass of wine is in one hand, the paperwork is on his lap. He is tugging at his left ear in the way he does when caught off guard and unsure of himself. Oh, I pray he doesn't resort to tears.

"What do you mean, 'like this'?" I venture feebly.

"What do you mean, 'what do I mean'?" Whit asks, holding up the sheets of paper. "This! It's *beautiful.* You're a real poet, and I didn't even know it!" He chuckles, perceives his quip as clever. "And I mean it! I am so sorry I have never supported your creative drive! Had I known, behind all that technical writing you produce, there was an *artiste* in waiting. . .

"But everything is alright, Sugarplum! Now I know and now I understand. And yes, *I forgive you.* Truly. I guess, I would have to say, I am almost glad you did what you did, given the, er, reality of things as they are now. None of it matters anymore anyway, Love. Your eloquent, sad verses here, we can cast to nostalgia, to our mutual memory. We have an eternity to enjoy now the happiness, the life, we worked so hard to build, to re-build. And everything will be better than ever before. That is what I have been trying to say. . ."

He is forgiving *me*?

"No, Whit. This isn't right. . . This doesn't make any. . ."

"Yes, it does, my love. It does. As I was saying, that spell of unconsciousness you suffered wasn't exactly what it appeared to be. I needed to have a way to introduce you to this. . . this here. . . our, um. . . well, I guess we can just call it our heaven. . ."

The rest of me falls to the floor, deflated, my soul cold-pressed and turned to mush by the crush of congealed love – and ominous confusion.

I then watch as I let go of my wine glass. Its contents spill all over the cheeseboard. The wine spreads to the table's edge, begins to drip onto the rug.

Deathly fear has taken hold of me, as does a surge of displaced energy. I lurch off the sofa, dizzy, just as I had felt this morning. I stumble towards the kitchen door.

Am I in search of a dishtowel or butcher knife? Oddly, it seems both have capabilities I could put to good use. . . including on myself. . .

The kitchen is in near complete darkness but for the borrowed illumination from the fireplace and candles in the living room, which cast sidelong stripes of soft gold into the galley. Wooden cupboards, which we had painted a milky white, reflect the paltry light, allow me easy enough passage to the sink – and to the butcher block worktable where the knives are stored.

My eyes adjust quickly, my pupils already being dilated due to the absence of any electrical lighting. With the cabinetry as pale backdrop, I begin to discern a humanoid form that has come into soft focus as I stand there. I wonder if my eyes and my mind are playing tricks on me. The being, about my size, appears to be seated on a stool near the stove. It is somehow made of shadows that have swirled slowly and gathered, much like that storm, to form a vague but familiar solid. I am reminded of the tornado, and how it had sprung from the loins of the clouds and molded itself into a solid, of sorts. The figure – slender, somewhat hunched over – appears in silhouetted outline, like some slightly abstracted human in a modernist painting. But for two gold-colored pinpricks wavering upon the oval plain of its face, its countenance is flattened out and featureless. These small lights are lined up and symmetrical, suggesting they are aimed straight at me. But like a pair of exhausted fireflies, the 'eyes' are dull, have no capacity to cast any illumination. The pinpricks simply behold me, motionlessly, as if contemplating me. Odd, but the being manages to remind me of me.

A voice breaks free from the center of its face. I am not afraid. I think it is because, wherever it is coming from, it is my voice.

Behold, Sugarplum, what you have here is all there is.

I am of no consequence. I am just a messenger, sent to clarify your situation.

What you have here – this and nothing more – with That One in there is all there is now. You two have this place, this house, and that is it. There is nothing else. Nothing beyond these walls. We disseminated a scenario to you both earlier today in a way we thought you might both comprehend the cleansing finality of your situation, which we need you to understand is final and unbreachable.

And you. You are here under these circumstances by way of That One. Him. In there.

For you see, it was YOU at the wheel.

No one here knows to what extent you willed it, intended it for either one of yourselves, nor whether you did it for – to – yourself or not, nor if you even knew what was – is – the real and true state of your heart. Or your mind. Or why you did what you did. So, meantime, it has been decided, it is by HIS wishes – not yours – that we will abide, and this, your joint here and now, is to be based on what to That One matters, and how He – not you – would want to spend His eternal hereafter.

Lucky for you, He wants to spend it with you.

For better or worse. Be it forever more, if necessary.

You two.

Together.

Are we understood?

Decipher what it actually was – is – in your innermost conscience, and your reward – or consequence – will be yours and yours alone to enjoy – or suffer through – on your own. Consider your options carefully; prices can be paid in many ways.

We are thinking, your yearning for freedom and what you perceive to be autonomy will guide you adequately enough to whatever afterlife is your ultimate and authentic destiny.

Heaven, Hell – it's all relative.

At the very least, come to terms with your truest motivations, and you will be spared spending eternity with one for whom you at best hold an unimpeachable ambivalence. Compromise, and you can still learn to make do. If that seems a punishment, that is on you.

Ironic, isn't it, that evidence now bears, He in His rather selfish way does indeed love you.

He truly believes He wants to be with you.

I am amused; but then, I have seen far, far worse.

Be consoled by that.

One can get used to much, much worse. . .

As the being concludes what I now know is my afterlife briefing, it begins to fade. It is like watching soot lifting from an old chimney flue. The humanoid form smudges at its perimeters and breaks apart, wafts into thin air. It is soon completely disappeared, and the dormant kitchen is magically rendered back to the tidy and undisturbed, faintly lit room it began as – and from all appearances, will remain.

Any attempt on my part to respond or protest goes wholly unrealized. It seems, I have even lost my right to a voice. I was only able to listen in complete passivity as my sentencing was made known to my failing spiritedness.

Evidently, *my potential for guilt* for something I may never put into words outweighs – whether I wish it or not – Whit's prior transgressions, as to the substance of our marriage commitment, and now, evidently, our afterlife as a couple. We had, yes, shared equally in our post-traumatic laissez-faire of the heart, each from our own, self-stunting perspectives. But because of something *I* had done – *may* have done, mind you – it had fallen to Whit to issue by strength of his core consciousness the edict by which I, we, now as one – co-joined so help me – would be made to go forward, just as we had in life.

No, strike that. In death.

Is this what they mean when they talk of Purgatory as a half-life? Is this a sort of Hell?

And would this be an eternal forever, or just some relative span of forever, given the unfathomable limitlessness of eternity? A set of months, or years? Perhaps some somewhat predictable increment; say, a second twenty-year span? You know, an eye for an eye sort of premise?

How I longed to have asked the shadowy visitor this question, for it might have granted me an iota of hope, that there might be a humanly documentable and finite price to pay, leaving us to then go our own ways, even in death.

But as I have noted, I lost the privilege to ask any questions. And just as the shadowy entity dissipated to become yet another, unfortunate memory, all I can do is add that to my tally and turn to go back into the living room. Better to try shucking the nightmare and instead seek to brace myself with the fortitude it will require, to figure out how to fake it, as they say, 'to make it' – for my sake. Well, both our sakes.

Back in the living room, when I see the table, with its picked-over charcuterie board, its empty bread platter, its bowl with just a smattering of figs, peppers, and nuts, and the absence of any spilled wine whatsoever, I realize, I am glimpsing through a nasty, little crevice of my whatever-this-is into *Whit's heaven*, and what he is making of it.

And then I see this:

Whit had some minutes ago set his wine glass aside, was rocking in his chair, gazing idly at the fire in the hearth and picking his teeth with a pinkie fingernail, one grown long for just this purpose. An amateur classical guitarist, having remained bereft of both time and talent, Whit had some time ago come up with the bizarre notion, to keep one fingernail grown-out and filed to a point for, if not musical performance, such as these miscellaneous, personal, um, "hygienic" activities. Stomach-turning.

He is momentarily engrossed in dislodging residual caraway seeds from the bread he had judiciously sliced and buttered for the both of us, and in my absence consumed. *His* version of a romantic repast for two.

Upon my return from the kitchen, Whit breaks from his studious revelry to let fall his eyes upon me in that telltale way of his as I cross in front of him. At this point, I have determined to acquiesce to the cosmos's final joke on me, and to commence with the eternal as I now understand it; for starters, by simply reclaiming my customary spot on the settee.

But Whit has other ideas.

My husband rises from that infernally quaint throne of his and takes the few steps required to place himself squarely in front of me, just as I am about to settle in, nice and cozy, to make ready for the first of what is – so help me – destined to be an endless string of innumerable evenings alone with him. When Whit next lets fall his right hand to the top button of his trousers to undo it, and when I see the unmistakable rise of fabric that makes instantly evident *what else* has been rectified in this custom-made afterlife of his, I know, by recollection of the fumbling and bumbling I had accommodated – endured – all those years with him, that *this* would now also be a part of the otherworldly dimension over which *he*, obviously, presides.

. . . in which I am nothing more than a prisoner participant, here to contend with what – or who – will be coming next. . .

†††††

Absolutely Everything

Utter and absolute Nothing surrounds me. I am either standing within the circle of a pitch-black drop cloth that has been hung about me to contain and quell me within its muffling confines, or, I stand facing an infinite void, which stretches out before me like a dead-calm sea on a cloud-enshrouded, moonless night.

Either way, the dark and the silence are thick. So profound, they are almost tangible, like some viscous liquid, coagulated. I feel the quiet could quash any echo, stifle even the smallest reverberation, would there be one. I cannot help but self-consciously test the assumption: I clear my throat, and the sound is immediately absorbed, cut short in the ether. My face may as well have been wrapped in a woolen shawl, wound twice, three times about me, in the way my mother used to do it when I was a child, right before pushing me out the door, into the pre-dawn midnighted stillness, to get me on my way to school. . .

. . . how long, that solitary walk into town, and from how far away that stillness would be broken by the school's bell monotone clang, there to pull me along, step by step, its cadence commanding me to keep pace. I would set one thin-soled boot before the other as I trudged over hard-packed snow that was never cleared from the back alleyways I preferred to take; I dodged drifts that would linger like tiny glaciers, guarded by chill shadows well into March. . .

We, Mother and I, also had Nothing back then; but, as she would always say, we at least had our health.

It is then I realize with a start, I don't feel any pain. None. None whatsoever. It's gone.

I feel its absence so profoundly, it too is a tangible Nothing, not unlike the mysterious gloom that surrounds me. But this is a wonderful Nothing. I am a-swim in such a velvety wave of, well, Nothingness, it is the most profound awareness I have ever experienced, to which not a single element of my recent past can be ascribed. I do understand – can remember – I have just emerged out of a state of prolonged and profound agony. It is as if a storm has just passed over, after having torn its way through my every organ, every fiber of my being, after having wreaked havoc on my soul and rendering of me a biological mockery, now leaving me in complete peace. I marvel in the way only those do, when presented with a gift of perspective, which surprises them for its exceeding *anything* they could have imagined. All that other stuff of misery – physical pain, that gut churning dry heaving, and all that chronic, expulsive retching, has stopped, utterly and completely. I am awestruck. A surge of gratitude washes over me in its wake.

Is this a form of joy? But there is no one to ask, no one with whom I can share my revelation, so the suggestion of happiness dissipates as quickly as it came on. Being that there is Nothing reflective, no mirroring surface to permit myself a glimpse of my own face, I can only imagine I might be seeing myself as I once was, before disease overtook me, deconstructed and consumed me. I can do Nothing, really, so I turn my focus back on whatever the here and now might be, and my solitary presence within it.

I stand – or so I believe I am standing – upon some sort of colorless firmament. It is neither hard nor soft. My feet seem slightly obscured, as if the air were a murky broth, my lower half submerged in it. I can see they are still shod in the same slippers I wore the last time I was able to get out of bed. Though I believe my eyes are open and that I am looking down at my own self, a part of me does wonder if I am merely asleep and dreaming, and still on my bed – my deathbed. Am I comatose, and peering into and through forgotten memories? The fabric of the slippers has been rendered colorless, a middling shade of gray. That is an aspect of dreaming, I think. I hold up my hands, arms outstretched, flex my fingers. My skin appears flawless, the scabs are gone. My fingernails, yellowed and split at the end, are smooth now, almost as if polished. But being that I am immersed in a sort of fog, what I can see of myself has been reduced to some non-color.

Yes, it does appear, I have my health. Or to state it more accurately, I have my health back. The absolute absence of discomfort of any kind, and the way my arms and hands look to me, it is as if I am looking upon a self from many years –

gosh – decades ago. But the slippers, my robe, and the pajama pants that I am wearing are clearly what they had dressed me in while in hospice. That said, the stains on my pajamas are gone. They look new, which is in keeping with this reconstructed state in which I am finding myself. I ponder a moment, realize the scenes of my final days are, in fact, also still fresh in my mind. They roll over each other: one, two, three days; more, totaling up to three weeks' worth of a drug-hazed slumber as the corporeal me shut down, one organ at a time, rotting me from my toes on up, from the inside out, until Death at long last came to call, to lay claim to the stalwart carcass that had housed the self-same me that is indeed standing here, right now. Yes, I suppose my body refused a little too long to relinquish the soul that was silently begging to be let go. It just hurt so terribly much, I clung where I should not have. Looking back, I can remember the waiting. The end could not come fast enough.

But now, here I am, soul intact as is, I believe, my body, miraculously repaired and resituated into a metaphysical version of what it once was, though with a solid amount of consistency to the continuum. The longer I contemplate the present, the more I realize, I might now be some *idealized* version of what I was, perhaps younger. I seem to be an of an age that connects me back to when I was not only good health but still able to look forward, when I could face without flinching an as-yet untapped future, try out the lesser paths, there for me to pick and choose as both whims and chance directed me.

Oh, I chose well, and I worked tirelessly to manifest the unknown into a reality that was milestoned and hallmarked with every material token I could grab along the way. Like those board games I cheated on as a child. Love, marriage, and any friendship deeper than an opportunistic acquaintanceship evaded me, all set aside with intention, endemic of the stoicism any self-centered, pathologically driven individual would be proud of. I knew what I wanted, and I got it. Goal by goal was ruthlessly met, rung by rung blindly climbed. Children were never more than a quaint consideration, whether within the boundaries of a committed partnership or accidental biological incident. Of course, I would have taken appropriate responsibility of any offspring, had they occurred. But having never been more than afterthoughts, my heart had never any cause to consider seeing life – my version of a universe – without me at its defaulted center.

In time, even obligatorily maintained relationships – extended family, the smattering of useful alliances I had seen fit to forge – were sidelined to roads not taken and back-alley might have beens. My work, my promotions mandated enough from me that, the more of the world I conquered, the less of its human inhabitants I even considered as worthy of my time or trouble.

When my mother, the only parent I ever knew, passed, she was five hundred, seventy-eight miles away, and it had been nearly five weeks, three and a half days from the last time we had spoken. And that last phone call between us, I had had to end it quite abruptly; too abruptly for her, for the questioning tone her voice clearly indicated. She did not, could not, register my hasty explanation for interrupting her story, some rambling narrative about an incident at her neighbors', and I do admit that my hanging up on her mid-sentence caught her fully off guard. I now wish I hadn't done that.

I find myself unable to remember what else we had talked about. I am trying to recall what her voice had sounded like. . .

My mother was an immigrant. Her accent and propensity for raising me with sayings were aspects of a cultural and linguistic legacy I realized I could still clearly recall, and I was glad that I could. The countless truisms she had plied me with back then seemed little more than easy-access quips posing as wisdom. How they irritated me, especially as I accrued what to my mind was success, with all its requisite markers: fine clothing, watches, jewelry, bigger and better cars and more of them, bigger and nicer homes and more of those. She would often parrot, "So long as you have your health, you have everything," which at the time seemed to me almost passively aggressive, intended to undermine all I had accumulated. The last time my mother said this to me, I actually told her to shut up. I had never used that hateful, little command with her before – it had left us both shocked into a momentary silence. I had always intended to apologize for that.

That particular adage about health, however, had felt less like a haphazardly borrowed bit of smarts as it seemed to me a simpleton's stating of the obvious. Had I been able to better understand the porous vessel that was my mother – never fulfilled, nomadic, adrift but somehow content with her lot in life – I might have been more tolerant, perhaps amused, perhaps warmed of heart.

Now, looking back from this vaporous perch, I look back also with an inkling – unfamiliar, disconcerting – of the selfishness with which I persevered. I was luxuriating in the sort of imperious disdain only the ignorant can hold over those they construe as fools, for having never known or experienced otherwise. I understand now, just like youth is wasted on the young, so is good health wasted on the robustly well. One never really knows its presence – feels its ill-turned absence – until one is forced to do without it, made to welter about amidst its ramifications, when biological nemeses like parasites invade to disintegrate, deconstruct, and befoul in the names of disease, malaise, and eventually, morbidity. It is when the

Grim Reaper's minions arrive to force you onto what at first appears as a cheery, little sled, perched on the crest of an innocent-enough looking hill that you really feel it, finally get it. You push off, are sent cascading downwards. At first the decline is a tolerable rush of stinging cold; but all of a sudden, you're bursting through drifts. You next find yourself crashing through fences, and before too long, you are heading full force into the face of a brutally unforgiving stone wall, which seems to have appeared out of nowhere. . .

Oh, the pain. . .

Mother was long gone before my own health issues kicked in. When it began to hurt, there was no one to sit with me, comfort, or distract me. By the time I lay supine and unmoving on the hospice bed, like some effigy on a formally situated dais, I was not only completely and utterly on my own, but alone. What had to pass as family to attend to me in my final weeks, my final hours, and then those wracking final minutes, were the on-call specialists and stern professionals who staffed the hospital. To be sure, my fortune secured my stay, and care, and no small measure of superficially respectful propriety, which was held out for me even in the face of what was a most inelegant exit at the very last. I was a mess. But there was no one to shed a tear, let out even a small sigh on my behalf. There was no one there, ready to smile back at me when in my final hours I would pry my weary eyes open to look around, see if I were still alive, still part of that waking humanity I had so willfully set aside, or if I had, in fact, crossed over into wherever it was I was headed.

She also used to say. . .

. . . funny. I cannot think of what else it was she would also say to me. Just that thing about health. Yes, as being everything. A little poke in the side, to point out to her only child, that for all the material possessions, all the successes, one's own, good health was wherein the real riches lay. That is what stays with me now.

Which is now, evidently, what I have once again, in droves. I am utterly and completely healed. Even what I used to call my fuzzy-headed scum on the brain, which had plagued me for decades (no thanks to that pernicious mix of stress induced insomnia and all those liquor-induced bouts of fitful sleep no nap could clear) has fully dissipated. I have not felt this clear-headed in – wow – forever. My eyes are relaxed, at rest in their sockets, the ringing in my ears has fallen silent, and that tension at the base of my skull has eased to a coolness that feels as soft as were a length of silk being slid across the nape of my neck.

To feel absolutely Nothing feels really quite *wonderful.*

But oh, it is dark here. Like the heavens at night, but not a single star, nor reflective cloud, nor moon. And it is so terribly, awfully quiet. . .

Is this some form of immortality? Am I now immortal? Nothing about this place feels heavenly, nor would I want what surrounds me now to be the stuff of an eternity. I certainly don't feel like any sort of angelic being. But surely, this cannot be hell. Or could it? I am loathe to consider either possibility conclusively, present circumstances being what they are, or are not.

No. I feel far too ordinary, too much like my "old" self. I am, for all this vague suspension (and yes, this blessed absence of any pain or even discomfort) still feeling quite the ordinary human, quite dispossessed of anything even remotely magical or mystical. I do wish I could see my face. While I never thought of myself as much of a looker, I wouldn't mind a taking a gander in a mirror.

I suddenly realize, I wouldn't mind seeing anyone. Anyone at all.

What else was it my mother would say? I grab mentally at any additional recollection, but images, words, little scenarios recede from my consciousness in commensurate speed at which I grab at them. They dissipate from my mind's eye as soon as I try to recall them. The pictures in my brain grow smaller.

I realize, I am trying to remember something else now, but can no more remember what it was I was trying to get myself to recall, nor why I was trying to formulate whatever I was thinking, or to what end. . .

That my past might be erasing itself from my consciousness shoots a cold stab of fear through me. Or might forgetting make this, whatever it is, easier?

The stillness that encompasses me almost feels like it is beginning to soak through me, as if it were penetrating my skin, closing in on my consciousness. I believe it is intentional – a sentient force? – and it intends to displace my memories, little by little, one at a time. The additional absence of hurt suggests a numbing I can tell I am beginning to regard more and more casually. Perhaps I ought not resist it. Perhaps I should?

For lack of anything else to do, I hold out my hands, arms outstretched, to admire them, again. Slim, paler that what memory suggests to me. Perhaps it is the lighting. But there is no light to speak of. No light source, no real shadows, either; no differentiation between firmament or the heavens. How is it then, that I can see myself at all? Are my eyes even open, or are they closed? Am I only imagining I can see myself? I gingerly touch my eyelids. Yes, they are open. I venture a slight touch to the outside corner of my right eyeball. It is slick and firm, like a fresh packed olive, extracted from one of those huge glass jars my mother kept in the cellar.

An olive. Food. Food?

The wine connoisseur, the gourmand, the globe-chasing bon vivant I had been now barely warrants a pause, barely ignites even the contemplation of a thought towards some culinary nostalgia, or residual craving. Life's simplest pleasure, having been with me (as it is with so many) a most haughtily and snobbishly pursued consumptive journey, no longer resonates with me, neither in mind nor belly. Aged bourbon, steaming mochas, a rare roast hot from the spit; tortes, truffles, oysters – they may as well be stale crackers to me now. These talismans of abundance, I see now, were there to fill psychological voids so deep-seated and complex, their true purpose is only further masked beneath layer upon layer of butter cream justification and big business rationalization. The simplest want; the original void. I recognize in me what I would describe as a complete and utter absence of hunger. Appetite per se is now relegated without the least bit of sadness to that of the perceived needs and appeasements I once prized, highjacked from the primal desire to net basic sustenance. Choice edibles and beverages took me on a life-long quest for the better, or purported best, which did not even wane once I was in hospice and could no longer swallow. I can still remember coughing out an order to my housekeeper on the last day she stopped by to visit, to go and fetch me a tin of foie gras like a good girl – which she did – which I never ate. I would imagine that blasted tin still sits in cabinet in my suite. . .

I am now rather caught up with this new capability of mine, which is to actually relish an utter and complete lack of hunger. Surely, this is some form of higher existence. . .

Will some answer to all this present itself? Will there be something to shine a light on my present unknowns, figuratively or otherwise? With no other options or choices or directives to occupy me, I decide to venture a bit of movement within the void.

I take a few, cautionary steps, but cannot tell if I am going anywhere. Dear God, it's dark. I might just as easily be lifting my feet only to replace them on the same patch of ground as before, with displacement of any kind being merely conceptual, of my imagination. It is as if I were on one of those new-fangled conveyer belts, like those hideous, rubberized walkways being installed in the warehouses when I last toured them, with me treading in opposition to their pull, going nowhere. I take a few more steps; this time, I think, in a different direction. I try to keep my back foot in place long enough to discern the displacement between the spot where I had last placed it to where it now stands, and though all my senses tell me I have taken a small turn, just as quickly, I see my feet re-aligned, come up parallel to each other, with no indicator I am standing somewhere other from where I had been a moment ago.

Nevertheless, I keep walking. I head in the direction I am facing, whatever direction that might be. What else is there to do?

I notice, oddly casually, the sound my footfalls make upon the non-descript surface flooring. Whether the noise is truly generated and heard by my own ears, or pulled forth as a peripheral, audial memory, I cannot tell. The sounds my steps make is that of ill-fitting boots scuffing over gravel. I am taken once more back to my childhood, my solitary walks to school. . .

I decide to turn my thoughts, so long as I have them, to nicer things. I decide to take a specific stroll through my life, more precisely, through some material components of my life, as a way to set a nicer sort of cadence with which I can keep time, since there is absolutely Nothing by which I can mark progress. Only what already resides in my head – life and what I had possessed whilst living it – provides me with anything of substance, which I can tap from within this vacuum. Something to tally, count, think back on.

I resolve to delve into my most pleasant recollections, which is to say Nothing involving human interaction; at least not directly, for it seems there was always some pesky housemaid lurking in the next room. True solitude was, as I liked to put it, red diamond rare. I decide to walk through the contents of my wardrobe, one garment at a time, glorious stuff housed in my private oasis, the vast suite of dressing rooms which occupied the entire third floor of the townhouse I considered my primary residence. I will go through my beloved collection of clothing as it existed on the days just before I was taken to the hospital. I wonder, casually, if it is still standing silent sentry, in ordered rank and file, cleaned and pressed, ready for duty, or if it has already been cleared out. Not that I really care. The massive wardrobes which housed the garments could themselves have served as a home for a small family. I had them built when I renovated the limestone manse I snapped up for a song, having rescued it from the descendants of a cash-strapped family of some inconsequential, foreign nobility.

I will try to maintain a steady pace with my reverie. What need is there to hurry, in the face of utter and absolute uncertainty, where neither journey nor destination are known? I commence on my journey of the mind.

First, there are the robes. Three, no, four of them, on their padded hangers. There is the hunter green velvet, with its shawl collar, its embroidered crest. There is the crimson brocade, with its silk-covered buttons and gold-trimmed mandarin collar. There is that exquisite Italian piece, made of an intricately quilted black satin, with its sash of. . . Was that leather? And then there is, there is. . .

I seem to recall a plaid flannel. Yes, of midnight blue. . . and gold, and um, some green. Was that also a robe or was that one a . . . Was it a . . .

Well, dash it. Onto something else. Forget the morning garb.

Memories of lesser fashions would naturally be more easily elapsed when compared to the far grander garments purchased for public appearances, status securing occasions where social standing could often be improved upon by way of broadcasting one's good taste. One's portfolio, no matter how it had been amassed, could always benefit by way of one's impeccability. How the sordid background financials of anyone got around to the extent they did, to serve as general knowledge for the entire herd of climbers I called my peers, I will never know. But I played along on all levels, competed, and won often enough. To be sure, I settled – albeit reluctantly – a few times as well. Onward then, I determine, time to recall the evening coats that were stored in the next cabinet over, grand garments I wore to shows (only ever on opening nights), to galas, and all those tedious fund raisers. . .

Yes. Hmmm. What would the first ones have been? I will start with the furs, of course. The furs, yes, and right next to them, the coats trimmed in fur. Boiled wools, an Austrian loden, that buttery leather number, all lined in fur. Fur collars, cuffs. . . Crikey. So much to recall. But I am getting ahead of myself. Back to the granddames *du gardes de robes*. There is the floor-length Persian Lamb, with its stand-up collar and rhinestone buttons. What a masterpiece, that one. Then there is the chinchilla. A cloud-like, silky delight, worth a small fortune all by itself. That piece I wore out only once. . . no, twice. . . the jist of it being, the coat was almost too fine a piece to wear outside of the protective confines of my third-floor quarters, where, yes, I would sometimes dress up for sole purposes of lounging, alone, on my chaise, cheroot in one hand, brandy in the other, surrounded by *my* finery, draped more often than not in Nothing but my beloved chinchilla, or that fabulous sable, and the skin I had been born in. Well, that, plus a few jewels about my wrist, a few rings on each hand. . .

. . . ah, but I digress. I realize, this revery was, well, adequate. I can still see the robes, the coats, I can still remember them. And how innocent the pleasure was, to play dress up with my hard won (yes, I had worked for what I had) treasures.

But just as quickly as I recall my pretty things, I lurch back into the present moment, to the utter and absolute Nothingness that is here, still draped about me, a diaphanous, colorless shroud in which I am wrapped – ensnared.

My reminiscences have distracted me, but for how long? Have I wiled away an hour, or a day, perhaps a week, or have only moments passed? I could swear, I just heard the creak of oaken floorboards, exactly how they sounded in my dressing room when I would walk across. . .

My musings are cut short by the sound of a voice calling out. To me.

"You! You there!"

A door on a far wall – a wall? – has appeared out of nowhere. It seems to have been quickly thrown open and casts a panel of golden light across the colorless floor. The bright beam stretches without fading into infinity. It skips over my slippers like a ray of sunshine, and for an instant, I can see my shoes in color. I had practically forgotten, they were. . .

And then I realize, someone – some humanoid entity – is standing in that doorway – tall, slender, silhouetted against a fire-bright backdrop so brilliant, all else is obscured. My slippers, and what color they are, were, and the light bathing my feet, are forgotten as I squint into the distance. Just how far away are they standing? Everything seems illusory, dream-like. I try to make out who this is, try to decipher any features on this *Scherrenschnitt* form that might better explain just who, or what, he, she is. The being just stands there, one hand holding the door open, the other propped casually against the jam. They are leaning into the void in which I stand, as if wishing to better see through the gloom, to see *me*. For me in return, it is a futile attempt. I am nearly blinded, can see only shapes. The being remains in shadowed outline and anonymous. Its features appear smoothed out, a bit too rounded on some places, a bit too tapered off elsewhere, pointed if you will, towards its extremities. The being appears to be a *representation* of a human, but their voice rings sure and solid, even affable in its inquisitive tonality:

"You!" The being says again. "How are you doing in there?"

I feel a lightning surge of emotion. It flashes through me, so powerful, it is all I can do not to cry out. I *know* I am feeling pure, unmitigated *joy*. I cannot waste one precious moment of this opportunity, and so I ignore my desire to burst out with useless sentimentality, know I must respond immediately and affirmatively, to not let this window – this absolutely and utterly wonderful, bright and shining and promising window – close without me having done what I could do to grab the chance, hold on to it, force an end to my solitude. I must answer *now*.

"Yes! Hello!" I shout at full throttle. My voice cracks. "I am right. . ."

And before I can finish this one small sentence, before I can ask for attention, or help, the being is sucked backwards into the lighted interior and disappears, and the door is slammed shut, as if by an unseen force, some non-existent gust of wind. Like everything else in this vacuum, there is no sound when the door closes. The wonderful, marvelous swath of light collapses to a knife edged, hairsbreadth of gold and is then also erased. My black infinity is resealed, and the absolute and utter Nothing in which I have been for who knows how long is once again as it was before, as if Nothing had ever happened.

I am stunned. I stand perfectly still, cannot utter a sound, cannot blink. That is, if my eyes are even truly open.

I am alone again. But I still have my good – no, perfect – health. I am without pain, without any discomfort whatsoever, still acutely aware of the sublime calm that reigns over every inch of my being, in the only way anyone can ever feel it once the storms of disease have run their course. I have my health within this anomaly, and so I have no choice but to carry on in the only way I can think to do it.

My memory seems to be failing me on smaller, seemingly trivial points, on what I had viewed of my earthly existence as meaningful. Looking back, it has not been difficult to re-jigger perspective. I had worked and earned and then spent and amassed an astonishing cache of superfluous things and stuff – and employed all the euphemistic terms of consumption to describe what I now understand to have been Nothing more than the appeasement of want, want, and more want. And, to what end? To no end at all. Aside from the hospice gown, a humbling scrap of clothing, and the slippers they had made me wear, I did not have a thing – a stitch, a trinket, a stick, a brick – with me at the end. I had in effect been forced to give up absolutely everything I had ever owned with my passing. To be sure, it had been one protracted and painful, drug-addled divestment. Breakdown by breakdown I was made to leave it all – including myself – behind.

But because I am finding I do not miss all that *stuff*, does this mean I now exist in some elevated state? Or am I subsisting in a lesser state, unable to *feel* anymore, as if my emotionality has been drained from my soul?

No! Of course not. I have just had the most amazing experience, and I have from it a brand-new, crystal-clear memory. And that experience had caused in me a surge of what can *only* be construed as joy. I now have a sublime memory of someone (or something) standing in a brightly lit doorway, saying something to me in a decently friendly voice. To my thinking, this could very possibly have been my first glimpse of *heaven*. That being, it spoke my language, and it inquired with as much invitation as anyone ever did with me while I was alive. It represented – represents – the *one* thing I want now, what I was bereft of over the course of my adult life: That of company. That of an ending to a solitude I had no idea would be mine alone to bear in this here and now.

So, my tally is a brief one. I have my health, and I have the infinity in which to own it. I will stick with that. And I can, and will, await a next appearance; but this time, I will be more ready for it, ready to pounce on the opportunity in the precise moment when someone or something presents itself to me. I rationalize that my astonishment during that first encounter was due to my having been too absorbed in the distractions of my materialistic remembrances. Surely, it cost me critical moments of immediacy in my response. To be better prepared for a next check-in means I need to be able to gain closer proximity to the door – any door – when it is opened again.

Then – and I am certain of this – I will be able to step through that door and join whoever, whatever is on the other side of it, and then I will truly have everything.

I realize, my reveries might sneak up, play me for the fool, make me repeat the errors of this new, immediate past, were I to delve back into their defunct and false solicitations. . .

No. I must remain alert and at attention and in active preparation for the next crack in the void.

What to do?

It comes to me in a flash. I will simply mark time, tally my moments as I know them, can grasp them, until the portal opens again.

I will count. I begin to count.

One, two, three, four. . .

†††

. . . four hundred ninety-eight thousand, five hundred sixty-five; four hundred ninety-eight thousand, five hundred sixty-six; found hundred ninety-eight thousand, five hundred sixty-seven. . .

†††

. . . two million, three hundred forty-four thousand, eight hundred sixteen; two million, three hundred forty-four thousand, eight hundred seventeen; two million, three hundred forty-four thousand, eight hundred eighteen; two million, three hundred forty-four thousand, eight hundred nineteen; Two million, three hundred forty-four thousand, eight hundred twenty; two million, three hundred forty-four thousand, eight hundred twenty-one; two million, three hundred forty-four thousand, eight hundred twenty-two; two million, three hundred forty-four thousand, eight hundred twenty-three. . .

†††

. . . fourteen million, four hundred eleven thousand, nine hundred, ninety-two; fourteen million, four hundred eleven thousand, nine hundred, ninety-three; fourteen million, four hundred eleven thousand, nine hundred, ninety-four; fourteen million, four hundred eleven thousand, nine hundred, ninety-five; fourteen million, four hundred eleven thousand, nine hundred, ninety-six; fourteen million, four hundred eleven thousand, nine hundred, ninety-seven; and I am wondering, if perhaps I might see my mother again; fourteen million, four hundred eleven thousand, nine hundred, ninety-eight; fourteen million, four hundred eleven thousand, nine hundred, ninety-nine; fourteen million, four hundred twelve thousand; fourteen million, four hundred twelve thousand and one; fourteen million, four hundred twelve thousand and two. . .

†††

There! There it is! I see something! I know I do! I . . . I . . .

No. No, I was wrong.

False alarm.

No, not a false alarm. I will prefer to call it a false ray of *hope*. If I happen to conjure up my very own St. Elmo's fire out of a desire so deep for company that even I cannot fathom how much I can now *feel*, well, I cannot help that. I am – was – merely human.

†††

Goodness. How long is it that I have been counting? Days? Surely more than mere days. Much more likely, weeks. Certainly. Months? How many months? Calculations like that are beyond my ken.

The thing is, I feel fine. There is no pain. And I am neither hungry nor sleepy. And I have Nothing else to do.

I can start again.

As one with eternity, here and ready to contend with it, to count to a million, ten million, or a hundred million, is not really at issue. What are but a few years to track, stay alert, and on call when the potential of reward might be beyond anything I could ever have imagined? I *know* there will be another check in, another calling out to me by either the same being that looked in on me that first time, or by someone, something, equally as familiar and promising to me as was that first one. I am sure of this because I have Nothing to lose, and Nothing to doubt. I am utterly and completely certain, someone will appear to me again, and when they do, *I will be ready*.

And I will anticipate this second coming with an unblemished and perfect earnestness. I am every child who has ever awaited their Santa Claus, any lover who has ever waited for their perfect other, every shepherd who over the ages has awaited their god. If I am alone at this infinitesimally unimportant, indiscernible point in time – which does appear to be the case – it is merely an interlude of solitude for one who, because I have perfect health, has just about everything.

One, two, three, four. . .

Infantile Troglodyte

If a nineteen-year-old could conjure the concept at the turn of the 19th century, then I in my ripe old age, with the help of all the high-tech bells and whistles that hallmark *this* era, can carry *this* to sublime fruition. Why, I can take it one better! *I* will begin at the beginning. *Mine* will start out small; hence, manageable. *Mine* will not only live, but grow. *Mine*, I will be able to teach. Train, if you would rather call it that.

My patchwork cherub, in pieces: skeleton, organs, muscle, connective tissue, a pliant, fresh skin in which to wrap my dear, little masterpiece.

Voltage channeled with artistic, microscopic precision, isolated heat and frigid cold applied as needed, monitors attached to track the slightest brain activity, regulators to ensure a wavelength's lilting flow; heartbeat inducing and acid generating implants sewn into place. . .

Whatever is needed to make my doll *tick*, I have done it.

Switches on, surges course. . . The lights, even these days, flicker momentarily as power is diverted. . .

I hope the neighbors don't notice; but then, all decent folk should be fast asleep at this hour.

Tha-unk, tha-unk, tha-unk. . .

There! From the depths of its small, heaving chest, arise the palpitations of twin lungs, laboring hard to expand, fill their stiffened recesses. A small drumbeat sounds from deeper still, a melodious, if muffled clockwork that signals to my ears, what the monitors in minute detail delineate.

My progeny, ignited, curls its tiny fingers, flexes its bubble toes, smacks its lips as were it tasting of its very own sweetness. A few more minutes pass, and I witness the slow lifting of flower petal eyelids. No doubt, it wants to have a better look. The babe wants to behold its loving and life-giving god. Papa.

I myself long to gaze upon my pallid child, and approach the bed from offsides, like the sun at dawn rising slowly, gently, to peek over the horizon's edge, to witness as the milk of life flows anew through its form, fills its veins, plumps its belly, tinges its skin with the soft hues of one newly reanimated. Pearlescent oyster grays give way to the blush of a blossoming rose, nigh on the verge of unfolding. . .

I hover like the noonday sun over my glowing child, afire with pride, but then watch as something else washes over my progeny. An edge hardens the lines of its winsome mouth. The scientist in me is transfixed as I next observe as something dark and primitive emerges, which causes its dimpled fingers to furl into a wee fist, round and hard as a river rock. I watch as the glimmer in its dew-kissed orbs transforms into a knife-edged glitter, focused not only on the blood-drained features of my crestfallen countenance, but pushing past it, as if in search of the visceral – my skull, my brain, the throbbing pulsation sounding a warning bell from within, calling me to a different attention:

All is not as it should be.

I begin to understand, I am no more a sun than I am the harvest moon, and this infant on the table is no more my angel as it is my hand-crafted monstrosity.

Its pupils narrow to obsidian slits.

The baby opens its mouth to cry, as any newborn would. A pointed tongue emerges, slaps left, then right, upon marzipan cheeks.

My progeny bares two rows of ivory tines and hisses at me.

Acid spittle stings my brow.

The babe rises, lifts itself up off the table like a freshly hatched viper. In its all-consuming hunger, it leaps at me, buries its tiny teeth deep into my forearm. It means to make a meal of me, or at least my appendage. The bite locks – I can feel the shift of its jaw – and when I thrash my arm about to shake it off, the baby flaps through the air, arms and legs flailing crazily, no more a precious doll but a limp-limbed, evil puppet, face planted into the fat and muscle of my bleeding arm.

Fantasies of picnics, of school lessons, of fairy tales I wanted to read by the light of the sun, spooky stories I wanted to tell in the dark, are dashed in the blink of an eye. I know what I must do, and though I am loathe to do it, I must give this, now, my all.

With my free remaining hand, I crush the infantile troglodyte's skull.

One, two, three blows. Preternatural strength, instinct driven, overtakes me, though several more strikes are required until the cranium finally pops, and my project explodes all over us both, and the teeth finally release their hold.

Under cloak of darkness, long before the tattletale lightening of the pre-dawn skies, I work frantically to undo what I have done. The machinery is dismantled, torn apart; I destroy the bed, trash the linens. Before the clock strikes the next hour, I will have bulldozed the shed and set fire to what is left. The promethean nursery is no more.

I next set out to do what I do believe I ought, but my ingenious malintent, which I cannot help, mandates nothing less than as melodramatic a disposal as I can manage.

That nineteen-year-old did, after all, come up with this, too.

I box the remains, still a-twitching, and resolve to deliver them to the cliffs, and from there into the unrelenting saltwater maw of the all-consuming ocean.

I stand at the very edge of the precipice, poised to cast the dismembered parts as far out into the air as I can, to let them fall into the churning waves, which will pulverize what is left of my poppet against the colossal mortar that is the rock-lined shore.

But in this moment, the beastling's teeth, its mandibles, resume their chatter.

Exhausted to my core, I lose my composure, and with it, my grip. The incessant gnashing is too much for even me. Before I can gather back up the pieces, perhaps to wrap, to burn, and then bury them as I probably should have done in the first place, they jump from my hands, land benignly in the tide pools below.

Let us pray, the barefooted bathers at yon beach tomorrow do not prove as tempting a dish as was I.

†††††

Gossamer Beast

I am loathe to rip my gaze from the window, from the cerulean immensity which has just now presented itself to me so completely and with such explosive fanfare, it is all I can do, to not break down into hysterical sobs. Tears of relief, tears borne of memories, of regret, all beg for release. They all but blow my eyes out of their sockets, so agonizing is the pressure of the soul that pushes against the backside of my cranium, seeks to cleave me in two. But the dam of my propriety holds, and any display of emotion is quickly suppressed, forced back down into the depths of my disease-ridden chest. I sit in silence.

I steal a glance at my pocket watch, tuck it back into the folds of my vest.

The moments, they crawl like slugs.

I exhale with intent, hoping to further calm myself. Emotive displays have never been my thing. Had not the heavens themselves sobbed so uncontrollably at take-off, I might have been inclined to permit a moistened eye, an audible sigh. Had not the bursting forth from the clouds been as profound an emergence into this pristine beauty as it was, our – mine and my fellow passengers' – escape from the rain-shrouded world below would have been far less profound than it just was. Still is. And now, with this razor-keen awareness, my diagnosis dancing about in my head, mocking me, constricting my heart, re-casting my life in nothing but shades evocative of decomposition, my – our – surroundings would have merely played adjunct chorus to my secret suffering. But not any longer. This is *heaven*, and I am in it. *We* are in it, astride a miniscule silverfish outfitted with a pair of makeshift wings Icarus would have approved of, on what will be my first ever – and last – airplane flight.

Since my diagnosis, I have shunned the sunshine, any brightness whatsoever. I have found myself longing for only dismal surroundings, to better connect me with a universe even more apathetic and indifferent than I previously thought it. I have even taken to staying awake through most of the night, doing my so-called living while others lie unconscious in their beds, then finally falling, drugged and exhausted, into my own bed at dawn, to sleep the sunlit hours away. Rather vampiric, but what use do I have for anything that smacks of luminosity, light-heartedness, light of day? When out and about at night, the sidewalks are emptier, the cafes devoid of those miserable cheery types; even the doormen to my apartment are then less engaging, more gauging and guarded when they greet me, as if the cover of dark has the potential to temporarily taint even the most familiar inhabitants they have been hired to usher in. I open my own doors.

I have from the get-go resolved not to tell anyone of my condition, nor how long the doctors at University had concluded I had already lived with the tumors, nor where those evil symbionts are located on my person, nor how long I was so coldly, so professionally, conjectured to live, per their calculations. What time has been purportedly left me will remain my secret. It is, indeed, mine to manipulate.

I know with clarity, thanks to the brusque meetings my physicians – some of them old friends, no less – had with me, that my situation had already progressed too far for any surgical fixes as are currently offered, which, if you ask me, are of no use to anyone. Chemical or radiation-based treatments for such as what I carry around with me are still so rudimentary as to rank somewhere between alchemy and phrenology. And so, for me it has been and will remain more a matter of seeking out and finding providers of comfort as the monsters inside me advance, grow, infiltrate new organs, and the rest of me. The doctor at University sent me away with a cache of pain elixirs and paper envelopes sporting massive, bitter-as-poison tablets (which to swallow with liquid is still a skill I have not mastered. I choke and sputter something awful), along with a letter of referral to an as-yet unretained medical professional I am to locate in my hometown, for them to provide me with, and eventually administer on my behalf, pain medications to help me through the last throes of what I understand are to be my final stages before succumbing to the inevitable.

In agony, depleted and withered down to nothing is not an implosion I wish to endure. Who would?

Ending it. I have, since packing and removing my personals from the flat I have rented for almost two decades, resolved this as something I would, in fact, consider. Suicide, that is. It has always seemed rather obvious to me, how I could so easily hamster away the various prescription medicines gleaned from the different medical professionals in the various locations I will soon find myself, with the basic intention to ingest them all at once, perhaps after having fasted for a few days, to let them take their merciful course. The potential for short-term misery cannot be as bad as what otherwise lies in store for me. Me being the stalwart fraidy cat that I have always been, I am deathly afraid to fail in even this; not only for the burden it would first place upon me, but also upon Old Carter.

And so, I have more or less resolved to fly home, live out my final days, weeks, whatever. To spend, as it were, what of life is left to me, under the blanketing expanse of the family estate, and with the drugs now in my possession and whatever else I can procure as I begin to need them. Like an old homing pigeon, I will land in the rooms in which my life began, reside within them as I see myself out.

Old school to the core, I have always been deathly afraid of flying. Still am. I long ago embraced an attitude of disdain towards plane travel and have often joked how I would never become one of those dare-devil passengers, strapped into some generic, sheet metal cigar. The military aces, renegade explorers, and boundary pushers can keep these contraptions for themselves. I was once forced to walk the hill at blustery Kitty Hawk. I pulled down my hat and with my muffler mummified my face against the cutting elements in protest against what, sure, I understand *others* chased. God-speed and good riddance to it, them, all. I am most content with my feet on the ground, both of them, and with my gaze shielded by the leaves of comforting trees spread far overhead me. I need nothing higher placed nor faster hurtled through space than my seat on a train car's upholstered bench, where the *rat-a-tacking* clatter of the rails sounds off from a comfortable few feet below me. Why, I have never even crossed the ocean, thanks to the healthy state of my hydrophobia, which has successfully prevented me from even setting foot into the murky, limb-swallowing depths of any shadowed green or graying body of water, whether a stone-clad pool or a secret-keeping, swampy old lake. Have shoes, will walk. Have needs, will soak in nothing deeper than the seas of my claw-footed tub.

I hope, I have not asked the stewardess too soon for yet another martini. But what is done is done. Medicinal.

One could, of course, convey thirst, and even a desire to permit oneself to sink into the slumbrous ease of a cocktail induced reverie without looking too desperate. Is that not a preferred condition in the air? A sedated passenger is a good passenger, no? I do happen to have a couple vials in my satchel, but the rest of my medications are packed into my trunk, which has been stowed in the airplane's belly. Charles had given me a fair assortment on my final visit before traveling home, which he did say I could take if I absolutely needed to, but in my ever more depleted condition (I am steadily losing weight despite my best efforts at consuming fatted calories to sustain my weight; nothing tastes like anything to me anymore), I am highly predisposed to falling into a sleep so deep, I might be impossible to rouse upon landing, which has the potential of great embarrassment, and the ensuing of invasive questions. And I am simply too tired and too saddened by it all, to even imagine mustering the creative energy it would require, to fabricate adequate answers by which to diminish worry, quash more inquiry, and God forbid, get anyone too close to the truth.

I extract my pocket watch and check the time.

I venture a look around inside the plane. All around me, fellow passengers are dozing off. The drone of the jet engines, the gentlest of undulations as the plane cuts through the air all make for a peace and quiet that should deliver this genteel collective far over the water with nary a disruption. Even the fussy child at its window seat has dozed off, having cried itself to sleep.

The last, last thing I would have ever wanted was pity. And attention for something I had no part of. The disease taking over my body is an invader, is not me. As such, I refuse to embrace it, make of it anything other than an evil companion. The specialist had warned me, that to remain in too much denial might be unhealthy. I chuckle even now at the idiotic audacity of his *professional* take on the matter. I have severed myself from the monsters.

I have had a decent enough life. It will have been too short; that much, I will admit. As one who has lived it quite successfully alone, it is my wish to carry on as such to the end. Perhaps from the private confines of a suite of rooms I shared with my late brother and sister, back when we were children. Old Carter will still be there, ready to do my bidding.

Old Carter, who outlived even my parents, or at least what was left of them after Edgar and Imogene. . .

Old Carter. I could, I imagine, recruit Carter to administer my medicines, including injections. An easy skill to acquire by one so astute, so trustworthy. There will be no need to keep any professionals around when time comes. . .

Old Carter, who, after he had pushed me into the back stairwell closet and packed me under a massive heap of household detritus until I could not move an inch, had then hissed to me:

Don't make a sound. Don't move. Don't' do anything until I come back for you. . .

Old Carter, who – I will never truly know – may have stormed about in that huge house of ours, may have been the one to crash about in the upstairs quarters. It might have been he who created some kind of bedlam the likes of which I had never before or since then witnessed, who may have forged false sets of tracks belonging to fictitious others, to the satisfaction of everyone involved to that point and going forward. For hours, it seems, I cowered in abject and oh, so innocent fear. For hours I whimpered and cried like some abandoned fawn until he, evidently satisfied with whatever it was he had set about to do, returned to the closet, and buried himself alongside me, underneath all those buckets and boxes and rags and bags, and put his arms around me. . .

Old Carter, who then sat with me, there in the dark for what seemed days on end, until the Constable finally found us – poor, poor us, without food or water for so dangerously a long time – imprisoned in our hiding spot during the heinous invasion and attacks, so subjected to fear and depletion, rendered by our hardship and trauma more unconscious than asleep. . .

Old Carter, who then tended to the house as I resurrected myself, as year by year I carefully reconstructed myself, increment by small increment, as adulthood gained its foothold within and upon me, as I progressed days, months, and eventually years from the nightmare that had played itself out at our family home, from which had emerged (aside from the two of us in our closet) the hollowed out and muted scarecrows that somewhat resembled my parents, from their own hidey-holes. They lived out their final, few years in a dazed haze of their own assorted elixirs, potions, and pills, which good old Carter ever so faithfully, so regularly, so generously, administered. . .

Old Carter, who when time came, packed my bags, took me to the train station, made me board that train to University, who while I accumulated one degree after another kept the house in our own version of a perfected and untouched condition; who, once Mother and Father had at long last laid themselves into their final beds under the live oak on the hill, waited within that big, old house for my eventual return. . .

. . . which time is at long last arrived. Which, understand, might, despite all this, yet never happen. . .

Today? Tomorrow? However one might wish construe the passage and demarcation of time, however one might choose to manage it, claim it for themselves. . .

Old Carter, who, if I were to present myself on that grand, granite doorstep, would let me in without question and without hesitation allow me to sequester myself in the nursery of my childhood years, in the farthest of the west-facing rooms on the third floor, from which I would not exit unless it were to be feet first and wrapped in my own, monogramed linens, on the last leg of a journey that would also, finally, place me back into the family fold, under the one and same, protective canopy of the live oak on the hill, neatly lined up with my more distant forebears, and the crumbling slush in the boxes seated to my right and left, what is left of my parents, my siblings. . .

Old Carter, who, as I made him promise, back when death had seemed so familiar as to be an invisible friend, that when came time for me, nothing less than a cradling bed of snapdragons should be planted over me, head to toe, nose to tail. I had always loved those flowers, with their fierce, eyeless faces and their petal-soft maws, which I could make snap-snap-snap at will, once having popped their itty bitty, infernal heads off their stems. Little Imogenes, little Edgars, blinded and crying, pleading, pleading, but not making a sound. . .

Maa, maa, maa, maa. . .

I used to drop them into the koi pond, push them under, watch their little mouths yapping for mercy, filling with scummy water. . .

Old Carter saw to everything back then; he will see to it now. Never an undue comment, never a superfluous, nosy question. That is dedication. Heart and soul. Old Carter, were he here with me in this airliner, perhaps right next to me in that unoccupied seat, *he* would be capable of seeing the beast, recognizing it for what it truly is, and he would be able to look out the window with me and see *this one too*. He would be able to discern its gossamer wings, and how it was coming right at us. Coming *for us*. And he would agree, what a wondrous and beautiful sight it was. That is how dedicated he is *to me*.

I take a quick look at my pocket watch, tuck it back into the folds of my vest. If my calculations are correct, we should be out over open water by now. The cloud cover is so thick as to be a solid quilt blanketing the entire world. Here on the sun side, it is a comforter of frothing, heavenly cotton. The ground and the towns and all of humanity twenty-thousand feet beneath us have been put to bed.

I look around the cabin and see here, too, humanity in its typically stunted, small-minded way is a-bed as well, oblivious to what lies immediately and all around us, way up here, at the very same threshold angels themselves stand upon, as they await entrance to their ever-afters.

I stand not among them, but very much *over* them. And my awareness, the lens of my very soul set to hyper-focus, permits me to look straight at the white-hot fireball of the sun itself. I am somehow elevated in a way even I could not have predicted. I stare out the window at a magnificence that is as pure and transparent as the robes of God Himself. And transcendent understanding which presents itself to me lets me know, I am at one with the heavens, with the angels who populate its vast stretches, not the humans on the ground nor those nearby me in the plane, strapped to their seats, empty glasses in hand, succumbed to the drone of the engines, and to the false sense of security to which most of Mankind clings.

I look out, see no fur-clad troll crouched upon the wing. What I behold is far greater, and oh, so much more lethal. Where an ape-like prankster may have served some paranoid subordinate, my apparition is derived from the mountains of Xanadu itself. For me, there reigns only the calm of one entered into the intimate presence of a divine beauty. I might as well be licking the cheek of the Nefertiti, or ripping from its flowerpot one of van Gogh's succulent sunflowers. I mark time, relish my reveries, think of my trunk down below as I continue to stare unflinchingly at infinity's potential, which beckons, beckons, and welcomes me. . .

And lo, there it is! A stirring swirl off towards the horizon. A disruption so marked, one cannot help but experience the gaze suddenly caught, then held. I see a whorl of clouds surge upwards and explode, much as a rogue wave might strike a breakwater and burst into a firework frond of sea spray. The explosion fractures into prismatic color play, then dissipates. But then, I see *it*; from the cloud's gaping wound, there is born what I have been waiting for: a gossamer beast, wings yet folded, like those of a newly emerged, titanic moth.

The beast yawns and shakes its horned head, brutally roused from its pre-birth somnambulance. It stretches its limbs – miles wide, they are – and I witness its wings unfurl, each appendage as broad and silky as a glacial lake. I watch as the beast wrangles itself free from its maternal cloud bed, see its nourished and swollen belly, its scaled legs, its clawed feet, and then, finally, I see its spine-laden tail fully emerged, undulating and whipping about with such dervish intent, the winds themselves are hurled our way. Seconds later, I feel the plane shiver in the eldritch currents.

The beast is from another time; it is *in* another time, though it is but a few miles – ten or a hundred or a thousand – distant. But the beast has detected the infiltrator, the silver rat which has breached its pristine playground. The beast smells it, smells us. The fetid fuel, the burnt exhaust, a hundred sweating armpits and half as many sticky groins; sheer nervousness, barely cloaked beneath the humanoid musk that cannot help but seep from frayed tweed jackets, stained lambskin gloves, from underneath stupid little pillbox hats, and filth-trodden shoes. The beast picks up the stench of all the alcohol this luxe-traveling collective has ingested, the milk souring on that brat's breath, the stale offal of burnt tobacco. It has even detected the rot in my chest, the curdling of my innards, and the tainted the blood I further spoil with teaspoons of this, doses of that. The beast recognizes, we in our communal putridity are not fit for this lofty arena.

And as such, we become the quarry.

Newborn and invigorated with an innocent's appetite for complete destruction, I can now only begin to imagine, how the beast launches itself from the gentle breast of its mother, to commence on a stealth approach in a perfect, perpendicular trajectory to the airliner, blind spotting a crew that in their own, abysmal and presumptive small-mindedness think they have the skies all to themselves. And the stewardesses, hiding out in the galley, with their coffees and Tattler mags and their gossip about who is pursuing whom, remain offsides and oblivious, so smug, so cozy, so tin canned are they. They don't know it, but they are all just waiting to be picked off. . .

I check the time.

I look across the row, to the window opposite mine, where a studious child has been reading and snacking on some small objects housed in a plastic tub for the duration of the flight. Everyone else is asleep, or at least pretends to be so. Blind to the miracle taking place outside, blind as a general matter, blind as a whole. Why should any one of them deserve another opportunity to live, to see, when all they would do is squander it? So much avoidance, such an all-encompassing apathy, not one damn thing will be missed by any of these sleepwalkers! Why are they even alive? What is there to miss when one slides through life like a worm, with blinders or mitts or mufflers bound, gagged, and restrained?

Redeem me, little one! Save the whole, paltry lot of you! Show me there is at least one other human aboard this steel trap that has the capacity to look, and then to see. Look not at me but past me, over my shoulder, then acknowledge that you have seen the beast too, that it is as real to you as it is to me. And then, perhaps, perhaps. . .

The child stares directly into my eyes. But it looks only at me, and then only long enough to stick its pasty tongue out at me. The child merely wishes to taunt me. Its eyes are dead already; its freckled cheeks already bear the leaden cast of a decaying dullard. *That* child is a beast. What is soaring towards us is by contrast sublime. Too good for the likes of this humanity to even behold, let alone be consumed by it. Were the little neanderthal across the aisle to look out my window, it would see nothing. Nothing at all.

Well, fuck you too, kid.

The beast approaches head on. It can see me through the window, to which I have pressed my face. I don't care if my flattened nose renders me as hideous as a wing-creeping mongrel. I see the beast and it sees me. It is taking direct aim at my core, which I offered up the day I decided. . .

On wings a millennium wide it soars, faster and faster, closer and closer. Outstretched, it splays a fluttering shadow the size of an island onto the cloud cover below us, which warbles and tumbles, violet-gray against the choppy, nimbus seas.

Eight, seven, six. . .

They say, one should wait until the whites of one's eyes are visible. That is when to shoot.

But the beast's glittering orbs mirror the plane, mirror my face, and all I can see is myself.

Four, three, two. . .

When the beast snaps its jaws down on the plane, when its fangs rip through me, separating my head and chest from the rest of me, when I see my bloodied torso falling down, into the clouds just before the blast changes everything to amber, then pitch black, I gape silently, a hooked trout seeking air but not finding any, going *maa, maa, maa, maa. . .* And I incinerate, and then I melt and become one with my fellow passengers and what was the machine that took us willing and arrogant hostages up, up with it, to raid the immaculate, heavenly lair of the gossamer beast and reduce us all to cannon fodder, be it for newsreel or folk tale.

We sink back to the dank plains of our Earth, a scorched batch of saw-toothed brittle and a charred handful of flowers.

††††††

For the late, great Richard Matheson, and Stephen King, specifically for "Cain Rose Up," which cemented the endocept, brought this piece together.

100 Word Horror

CHOOSE WISELY

Darling, you mean it? I am to be a *father*?

But what is this? A basket, five eggs? So colorful, so beautiful!

Not Easter eggs – what then?

Oh, I see – they stir, they crack, and split. . .

And from their shards scamper our. . . *our offspring*?

Human-headed, beetle-bodied critters?

How fast they are! But why, oh why, do they crawl up my arms, their wide, faceted eyes affixed on my neck?

I see. . . They must attach themselves to me, and like ticks, drink of my blood, until bloated and weighted, they drop off and morph into their next state?

You could've warned me.

VENGEANCE

Even in death, I sought to ensnare him, usher him into my realm. I wrought terror: heart-stopping attacks, blood-curdling screams, lurid whispers, icy strokes ’gainst the backs of his hands. I broke him down; certain our time would soon come.

But when I materialized on the landing, causing not just him but *her too* to fall down the steps, ’twas not his skull, but hers, that cracked.

And thus, I am left running, trying futilely to hide from the vengeful spirit that is hers, here in this labyrinthian house we are now consigned to call our miserable – and eternal – home.

HARDEST GOODBYES

The hardest goodbyes are those where love's loss is as vast and deep as the seas.

Just how far she had fallen was made clear on that night when he told her, between them it was over.

He watched her sigh and close her eyes, mistaking her calm for acceptance.

But still waters run deep, and tempests claim their victims. For, as she sank into the divan, from her chest burst her heart. Like a firework it ignited, then exploded. And like the tides, it washed o'er them, and with blood it anointed.

Engulfed forevermore, in coral they are enfolded.

BROTHERS, SISTERS

Look at us! Once family, now foe; she spilling out all over the floor, me flowing unfettered, seeping out the front door.

What a story they'll write when they break in and find us both!

Until then, here we'll lie, in our co-mingled pools of bad blood, facing away, loathe to look upon the expiring other.

Let us hope, if Hereafter is made manifest, it's played out in separate realms, for to lethal blows we were each finally driven, each having sought out the one who wanted most to kill us; coincidentally born, then later formed, the other's mortal enemy.

THE WELL-SPOKEN

The murd'rous prisoner, who'd mistaken his life's worth by the count of all the others' he had taken, looked out upon the audience, whose stony eyes beheld him.

So, he drew a deep breath and spake: "Live, so that when thy summons comes to join that innumerable caravan. . ."

But the faceless officer stopped him short.

"Why, Buster," said he, "these good folk aren't here to witness your *elocution*; they're here to witness your *electrocution*."

And before the well-spoken killer could utter another lyrical word, the officer tripped the switch, made the killer dance until his brains were fried.

So live, that when thy summons comes to join
The innumerable caravan, which moves
To that mysterious realm, where each shall take
His chamber in the silent halls of death,
Thou go not, like the quarry-slave at night,
Scourged to his dungeon, but, sustained and soothed
By an unfaltering trust, approach thy grave,
Like one who wraps the drapery of his couch
About him, and lies down to pleasant dreams.

from, THANATOPSIS "A consideration of death" by
William Cullen Bryant

BLACK BUTTERFLY

Yon black butterfly, silk scrap skittering, a lace fan tossed skyward by some bella donna, folds its wings as it descends, lights upon my hand, ascends my finger, comes to rest upon the tip.

Making ready to resume flight? No.

It unfurls its curled ribbon tongue onto my skin, and then bites, piercing me like a thorn, which burns, leaves that odd taste in my mouth. . .

When it begins to sip a drop of me, I know the butterfly is not of the Spring, nor the life it brings, but of Autumn, and all the death it foretells.

BRIDE'S HEAD

Die junge Braut revealed what was left of herself with a silent, refined air, one of slumbrous, bygone elegance, bravely, stoically feigned; her ambered lace gown billowing, fabric nearly spilling o'er the edges of her age-blackened bed, there on its shelf in the crypt, at the back of the church.

'pon lifting the lid, a cake plate skull fragment was all that remained of her head. We were told how vandals had stolen it from her shoulders some long years ago, and that all they could find to return was this shard.

I found myself feeling no horror, only sorrow.

This is a true story. Our tour guide was a classmate from my mother's childhood, and at the time, the church organist. The 'Kirche' is in Germany, not far from Frankfurt. To open a casket like this may seem a crass gesture, but the story was told with respect and regret. Considering all the churches, crypts, and age-old artifacts of final repose I have visited and studied, the reveal and sharing on the vandalism has kept this memory clear and separate from countless others. I can, therefore, maintain a singular regard for this woman, to help counterbalance the premature demise and subsequent defilement she endured.

Poems

MY LORD

My Lord
By the lowering gift of your pain-filled kiss
What were once mere days
Are now wholly nighted
For I have willingly bathed
In the pestilent haze
Of the hand in death you have offered

My dark beloved, all that I ask
Is if just tonight
You would make some small room
In that old, wooden box
that serves as your womb
So together we can be kept
From the sun's hot, hateful, and prying eyes
And from there as one await
The blue moon's cool and gentle gait
'til we can next sense its soft command,

"Come, my loves, arise!"

MIDNIGHT CAFÉ

Seated here at the midnight café
Amidst cheerful banter
Genteel laughter besprinkled
Knives flashing
Fangs glinting
From sly grins, all-knowing
And the garçon, bowing elegantly
Asks of me most deferentially
"How, madame
Do you prefer your blood tapped,
Hot, panic heated,
Or tepid, calmly spent?"

ONE SHORT HOUR

Here I lie 'pon my lonesome bed
With nothing but a spate of soil
To cradle my aching, wakeful head
For to await
The sun's last call
So at long last my feet can fall
'pon the bloodied carpet
Where 'twas I so cruelly castigated
By none other
Than the murd'rous lover
For whom in one short hour
I will come
To do to him
What all he did to me

ORPHIC LAMENT

I try my best
To breach the thresholds of the ordinary
To touch to grab to hold, re-craft
Orphic and poetic alternatives
To paying bills
And making do
Working sleeping working sleeping
Exacting small prices ’gainst countless costs
Full-on resound the stinging slaps
First, one fallen cheek
And then, as always, the other

Is this what’s left
Beneath the context of my everydays?
Or am I to shrug off
Everything
And everyone
I have ever known and sought and been
So as some disembodied afterthought
I can fly past the knife-edged, jagged sills
Of that wide and open window there
And once I’ve breached its constructs
Undo the crippling ties that both
Have blinded and bound me
To life as Man has long defined it
To taste instead of the After
As the sun god himself once taught it?

SAY IT

My muse came crawling
'cross the floor
Nails dragging knees shredded and bleeding
Let me have it, she pleaded,
I can take it

How blessed, to be this familiar
With what cuts clean and deepest
With what shines even the smallest light
On all that might
Remain better or best left unsaid

Say It

Lay to paper
Greed and gore
Tears 'til blood-filled as rivers they flow
Unfettered unchecked unfiltered
Rent and torn, incessant scratches
Weakened, flinging rusted hatchets
Lined up as martyred sentinels
Held fast by hooks in morbid hesitation
Means to ends 'midst starkest truths
Dark, decrepit recitations

How hard to sow with soul unearthed
How sorrowful to slog when left unbirthed
To claim alone
And lay one's stone
To seek the unrequited hurt
My own, blood-thirsty audience lurks
But needs first to be invited in

How ironic
The beauty of the day shines that much brighter
When by dark mortality contrasted

I wrote a horror short the other day
As grim as I could make it
But then I heard the news this morn'

I've got nothing on the commonplace

Words parading as…
Deeds posing as…
Good intentions, too quick to warp…
Reversed, inverted banners flown
Hanging high and wide and proud
Gathering?
No,
They are tearing, weeping, wreaking, sowing…

And still, too few see these things for what they are
Fewer yet can

Say It

Say also this:
Mourn those lost
The innocent
For, in equal measure
With their killers
they are now of the past, and gone
As one, they have been reaped
As one, they have been gathered

DELECTABLE LIGHT

Coral embers bleed to grey
as cast by desp'rate, cutting seas
and lavenders are mere memories
of a long-aged past, how they in turn do linger
distinctive, but vague, hauntingly beauteous
borne of quick-fire caresses, all that boundless cosmic fallout
we have come to simply call "*Color*"

The waning blue of a brief day's fleeing
is the wash with which I'd paint the tears I once did weep
could I but gaze into a mirror to see them
to know where, and how, to record them

The riotous skies, yes, they'll keep a-dying
just as they always do
as we all have done, as I have, too
but while they yet slumber
I shall be made to rise
For I must instead forever dive
into the dregs of down-trodden days
reduced to the monochrome of night

Oh, how I miss her bright, life-giving kiss
How I am loathe to quell this remembrant bliss!

But I must now find for myself some sun-soaked, sweet, and tender fool
on which to feed, satiate once more this damnable need

If for no other reason than to partake
of the smallest, little bite
of that benevolent and blessed, delectable light

. . . six hundred, sixty-six million, six hundred sixty-six thousand, six hundred sixty-six; six hundred, sixty-six million, six hundred sixty-six thousand, six hundred sixty-seven; six hundred, sixty-six million, six hundred sixty-six thousand, six hundred sixty-eight; six hundred, sixty-six million, six hundred sixty-six thousand, six hundred sixty-nine; six hundred, sixty-six million, six hundred sixty-six thousand, six hundred seventy; six hundred, sixty-six million, six hundred sixty-six thousand, six hundred seventy-one; six hundred, sixty-six million, six hundred sixty-six thousand, six hundred seventy-two; six hundred, sixty-six million, six hundred sixty-six thousand, six hundred seventy-three; six hundred, sixty-six million, six hundred sixty-six thousand, six hundred seventy-four; six hundred, sixty-six million, six hundred sixty-six thousand, six hundred seventy-five; six hundred, sixty-six million, six hundred sixty-six thousand, six hundred seventy-six; six hundred, sixty-six million, six hundred sixty-six thousand, six hundred seventy-seven; six hundred, sixty-six million, six hundred sixty-six thousand, six hundred seventy-eight; six hundred, sixty-six million, six hundred sixty-six thousand, six hundred seventy. . .

. . . *wait*. . .

YES!

"Over here! I am here! I am here! I am. . ."

†††††

Earlier versions of the following published elsewhere:

"Joined with the Seas"
Crow's Quill zine, Eldritch Seas, Quill & Crow Publishing 2002 & NEITHERIUM, K.A. Schultz 2022

"A Killing Repose"
Crow's Quill zine, SNOWED IN, Quill & Crow Publishing, 2023

The Santa Domnia canticles were derived from "Santa Domnia,"
NEITHERIUM, K.A. Schultz 2022

"Say It" & "My Lord"
To be included in the forthcoming poetry anthology, FRISSON Ravens Quoth Press

"At One With Mere Ashes"
To be included in the 2024 forthcoming issue #64 THE SIRENS CALL zine WHEN HELL FREEZES OVER, Sirens Call Publications

Made in the USA
Middletown, DE
01 September 2024

60300512R00116